STRINGS

THE STORY OF HOPE

STRINGS

THE STORY *of* HOPE

A NOVEL

PATRICIA ANN LEDFORD

First Edition: May 2019

ISBN 978-1-7335242-1-6 (paperback)
ISBN 978-1-7335242-2-3 (ebook)
ISBN 978-1-7335242-0-9 (hardcover)

Subjects: United States - Revolutionary and Cherokee-American Wars, 1776-1804 – Fiction. |

BISAC:FICTION/Historical. | FICTION / Romance. | FICTION/Generational. | Sagas. FICTION / Romance. | FICTION/ Historical American. | FICTION / Women. GSAFD: Historical Fiction | Romance Fiction.

Printed in the United States of America

For Alexandra Avaleen

In July 1776,

Cherokees attacked a small settlement in northeast Tennessee.
Militia forces from Fort Caswell retaliated
by destroying a nearby Cherokee village.
The attacks came on a dark night in drizzling rain.
But the rain was not enough to save both the village and
the settlement from complete destruction.

Chapter 1

Anna Hope O'Connor prayed silently as she watched brilliant purple and crimson hues sweep the sky. Suddenly, the sun dropped behind the mountains. *The Lord's warm colors bring darkness ...*

It had been a light-hearted afternoon of riding -- until they heard the news. *Last evening's attacks were only the beginning.*

Patrick O'Connor's thick, Irish brogue interrupted her thoughts. He gulped to swallow his fear, then forced a wide grin. "My princess, my pride and joy ..." He paused to take a long look at his daughter. A daughter who rode her horse Isaiah with a free spirit, never wearing a cap, relishing the breezes as they crossed her face and twisted her hair. A daughter whose knowledge he had closely guarded, perhaps protecting her innocence too fiercely. The Bible had been her main source of information, along with carefully selected books for reading as she grew older. She was just fifteen and he now wished he had told her more about the dangers that lurked beyond their home, a fine home for certain, but a home surrounded by many acres of land, shielding her from interaction with anyone who might be a bad influence.

Tangled ginger-red curls framed the freckled face he cherished. He couldn't say what he was thinking: *Dragging Canoe is coming. This may be our last time together.*

He reached out to halt her horse's movement and spoke in a solemn, rushed tone. "It's getting dark and we don't have much time. They could be watching us now. Your haversack's in the cave. And remember what I told you about Hawksbill Mountain. Its arched peak sits high above other ranges!" He checked to ensure his treasured gemstone was still in his pocket. *No. Not now. I'll keep it safe for later.* With a swift kick to his horse, he nodded in the direction of their home. "Hurry! Your mother needs us!"

They raced home, quickly dismounted, and threw the reins loosely across the trough's rail. Hope followed her father inside and rushed over to give her mother a hug. Seconds later, flaming arrows hit the roof. Shards of burning shingles rained down on the floor. Hope ran to hug her father, but he pushed her away.

"Get out! GO! -- NOW!" Using both hands and the full weight of his body, Patrick shoved his daughter outside, then rushed back through the flames to find his wife. Timbers crashed down, blocking the doorway. Screams merged into one loud screeching noise. Stumbling backwards, Hope reached the railing behind her to regain her balance, then turned to call her horse. She heard his panicked snorting, then saw him rearing up and striking his hooves in the mud. His panic forced her to stay calm enough to get closer and grab his bridle. Holding his bridle and mane, she settled him enough to pull herself astraddle. Another loud crash. Isaiah bolted. Hope held on as he galloped wildly through the burning maze -- away from what had once been peaceful, happy memories. She gave Isaiah free rein until he was calm enough to let her guide him toward the cave. Within seconds she found the haversack, threw it across his back, and rode into the night.

Days later, the smell of smoke lingered. Screams surged through her mind. Many miles from home, Hope was tired, mud-spattered, and completely lost.

Now, Isaiah was all she had. She had ridden him hard, following deer trails blindly through thick brush and pine needles until the trails opened into unshaded fields. It seemed she had been riding for years instead of the few days since flaming arrows struck her home. She pressed her knees into Isaiah's ribs, pushing him harder to gain distance from the terror. She was frightened and distressed. *I'm fifteen and alone -- possibly forever.*

The sun's harsh rays blazed through her damp hair, burning through her clothes to blister her back. Salty beads of sweat streamed into her eyes, blurring her vision. All she could think of was the unbearable heat. She peeled her sweat-soaked kerchief and shift away from her skin. Visions of crashing embers seared through her mind. *The scorching fire. Screaming.*

Isaiah's pace was lagging, his flanks glistening and slippery. *We'll die if we don't find shade. Water. Dear God. Where are the clouds? Get us out of the sun! Please!* She collapsed forward onto Isaiah's soaked neck and fell into a deep daze. Isaiah continued slowly making his way across the wide and endless field, then he stopped and gently shook his head, waking his rider. Hope nuzzled her nose in his mane, wishing not to move. A cool breeze softly caressed the back of her neck. Isaiah snorted loudly, shaking his head harder, forcing her upright. They were no longer in the field. With a slight kick, Hope nudged them toward what sounded like tumbling water. "Isaiah! Look!" In a ravine below, water rumbled downhill through fern-covered rocks. She steered Isaiah into the woods. Branches scratched her face. Isaiah's hooves slipped as he struggled to navigate the rugged terrain.

"It's okay." Hope whispered as she carefully dismounted. "I'll help you." She placed her hand on the side of his neck and slowly led him down the rocky hill, pushing her feet into the leaves to steady herself until Isaiah was close enough to make his way to the water.

A slight breeze rushed past her as she continued toward the rippling sounds. It was getting cooler. She lifted her petticoat and waved it swiftly up and down to dry the skin beneath her damp clothes. The quiet music of the rushing water calmed her spirit. Wind played games tossing strands of her hair as the river lured her closer. She tossed her kerchief, loosened her apron, unpinned and removed her short gown, unlaced her stay and threw it behind her, then untied and dropped her petticoat. One after the other, she pulled off her shoes. The cool water would bring relief from the heat.

Reaching her arms toward the sky, she thanked the Lord for His guidance. Yet her heart hurt. Tears trickled down to meet sticky sweat stains on her cheeks. Still in her shift and stockings, she stepped out of the pile of clothing and ran as fast as she could toward the water. Twigs slapped her face, stinging, but not slowing her thoughts or the swift movements of her legs.

She didn't see the log at the edge of the bank -- nor did she hear the rustling of the brush nearby. Tumbling toward the river's edge, she landed hard on something sharp. Unbearable pain tore through her left leg -- *God! it hurts*! The pain flashed up to her brain and back to her throbbing foot. The water was moving rapidly. She felt herself being carried along with the current, bouncing against rocks like a broken branch that had traveled its path for days. She reached out for a log, a rock, a tree -- anything that could stop her. Suddenly, she felt a hand grabbing her hair.

Oh thank God -- father found me … But what was he doing? Her knees and thighs, her stomach pounded against the rocks like an old sack as she felt herself being dragged to shore. Opening her eyes she could see a blur of long dark hair hanging over the largest, darkest eyes she had ever seen. She tried to scream, but no sound could she hear. She felt only pain. Her flesh burned from being dragged over the brush.

A huge brown hand moved toward her mouth, against her face, fingers fumbled through her hair. She was trying to say thank you for saving me -- but the words were blocked by the sudden surge of more pain as hands twisted her hair, jerked back, then dropped, bouncing her head along the ground -- until he stopped, pulled her up toward him, then threw her down on her back. The agony was unbearable. "God! Help me!" she shouted, praying the pain would pass.

At first she could see only his long black hair, but as he moved closer she noticed a thick scar running across his cheek from his left eyebrow to his nose. She was dizzy -- frightened. She tried to kick her legs, but they were pinned down by even stronger muscles. She tried to shove her feet up against this strange, dark body. Another hand grabbed one leg and pulled it sideways. A knee pressed against her inner thigh. Something hit her between her legs -- another hand. No. It hit her again and again. It pounded until it thrust inside her. *God help me*. The piercing stabs were unbearable -- she felt her flesh tear, burning, a rush of water -- or was it blood. And that was all she remembered before the heat rushed to her brain, passing the pain as she fell unconscious.

Chapter 2

Hope was dreaming, her bed was wet and crunchy. She felt something in her ear and reached to pull it out. Slowly moving her arm along the wet crunchy bed. The dream faded.

"Isaiah", she whispered. She clicked her tongue,"tchk, tchk," making the familiar sounds to call him. All she could hear was water rushing near her muddy mattress. She pushed against the mud to raise herself. The pain took over. She rolled to her side and opened her eyes. Daylight's brightness hurt too much. She closed them again. *I'll sleep ... just a moment more. This is better. But no! Isaiah is running away.* "Tchk, Tchk!" She moved her legs to catch him. Searing pain woke her again. Alarmed, she realized she had no clothes except for the stockings that still covered her feet and legs. She was too dazed to remember why. The pain was unbearable.

She fell unconscious again. Dreams of home returned. It was her thirteenth birthday. Her father whispered as he rubbed the wide zig-zagged blaze down the horse's nose. "He's a red dun mustang. As close to the color of your hair as a horse could be. He'll be your best friend -- always." She had named him Isaiah, after her favorite prophet, the prophet who passed down the stories of God's children, their struggles and their blessings. She was riding Isaiah across the field and into the woods. So fast they were floating. Then she fell, tripping on a big log.

The water was cold. Tossing through her dream, she had rolled into the rushing water. This was no dream.

Shivering, Hope dragged herself back to shore and struggled to stand. The morning sunlight sprinkled through the leaves of the forest, but provided no warmth. Every inch of her body ached. Her muscles trembled from weakness and she felt sharp pains shooting through her left leg. She tried to stand. Intense pain pushed back against the force of her foot. She grabbed the trunk of a tree, pulled herself up, and leaned against it to get her bearings. Grabbing the tree, then a branch, and then the next, moving forward using her right foot and dragging her left, she staggered up the hill. She saw her clothes scattered along the hill, then slid back to the ground. Using her forearms and elbows, she dragged herself uphill, reaching along the wet leaves to pull each item toward her until she thought she had everything, then she rolled onto her back and pushed herself into a sitting position. *My stay. Where is my stay?* Looking around she spied it further up the hill. *It's too far away. And I am too weak.* She tugged at the hem of her shift to straighten it underneath her, then tied on her petticoat. Pulling her short gown closer, she placed her right arm through its sleeve, and rolled over to pull the other sleeve over her left arm. With no pins in sight, the gown now hung open at the front. *Keeping it loose will be cooler.*

She stretched to pull her apron closer and used her teeth to rip the tie ribbon off the waistband. This took all the strength she could muster. Once it was separated, she rolled over to grab a large stick, breaking it to the length of her lower leg to above her knee. She then set the limb against the back of her leg, tightly wrapped it with the apron cloth then looped the ribbon around as tight as she could. With her apron finally attached to her left leg, she pushed her right foot into a shoe. Her left foot was too swollen for a shoe, but fortunately her blood-stained stockings would provide some protection. She pulled herself to another tree and tugged a branch until it broke loose. *This will be my walking stick.* She placed it in front of her and pulled herself up to stand.

Isaiah. He must be close by. Clicking her tongue "tchk, tchk" and again "tchk, tchk. Isaiah," she called. Isaiah had bolted, but had finally headed toward her that terrible night they fled the burning homestead together. *He'll come now.* She called again, this time louder. "Tchk, tchk. Isaiah!" She closed her eyes, her heart breaking through the silence. *I'll find him along the way.*

She could barely move her left leg, depending on the tall stick for support. She fought back tears and looked up through the trees to the bright yellow fire burning in the sky. *God's morning light.* Her thoughts turned to her faith, *fear thou not: for I am with thee: be not dismayed: for I am thy God: I will strengthen thee: yea, I will help thee.* With these words and determination, she began her journey.

She had no idea where she was but the river seemed her best way forward. At least she would have water and the sun would guide her direction. She headed east toward the mountains, recalling her father's stories. Visions of waterfalls. His family's journey from the north to the Watauga Valley. Nearby hills filled with gems and minerals. But the most treasured tale was of Hawksbill Mountain. The distinct hawk-bill like shape of its peak. *If he survived he'll go there. Maybe, just maybe.* "If " was all she had. *I will find Hawksbill Mountain.*

Right leg forward. Setting the tall stick to her left and holding it with both hands, Hope began pulling herself along. *Right foot forward, drag left foot to meet the stick. Repeat.* Slowly and painfully, she navigated the rough terrain along the riverbank.

As days passed, she nibbled on berries and found sleep in mossy glades near the river. Her mind began to clear. She had ridden east from the settlement and now she was on foot, slowly navigating her way further east. The river was shallow much of the way, making it easy to access whenever she needed to cool off or quench her thirst. *This must be the Doe River,* she thought, convincing herself. *This river flows from our settlement to the mountains beyond. Hawksbill Mountain. Right foot forward. Pull …*

Chapter 3

Maska's anger subsided as he stood looking at the broken girl before him. He felt no remorse as the memory of his mother's screams continued to rage in his head. It was as his father taught him. *Take what is yours. Take what is theirs.*

His father named him Maska, meaning strong, to remind him what he was to become. But during his early years, it was Maska's uncle who was tasked with teaching him the ways of their people. He had pushed Maska into rushing streams that poured over tall waterfalls, forcing him to fight for survival against the currents. His uncle would then demand Maska bring a large rock from the river to mark his journey. And with each rock, he grew stronger.

But waterfalls were also surrounded by slippery rocks. One fateful day, his footing failed. Tumbling downstream, his face hit the razorlike rocks, cutting a gash in his cheekbone from the left side of his eyebrow to his nose, narrowly missing his eye. His uncle made it a point to put him to work as soon as he returned to the village, thus allowing no time to tend to his wound. The wound healed into an ugly mark, for which he became known throughout the land. He now considered it a mark of strength, often running his thumb down his scar to show he had no fear.

His uncle was gone now. But Maska still had the skills his uncle taught him. And he had his grandfather's knife, with its handle of smooth deer bone carved to form the head of a screaming eagle at the end. Whenever he held the screaming eagle in the palm of his hand, it became a part of him.

I am strong, One day I will be chief. I will conquer the white man to end our fear. My people will rule. White man will fear us. White man will leave our country.

His thoughts turned to where he was. He had run east of his burning village and followed the river until he saw the girl with hair reminding him of flames destroying his home. Revenge was his. He wanted to destroy the white man. *Now I must find my people.*

When the white man's raids of his villages began, he heard that many of his tribe had headed west toward the Great Island, Mialoquo where the legendary Chief Dragging Canoe was leading revenge attacks on the white men and their women.

He turned each way to get his bearings. Stepping back, Maska saw the horse upstream. He quietly approached Isaiah, grabbed his reins, pulled him back up the hill, mounted him with a swift kick, and began riding toward the sun. Far ahead he could see the shaconage, mountains of the blue smoke. Mialoquo lay on the other side of the shaconage near the three rivers, Callamaco and two others. His new horse made the trip easier and they continued toward the setting sun. The sun would set three times before he reached Mialoquo, the place where he hoped to find his people.

As he approached the village, he dismounted to walk his horse quietly toward his people, hoping not to startle anyone. As he got closer, his heart sank. These brown men were not his people. They were a very different tribe.

Chapter 4

Mosquitoes or ticks? Both. She was certain. It was now impossible to count the many bites coating her itching body. The pain from her left leg had long ago turned to numbness.

The moon was full, helping to guide her way, shining down through the thick leaves of the forest. *Fairy lights,* she thought, recalling her father's name for the shafts of moonlight bouncing across the water. Up ahead, she spotted a large, smooth rock hanging over the water. Using tree limbs to balance herself, she climbed up the river bank, then crawled onto the rock. Exhausted, she lay down close to the edge, resting her head on her arms so she could watch the fairies bouncing on the deep pool of water below. The water looked to be twice as deep as she was tall. She consoled herself with thoughts of what looked like a path from the rock to a shallow edge where she could ease herself into the pool after a little rest. Weak and nauseous, she succumbed to exhaustion, and drifted into a deep sleep.

The nightmare of three nights ago dominated her dreams. Startled by her own screams, she opened her eyes. Bright sunlight peeked through the trees, blinding her for a moment. Then she saw movement. *Another deer,* she hoped. But these were different figures moving toward her.

"Look! Thar's someone on our divin' rock!," the young boys yelled. "I heard screamin'!" shouted Jake. The boys ran toward Hope as she sat frozen in fear, helpless to run or even move.

On their rock sat a frail girl, wearing more mud than clothes. "Here! Don't be 'fraid girl!" Jake squealed. "Ya 'kay?" He approached her cautiously, tiptoeing as though the sounds of his feet on the leaves might scare her.

She stared at the young boys. *They can't be more than ten or eleven years old,* she thought. Hope nodded, then began sobbing. Happy and scared, she tried to speak. "I can't walk fast, my leg's broken," she whimpered.

Jake scrambled out onto the rock and sat beside her.

Realizing her clothes were torn and loose, Hope struggled to close her short gown to cover herself enough to be presentable.

"Try to stand. I'll help ya," Jake whispered to Hope. "Jared, come here n' help me!" he yelled.

Jared crawled onto the rock, then stood holding out his hand, pulling Hope toward him while Jake lifted her right arm over his shoulder, whispering. "Slowly now. We kin do this. Just lean toward me."

The two boys placed her between them and lifted her up so that her legs hardly touched the ground. "We live just up th' hill," Jake said.

Hope's head slumped forward as she fought the shooting pains that came with each movement, then she fainted.

"My, my girl! What happened to ya?" Hope opened her eyes to see a silver-haired woman with eyes as blue as the sky. Matilda whispered, "Dah boys brung ya here n' ya been asleepin' fer hours. I tried to clean ya up a bit. Ya were caked with blood, mud, leaves, n' covered with ticks full nigh to poppin! Ya needs a good bathin' but first let's git ya some grub.

"I made chicken stew. Ole Nan had laid 'bout all th' eggs she had in 'er anyhows," the woman chuckled as she placed a large spoon to Hope's mouth. Hope sipped the hot broth cautiously, then opened her mouth wide to suck in the soup, relishing the hearty stewed chicken on her tongue before sliding it between her teeth. She closed her eyes as she swallowed the first few pieces, savoring the first real food she had eaten in almost a week.

"Wut's yer name hun'?" the woman asked. "Hope," Hope whispered, taking the stew pot from Matilda and hungrily slurping another spoonful of stew.

"Mine's Matilda. I'm thar granny," the silver-haired woman said, nodding toward the boys who were now peeling potatoes just outside the door. "Th' older boy's named Jared, his lil brother's Jake. Their mamma done gone to heaven a year ago n' my son, their papa, is somewhar' yonder huntin' for food n' Imma hopin th' Indians don't find him." Matilda turned toward the door, shouting, "Boys go fetch some water n' build a far under th' tub. We's gonna git this purty gal out of 'er dirty clothes n' muddy stockin's n' into one of yer mamma's shifts. Glad I saved 'em." She turned to Hope and said, "Sarah wuz her name. She would light up th' room, purty as sunrise o'er a meadow of buttercups, but th' winter's cold grabbed her lungs n' took 'er away."

Once the water was ready, Matilda helped Hope into the tub. Hope sunk down into the warm water, happy to feel the stinging as she soaked her wounds. Matilda gently washed Hope's back, then gave her the rag and soap, urging her to do what she could to wipe the soap across her cuts and bruises. She could now see her left leg and the splintered shin bone. But the warm water not only soothed her aching muscles, it soothed her soul. And, with the pain melting into the water, her thoughts turned to relief and gratitude for Matilda and the boys. She almost felt safe again.

Chapter 5

Hope woke to shouting and the sound of logs hitting the fire. She sat on the edge of the bed she now shared with Matilda, tried to stand, and realized her left leg was freshly bandaged, revealing only a stain of blood on the cloth above her shin. She pulled herself up along the short rock wall that separated Matilda's bed from the main room and hobbled over to peek around the corner to see what the shouting was about.

A tall, thin man with a shock of yellow hair was screaming at Matilda, waving his tightly muscled arms and shaking his fist. "Ya killed me Nan!" he yelled. "What wuz ya thinkin'? Now we jest have a rooster n' no chickens! We's jest gonna starve to death!"

"Now, now," lulled Matilda. "Thar's plenty of turkeys in them woods. All ya have to do is shoot 'em. Now calm yerself, we's got a guest still asleepin'." Matilda tiptoed around the corner toward her room and was surprised to find Hope sitting on the bed, fully awake and pulling a thin blanket over her shoulders.

"Last evenin' ya wuz screamin' in yer sleep n' ya didn't stop or wake up -- even when we wuz fixin' yer leg," Matilda's voice was as soft as a lullaby. "I won't ask ya about yer dreams, but ya kin trust me to keep yer secrets. Now, come sweet girl an' meet me Henry. He jest come back this mornin'. Here, let me brang ya one of Sarah's short gowns, n' a petticoat n' apron to cover yerself."

Matilda helped Hope put on Sarah's clothes, then pulled Hope's arm around her waist and held her as she hobbled into the big room. Henry was lighting his pipe by the fire, his long nose almost touching the pipe's bowl. With a puff on his pipe, he turned to see Hope, immediately taken by the flaming shock of hair piled high. Long strands fell loosely around her freckled face. He sighed, realizing her eyes were getting larger as she appeared frightened at the sight of him coming closer to her. He paused. "Howdy!" he said hoarsely, clearing his throat. "I 'magine ya had quite th' journey gittin' here Missy."

Hope tried to stop trembling and pulled herself closer to Matilda, wishing to distance herself from the tall man with the booming voice. The smoke from his pipe made her sneeze.

"Well, young'uns, let's see if I can't scramble up some fixin's fer breakfast," Matilda chimed. "Sit!" she said, guiding Hope to the long bench by the hand-hewn table. Hope put her face down into her hands, resting her elbows on the heavy surface. Henry seated himself across from her.

"Name's Henry Greer, n' yer Hope, I hear," he said. "Lookin' like ya gonna be around awhile til ya heal up, ain't ya," he grinned, taking another puff on his pipe.

Hope peeked through her hands to acknowledge the man speaking to her. An even wider grin crossed his face as he took in the sight of the young girl in his wife's clothes -- and the stark fern-green eyes peeking through her fingers.

"This here table's me handiwork," said Henry, tapping on the table's smooth wood finish. "Me Sarah insisted on havin' a fine eatin' table. Took me nigh to three days to build it. Cut down two oak trees to git jest th' right planks fer it. Cut th' planks three inches thick so's to make it strong n' solid. We were married twelve years afore she passed on. Many a good meal she cooked."

Matilda set a pot of porridge, along with some corn cakes on the table. She handed Hope a pewter spoon and wooden porringer then used a long gourd to scoop a good helping of porridge to Hope's bowl. Henry grabbed the gourd and scooped himself most of the remaining porridge. The boys then took the pot to the end of the table and used corn cakes to shovel out the remains.

After gobbling down his porridge, Henry stood. "Gotta go find somethin fer our next meal," he said grabbing his musket and stepping out into the day's brightness. He shoved the leather-hinged door to close it behind him.

Matilda took up the pot and remaining tablewares nodding to the boys to help her. Arms full, the three headed out the door toward the river pool to wash the wares.

Hope took in her surroundings. The table was definitely the main piece of furniture. Matilda's cookware was piled on a clapboard shelf atop stones, next to a waist-high tree stump which she used for a carving table. The boys' beds were leaf-filled pillows on the dirt floor in a corner near the fireplace. Henry's bed was made of sapling planks stacked on some rocks across the room in the other corner. Matilda's room was in the other corner, just large enough for her log bed that sat on knee-high posts. But it was a bit more private, protected by a rock wall about Matilda's height and as long as the bed and then some. It was just tall enough and long enough to separate the two rooms, but it had no door, the opening was at the foot of her bed.

Hope placed her head down between her arms on the table and thought back to her own home with its wood floor and a loft for sleeping. But the loft quickly collapsed onto the floor in flames. She opened her eyes to erase the image, then closed them to ease the pain. Every inch of her body still ached.

"Quiet boys," whispered Matilda as they scrambled back inside. Hope raised her head to see the threesome slowly opening the door and pulling it to as they hauled in the dishes. "Didn't mean to wake ya," said Matilda. "Boys ya got chores to do. Now git on wit''em."

"Can I help?" Hope pleaded. Matilda plopped a sack of potatoes and a knife onto the table, without saying a word. Hope commenced to peeling, painfully and slowly, but with a slight smile turning up her face causing a peaceful sensation throughout her sore body. Eight peeled potatoes later, Matilda gave her some snap beans which Hope happily stringed and snapped for boiling with the potatoes.

Henry popped in and out to let them know he shot a turkey and was gathering the boys to help him pluck and clean it. Soon, the turkey was pierced and roasting over an open flame not far from the tub outside. Matilda set the pot of potatoes and beans on the fire below.

Matilda propped the door open and unlatched the small window across the room to garner a breeze. Henry stepped in to grab his fiddle, stepped back outside, and began playing a lively tune. The boys did a little jig outside beyond the roasting fire.

Hope bowed her head to thank the Lord for these kind folks who saved her from what would have surely been her demise if she had continued her slow journey to find Hawksbill Mountain.

Chapter 6

Now alone in the dark, Maska rubbed his scar, mulling over how to approach this strange mix of natives. He decided to retreat to the river and wait until dawn to enter this new village. The men he saw were not of the same skin. Some had shaved the front part of their heads leaving one thin braid hanging over their ear, their back hair short, barely touching narrow bands around their neck. Others had no hair except for a scalplock braid rising from the top middle of their shaved head to form a braided tail that extended to the top of their back. Still others wore elaborate long hairstyles and walked in a proud and vain manner. His hair was long, straight and black. He wore no feathers or headband to mark his legacy as he had been awakened in the middle of the night by the attack and had run, wearing only his breechcloth. His feet were tough and he ran with only his knife, relying on strength earned by carrying rocks and swimming in rough waters. The horse was a blessing from the broken white girl. He assumed she was dead and would not have needed it anyway -- not that he cared.

He tied Isaiah to a tree near the stream and lay his head near Isaiah's feet. His strong body had endured three days of riding, only stopping occasionally to water the horse. His anxiety melted into exhaustion and he quickly succumbed to sleep.

Dragging Canoe woke before the sun rose. This was his privilege and his pleasure, wanting to be the first out each day as the leader of this mixed breed, plus he relished his quiet time in the morning mist.

His name, Dragging Canoe, was not one of strength, but one of legend. He had survived smallpox at a young age, which left his face marked, and his body weakened. When he was just seven, and wanting to join a war party moving against a neighboring Shawnee tribe, his father told him he could stay with the war party as long as he could carry his canoe. He had tried to prove his readiness for war by carrying the heavy canoe, but could only manage to drag it. Thereafter, his father called him *Tsiyu Gansini*, 'he is dragging his canoe'. The name stuck and it, along with his scarred face, differentiated him from any other. His story also made him a fighter as no one dared tease him about his name. He had carried many a canoe since he was seven, holding it above his head and running ahead of all others, then throwing it back at ones lagging behind. *My name should have been 'Powerful One Running with Canoe' or 'Throwing Canoe',* he thought, chuckling to himself.

He grimaced and tried not to limp as he headed toward the river. His leg was healing slowly from the wounds he had incurred during the battle at Long Island Flats. The musket ball had pierced both his thighs and he had been carried to the rear on a litter. It had been a well-planned attack, but one that was not a surprise to the enemy. Over a hundred of his men were injured and thirteen killed. He had been forced to order retreat.

After Long Island Flats, his followers had fought hard at Fort Caswell launching many attacks in a two-week siege, only to lose even more men. The surviving warriors had retreated back to his stronghold in the west. It was getting harder to find victory over the white man.

Isaiah snorted and jerked at his rope, startled by the stranger coming toward him. This woke Maska, who jumped to his feet to face the tall man looming before him.

The hard body held a chiseled face of high cheekbones and stark, piercing eyes unlike any he had seen. *I dare not challenge this one*, he thought.

"Come. Bring horse," ordered the tall man. Maska took Isaiah's rope and followed Dragging Canoe down to the village.

"The white man calls me The Dragon," Dragging Canoe said. "That is because I leave their settlements dark and bloody. The white man is taking away our hunting lands, our food. I will not stand for this. We will continue to fight the white man. We will drive them out of our land."

"The white man destroyed my village. And killed my mother," Maska said. "I am your fighter and you will see I will be your most ferocious warrior."

Chapter 7

Henry Greer was extremely busy in recent days. He had ridden into the Watauga settlement and traded some furs for a new saw and other supplies. He even traded a baby goat for six baby chicks which they would keep inside until they grew enough to lay eggs.

Old familiar and some surprising feelings stirred within him. It had been many weeks since the ginger-haired girl came to their home. He had carved a tall cane with a rest for Hope's arm and she was becoming stronger. The cane enabled her to move about and she was now seated on a stump outside, mending her short gown. *She is thin, but has some nice curves about her,* he thought.

When Sarah died, a piece of Henry's heart went to heaven with her and he had not sought or even thought about seeking companionship outside of his own home. His widowed mother, Matilda, had moved in to help with the boys and, since she had left her own home behind, he gladly built a wall to give her her own space. He thought more and more about that space and though there was no complaining ... *Matilda an' Hope must be gittin' a lil uncomfortable sleepin' in that small bed.*

"Hope!" he shouted cheerfully. "It's time a got yer own space. I'mma gonna build ya yer own home! I've talked it over wit' th' boys n' they's gonna help me! It ain't gonna take long -- maybe a week er so. It'll be small but then ye n' Matilda won't no longer be crammed into that small lil bed. What d'ya think?"

Hope tried to control her emotions, mustering a smile and trying not to reveal the mixture of shock, excitement, and genuine gratitude that overcame her. "Why Henry, I don't know what to say," she said, holding back her wish to squeal with joy. "You, Matilda, and the boys have been a great blessing to me, but I don't want to put you to any more trouble. I should move on so you can get back to your life as it was."

"Nonsense!" Henry exclaimed. "Why! Ya knows it's gonna take nigh a year fer ya kin walk any distance to speak of. N', I only got one horse. So, ya jest gonna have to stay put til ya heal up. If ya still feel ya gotta leave one day, that's fine. Then I'll just give yer home to Matilda. But, fer now, it's only fittin' that ya have yer own space. N' that's that!"

That afternoon, Hope heard axes hitting wood and trees falling in the forest. Then she watched as the boys hitched their sapling sled to the horse and returned pulling large logs toward the plot. Days later, they cut the logs into sixteen foot lengths and barked them. They worked day and night notching the logs, cutting some in half to make the front and back walls, notching, then staggering them to criss-cross at the corners. A few summer downpours helped them amass some mud and they brought moss up from the river to fill the gaps between the logs. They then cut the bark from the logs into squares for the roof.

She was growing especially fond of the two boys. The boys never seemed to complain and she guessed they were accustomed to the harsh weather's affect on their skin. Watching them, she mulled over the differences in their appearance. *Jared, the oldest, a bit taller, and of stockier build than his brother. Jared's light brown hair is streaked with the tawny color of acorns. Unkept hair that usually hangs in straggly ribbons across his face to frame his sky-blue eyes … Jared is strikingly better looking than his brother, Jake.*

Jake's hair is the color of corn husks in the fall, and much neater -- always tied back with a leather strap. And his face and frame is thinner, built more gangly like his papa's, and his eyes -- a light green -- definitely not from his papa. She wondered if these were the eyes of his mother. But Jake's nose was clearly his most striking feature, slightly crooked with a boney bump across its bridge. She made a mental note to learn the story that made it that way.

Hope had not appreciated or even thought about the work it took to build the home her father built after he and her mother married. She was born many years later. That was fifteen years ago. She admired the tenacity of Henry and the boys as they towed stones up from the river and placed them carefully to build her a small hearth and chimney. They had even found a large flat rock to make her stoop -- one she could sit on to watch the sunset and the stars. The last project was the door, or so she thought.

Early one morning, Henry finally gave the okay for Hope to enter her new home. He held her left arm to walk the short distance. As they approached the door, he put his arm around her waist to help her up the stoop. There were two windows across from each other not far from the fireplace, just like in his own place. This let in enough light so that she could see the whole room. Henry was still holding her, his arm around her waist. "Now, thar's jest one more thang I'm agonna do fer ya," he said softly. "Gonna be a surprise n' I'll brang it this evenin'."

The boys ran in carrying a log stump. "Here's yer first chair!" they exclaimed, bursting with pride as they helped her sit in front of her hearth. "We'll git yer far started in a few. Jest set here fer awhiles n' enjoy yer new place," Jake said.

Hope took a deep breath, savoring the breeze that flowed from her door to the window. She then used her crutch to go outside and sit on her stoop, taking in the view of the field that surrounded what was now her home. She could even see the corn crop growing in the far field. It would be ready to harvest about the next full moon. The sun was setting as the boys came in with flint, a striker, kindling, and some logs to get her fire started.

Against the red and yellow hues of the sun, she saw a tall shadow, recognizing it was Henry walking toward her, carrying several short boards. He nodded his head to her with a smile, as he stepped around her to go inside. "Don't look yet!" he said. She heard some hammering and scraping of boards near the wall at the far end of the room. "Not yet," he said, stepping back outside.

Then he returned carrying what looked like a large pillow. Matilda followed carrying a blanket. "Matilda helped me make ya a straw-stuffed pallet fer yer bed," he said. They walked past her, then he returned to help her stand up from the stoop. "Come on in," he said. "I made ya a comf'terble bed - with Matilda's help, of course."

Hope couldn't believe her eyes. There was a bed, raised on legs sitting about a foot off the floor. It was the size of Matilda's bed, only quite a bit wider.

Hope took great pride in her new home and the Greer family thoughtfully gave her privacy, not entering without Hope's invitation. Henry built her a small table, Matilda gave her an iron pot and a wooden spoon, so she was now able to heat mush and make cornbread for breakfast by placing her carefully shaped cornmeal patties on a rock inside the hearth. As a housewarming gift, Matilda gave Hope Sarah's Bible. Thereafter, Hope spent each morning reading the Bible, and giving thanks to the Lord for her many blessings.

In return for their gifts, Hope insisted on doing all the mending for Henry, Matilda, and the boys. She would spend the day mending, taking the repaired clothes over to their place when she joined them for supper. She also began gathering scraps from worn out clothes to make a quilt. She only had one piece of clothing that was her own, and that was her short gown. Matilda burned all the other clothing saying it was too stained, insisting it was best to let the bad times burn and turn to ashes.

Most evenings, Henry would linger at the supper table while Matilda and the boys went to the river to wash the pots and plates. He relished this time with Hope, savoring her stories about her childhood, and her horse Isaiah. She always stopped her story with that fire-filled, smoky evening when she and Isaiah managed to escape the horror of the Indian attack. When asked how she was separated from Isaiah, she held back tears, sometimes breaking into sobbing, unable to stop for many minutes. Henry soon learned to avoid asking about Isaiah.

And Hope listened to Henry's stories about meeting and marrying Sarah, the birth of the boys, and was careful not to ask about Sarah's illness and death. Over the days and weeks, she began to look forward to each evening, and especially enjoyed the nights when Henry played his fiddle. Sometimes they would sit outside on her stoop while he played, increasingly making melodies she had never heard. His stringed tunes were often soft and soothing, and as each evening passed, she wanted to linger longer, feeling closer to him as the music seemed to pour from his heart.

One evening Henry stood to face Hope, playing her favorite of his original tunes. She was captivated, her heart filled with a joy she had not experienced. Suddenly, Henry stopped, set his fiddle on the ground, and knelt before her. "Miss Hope," he said. "We've gotten close over th' past many weeks, n' I confess I feel closer to ya ever' day. So close, in fact, that I can't think 'bout a fall, n' then a winter, n' a spring -- or anytime ever, without ya close to me." he paused taking both her hands in his. "Preacher Jonas is comin' fer supper tomorrow n' well, I think it's time we get married."

Hope was silent. Since she came to the Greers' homestead, she had not seen any people other than Henry, Matilda, and the boys. And, she loved the boys. They were like angels to her, just as Matilda had become like a mother. This was her new -- and perhaps her only family. This tall, thin, yellow-haired man was now her closest companion. His sky-blue eyes held a captivating, pleading look as he squeezed her hands, signaling for an answer.

"I will marry you Henry Greer," she said smiling. Henry held her hands tighter and pulled her up to him, kissing her hard. "That hurt!" snapped Hope. "If we marry, promise you'll never hurt me ever! Not ever in any way whatsoever! You are a kind man and I only want to marry your gentle side."

"Okay n' I promise," said Henry, pulling her close and holding her tightly, but not too tight.

The next morning Matilda found Hope reading the Bible and crying. Matilda placed her arm around her and hugged her gently. "Now, now," Matilda whispered. "This here's a happy day. Yer gonna be me daughter n' I know ya's gonna make me Henry very happy. N', in time, ya'll be laughin' more'n cryin'. Ya'll have a child of yer own. A baby brother or sister for Jared n' Jake. N' that child will be yer best friend fer'er," Matilda said. "Now! I've had th' boys build a far n' fill the wash tub so ya kin get cleaned up if ya want. Yer gonna be a beautiful bride."

Hope stepped out to see two sheets and a quilt blowing in the wind. They had been strung across a rope surrounding the wash tub. She was now able to step between the draped sheets and into the tub. Four daisies were floating in the water.

"Them four flowers is from each of us Greers," Matilda said standing several steps away from the tub. "I'm brangin' ya a dress I wore when I married Henry's father. I wuz 'bout yer size back then. Take yer time n' enjoy yer bath. Preacher Jonas won't be here til much later today n' I'm makin' a special meal of fresh trout th' boys caught in th' river early this mornin'. After they brought th' fish, I packed 'em a snack n' chased Henry n' th' boys back to th' river. They's been told to stay away until they hear Jonas a comin'. Henry has his clothes n' he's gonna bathe in th' river so's he kin make a clean husband fer ya. Lord knows it's been many moons since that man took time to clean hisself."

After Hope indulged herself in the large wooden tub, Matilda brought her a bucket of clean water and helped her rinse her hair. It had grown to her waist and Hope took pride in its bright flaming color, tossing it forward and taking advantage of the noon sun to use her fingers to comb it dry until it was silky and smooth. Inside her home, she saw Matilda's beautiful dress laid across the bed. Hope lingered, staring at the bed wondering what the night would bring. Her own mother had been a distant woman, keeping to herself most of each day, focused completely on her chores and only giving Hope time enough to teach her how to sew. Hope's father spent most of his free evenings and Sundays with Hope telling her stories about his Irish homeland, their farms, and insisting she learn proper English as it was taught to him when his family first came to this country. He spent very little time with her mother, saying, "Your mother prefers to be on her own." So Hope knew nothing about what happened between a husband and wife, except that their time together could somehow create a baby. So, she figured, her mother and father had been together that way at least once.

Matilda came to the door to let her know that Preacher Jonas had arrived. "Henry took Jonas o'er yonder past th' cornfield hopin' to find a ripe watermelon fer dessert," said Matilda. "Here, let me tie th' back of that dress fer ya. My! My! Ya's such a beauty! That hair, them large green eyes, n' that turned up nose. Matilda paused, lifting Hope's hair to place gently over the back of the dress. "Now ya stay here til we's ready for th' wedding." Hope sat on her stool by the table, and took her Bible, holding it close to her chest.

Soon, with another familiar knock on the door, Matilda entered. "It's time," she said, taking Hope by the hand and leading her outside. "This here's Preacher Jonas," Matilda said. Preacher Jonas took Hope's hand to greet her and gently held her arm, "I'll help ya walk that way," Jonas said, "As I hear yer leg might still be troublin' ya a lil." Hope took a deep breath and clasped Sarah's Bible tightly with her right hand.

Preacher Jonas slowly led Hope toward Henry who was standing by the oak tree at the path to the river. He helped her turn to take her place by Henry's side. Henry took her hand and Jonas stepped to the front centered between them. Matilda stepped to Hope's left side and placed a bouquet of cut daisies on Sarah's Bible. Jared and Jake stood to Henry's right. "What a beautiful family ya is. A sight to behold indeed," said Jonas as he opened his Bible. "I come fer supper, but am honored to join this man n' woman in marriage. I'll post th' notice of yer marriage when I get back to town day after next." Looking to Henry, he said, "A man shall provide for his family to keep them fed n' provide them shelter, as I can see ya done well, Henry. Henry, do ya agree to provide for yer family?" Henry nodded and said, "I agree." Opening to a marked page in the Bible, looking to Hope, Jonas read "Wives, submit to yer own husbands, as to th' Lord. For th' husband is th' head of th ' wife even as Christ is th' head of th' church, his body, n' is himself its Savior. Now as the' church submits to Christ, so also wives should submit in ever'thang to thar husbands," and then, looking up from the Bible he said to Hope, "Hope, do ya agree to this vow?" Holding her Bible tightly, Hope nodded first to Preacher Jonas, then to Henry. Jonas continued,

"Wherefore they's no more twain, but one flesh. What therefore God hath joined together, let not man put asunder. Henry n' Hope, ya is now wed."

Henry leaned over, placed his hands on Hope's face, pulled it to him and kissed her gently on the lips. "My, my that's th' sweetest taste I ever had!" He then stepped back nodding to all. "But I'm starvin'," he said. "Let's git to eatin' some of that fresh trout I smell cookin' o'er th' fire." He grabbed Hope around her waist and led her to the table in what was now Matilda's home. Preacher Jonas, Matilda, and the boys followed. "I've saved us some of th' cider we drank last time you wuz here Preacher Jonas. N' if ya git to feeling light-headed, they's an extra bed here, if ya want to stay th' night, as I'll be settlin in wit' Hope here n' makin' her home me own beginnin' tonight," Henry grinned.

Hope sat quietly listening to Jonas and Henry telling tales and watching them toast each with the cider. Henry looked to her, handing her his cup of cider. "Hope, ya only ate few bites of th' trout n' a little helpin' of Matilda's sweet potato pie. Ya need to drink some of this cider t' help us celebrate our gittin hitched." Hope took a sip of the cider and pursed her mouth as it burned on the way down her throat. "Here, take another sip," Henry said, "The more ya drink, the less it burns!" After a few more sips, Hope grinned. "It's making me feel warm and my leg's not hurting now," Hope giggled.

Preacher Jonas and Henry kept telling tales while Hope watched and listened, giggling as she sipped more cider. Matilda took the boys to the river to wash the dishes. There was a big thunk as Jonas' head hit the table. "Guess he's sleepy. It's been a long day fer him n' it's 'bout time we went t' bed ourselves," Henry grinned, lifting Hope up off the bench and carrying her in his arms toward the open door of what he now considered his home. "I'mma gonna carry ya across th' stoop as it's tradition fer good luck once ya git hitched," he said, stumbling and nearly tripping up the stoop into the doorway. He carried her over to the bed and set her down, then leaned around her back to untie her dress and pull it over her head. "Just relax my dear, I'll be gentle," he said as he removed his shoes and pants. He pushed her gently back onto the bed and began kissing her first on her lips, then he pulled her shift over her head and began kissing her breasts. Hope had never felt the warmth that flowed through her body as he kissed her. She guessed it was the cider that was making her feel so warm and light-headed. He took off his shirt, slid out of his pants, and gently pressed his hairy chest against hers. His hands moved between her legs and he placed himself inside her, moving back and forth for just a few moments, then with a heavy sigh, he squeezed her tight, and uttered, "Ahhhhh!" Then the snoring began as she realized he was sound asleep on top of her.

Over the next few weeks, Henry and Hope worked together to make their home more comfortable, preparing for winter. He made frames for two rocking chairs. Hope weaved ribbons of bark to make the back and seats. As the nights got cooler, Henry would add birch to the fire to make it dance with different colors while he created new tunes on his fiddle. Hope enjoyed putting words to his tunes as they sat rocking in front of the fire. More and more often the evenings ended with rocking chairs abandoned in favor of cuddling in their bed, and touching each other in the places that gave pleasure.

Hope was always the first one up in the morning, making coffee, and stepping outside to watch the sun rise. This morning, she smiled, taking a deep breath of cool air, damp with dew. She could now see several mountain ranges beyond their valley. As the warm days turned cooler, the mountains had been painted with many colors and the sunrises were bright reds, purples, and oranges popping against the crisp blue sky. Now, the trees were bare, opening up to reveal vistas that had previously been lush with green. She closed her eyes embracing the wind as it blew her hair across her eyes. Brushing back the strands, she thought fondly of the months that had passed here in her new home. Many colors flashed through her mind. Though she was inspired by God's colorful work throughout the fall, the field of blue flax was her favorite. The blue field, large and lush when she first arrived, reminded her of the fields at home. Those home fields were burning when she and Isaiah fled. But once she had been able to go outside in this new home, she embraced the sense of calm the flax gave her as it moved slowly back and forth, making waves with the winds of the valley. Now the field was barren.

She had watched from Matilda's stoop as Henry, Matilda, and the boys harvested the flax during her first few weeks at their home. They had tied about half of the flax into sheaves and stacked it in stooks to dry and save for later use. The rest had then been retted near the spring where the creek met the river. This retting had taken about three weeks. They spent many more hours preparing the flax, twisting it and folding it in half being mindful to mark the root and blossom ends so that it could be used for weaving. The seeds were stored in a large gourd for use in baking. Matilda mentioned they might even have enough extra seed for Henry to sell when he went into town for supplies.

Hope cherished the flax, not just because it now provided food and clothing. She savored the memories it brought her. As early as she could remember, her father read to her, eventually teaching her how to read and write using the words from the Bible. It was from his readings that she first learned of flax and the ways of God's children. She must have been about six years old when her father took her into their home and showed her flax fibers laid out on a table. Taking ten strands of fiber into his hands, he taught her how to braid them and then weave a cradle, making a sling. He told her a sling had a longer range than a bow and this was what David had used to slay Goliath. From that time forward, her sling was always with her and she was constantly scouting for just the perfect rocks to stuff in her pocket alongside it. She taught herself how to knock squirrels out of trees and once had even slain a snake with her weapon. Unfortunately, her sling was lost when she tossed her clothing that fateful day she had tripped toward the river. In the past few months, she had set aside enough flax to make a new sling for herself. It was now in her pocket. Today, she planned to weave two more slings for the boys' Christmas presents.

She was so caught up in the sunrise, her memories of her father and the flax, she didn't see Matilda approaching her at the stoop as she often did for morning coffee. "Yer almost back to normal, I reckon," Matilda whispered, gently taking Hope's hand. "Let's walk down to th' chicken coop to gather some eggs. I wanna know how yer feelin' these days. We's always talkin' 'bout chores n' th' next task, but today I wanna talk 'bout you."

Hope stood up, wrapped her shawl tighter around her shoulders, pulled the hem of her shift toward her knees with one hand, and set her coffee down on the stoop with the other, "Okay. You know I don't like to talk about myself but since you asked, I'm definitely feeling stronger and my leg only hurts when I use my left foot first, like this," she said, stretching her left leg forward then rolling the balls of her feet forward, then using her heel and entire foot to move her forward. "I know I have to keep moving it this way, and I try to push by the pain. That's the only way my leg will get stronger. My left leg is definitely thinner than my right leg because I haven't used it as much as I should, but I'll try to do better."

Matilda let go of Hope's hand and walked slowly alongside Hope, so she could move using her own strength. "Well, how ya feelin' elsewhar? Yer lookin' purtier ever' day. Is yer tummy okay? Ya feeling a bit light-headed now n' then?"

"Well, I've been more tired and sleepy than I used to be, but I know that's just because I'm healing from my injuries," said Hope.

"Ya seems to have gained some weight lately. Aint yer shift gittin' tighter?" asked Matilda.

"Yes, I think I am a bit fatter. You're a great cook, and I appreciate how you've been showing me how to make some of Henry's favorite dishes. He really loves your pies."

They had reached the chicken coop. Matilda gently grabbed Hope's arm to stop her from opening the gate. She turned to Hope, placing both arms around her, giving her a big hug. "Yer like me own daughter, ya know. N' I'll always look out fer ya. But I's been noticin' little things ya may not have realized. I see ya different from how ya see yerself, I reckon," Matilda took a breath. "Hope, it's time ya told Henry ya's with child. Ya's fixin' to have a baby!"

Hope stumbled back a bit, grabbing the coop's fence to catch herself. "Oh my! I didn't know. What makes you think that? What? I knew that women sometimes got pregnant after they married, but I, well I… my mother never told me how or how to know. I was close to my father and he would never tell me anything except to stay away from boys. I know Jesus' mother was with child, but that was God's son. Oh my!" Hope exclaimed.

"Let's go sit on that rock under th' trees," Matilda said, now leading Hope by the hand and helping her to ease down on the big rock across from the chicken coop. "Hope, I'll jest get to it. When ye n' Henry sleep together, but don't sleep before ya connect with each other, ya could be makin' a baby," Matilda said. "Have ye n' Henry been connectin' that way?" Hope nodded. "N' sometimes he leaves behind a lot of wetness?" Hope nodded. "That wetness carries seeds that makes babies. So when'er that wetness stays inside ye, th' seed kin attach itself n' grow to make a baby."

"A baby! Henry's child! The boys are going to have a sister or brother?" asked Hope. Matilda nodded.

"I don't know what to do! What do I do?"

Matilda went on to explain, "When ya were at yer homeplace, did ya see neighbor women get fatter wit' babies inside 'em?"

"I saw one who looked bigger every time I saw her. She lived down the road apiece. And then about a year later, I saw her with a baby. Oh my!" Hope's eyes got wider as she looked out to the mountains as if she could see the woman in her mind. Then she looked back at Matilda. "So, I'm going to get that fat?"

"Yep. Yer gonna git much fatter after Christmas, after several snowfalls, n' then when it starts to git warmer, one day in th' spring you'll feel a rush of water down yer legs, n' ya'll get terrible crampin' between yer legs. Then th' baby will come. Don't worry, I'll be here ever' minute along th' way. I helped Sarah, n' now I'll help ya ever' day as th' baby grows until th' day ya bear me grandbaby. Then I'll help ya raise it to be as sweet as Jake n' Jared." Matilda paused and took both of Hope's hands, looking straight into her eyes. "Now, when ya gonna tell Henry yer havin' his child?"

Hope stared again at the far off mountain ranges, then stood and wiped her shift, moving both hands back and forth lightly across her tummy. She walked to the coop, opened the gate, stepped in, and began gathering eggs, making a cradle out of her shawl to hold them. "I guess I'll fix him a special breakfast before he does his chores."

Henry was returning from the small shed where he took his morning ritual when he saw the two women walking toward the house. Hope was doing well, he thought. She could now manage many outdoor chores on her own. He saw the eggs in her shawl. "I betcha we're gonna have a mighty fine breakfast this mornin'," he shouted.

"You betcha! And I've got news!" Hope screamed.

Henry took the news with great glee. The thought of a new child in his life gave him boundless energy. As the months passed, he made preparations for his growing family, slaying two hogs and putting them up in the smokehouse. He and the boys cut trees, then used his saw to cut the logs into boards to build a plank floor. Despite several hard snowstorms, he had also managed to fell two oak trees, which he cut, dried inside by the fire, then scraped and whittled to make a smooth surface to craft the baby's cradle.

He took great pleasure in patting Hope's growing tummy and in the evenings, he snuggled closely with his ears to her belly, listening for the baby's heartbeat, jumping back with a shout when the baby kicked up hitting his ear. "It's gonna be a lively, fair-haired lil one fer sure! Or, it'll be a purty ginger-haired girl like 'er momma, or a fair-skinned boy like its brothers!" he would say. "Ever' one of us here gits freckled in th' summer, but none as much as Jared," he would say. He counted back to the day of the wedding. It had been fall, so he expected the baby to come in early summer. He hoped it wouldn't be too hot on the blessed day his child would come.

Matilda and Hope spent many days gathering the last of the potatoes, onions, beets, and carrots and storing them in the root cellar. Both cabins held up well throughout the winter. At Christmas, Hope gave the boys their slings and met them outside on warmer days to teach them her tricks, whipping the sling round their heads til the force was strong enough to throw the rocks they had carefully gathered under her guidance. The rough winter finally faded into warmer mornings, harsh winds bringing rain instead of snow. Hope could again take pleasure in the sunrises as she sat outside on the rock where she had first learned the ways of baby-making from Matilda. The buds on the trees were turning into leaves and the dogwood tree revealed blossoms signaling spring was here. The dogwood blooms reminded Hope a year had passed since her fifteenth birthday. She was now sixteen.

Her leg was now completely healed and that was good as her tummy had grown so large she could no longer see her feet. She had borrowed Matilda's moccasins to make it easier to slip into something to protect her feet from the occasional stone in the path to the chicken coop. The boys were so excited about the new baby brother or sister to come that they doted on Hope, often skipping in front of her to inspect her path to ensure there were no obstacles that would cause her to stumble.

Today she woke much earlier than usual, feeling a burst of energy like she never had before. She made coffee, set the table, stoked the fire adding some logs, and started heating some porridge, aiming to have everything done before Henry was up and about. She went outside, gathered some sticks and added logs to start a fire in the rock pit, filled a large kettle with water and set it to boil so she could heat rags to scrub the table after breakfast. Now, being extra hungry, she headed down the hill, past the barn, to the chicken coop to gather some eggs. As she unlatched the coop's gate, she felt a sharp pain beneath her large belly.

Suddenly her legs were soaked with rushing warm water and the moccasins on her feet were wet. She stepped aside to see a puddle of water where she had stood. She rubbed her belly to reassure the baby and calm the pain. When the pain passed, she waddled over to the coop, grabbed eight eggs, stuck them in her pockets, and headed back toward the gate. Another pain hit her so hard she screamed. *It must be time,* she thought, recalling the stories Matilda had told her about when babies decide to enter the world. She grabbed the gatepost to steady herself and headed back toward the house. Another pain hit her hard. She could hardly breathe. The pain left long enough for her to make it to the nearby rock where she and Matilda had spent many a day planning for this moment. Their plans had always anticipated this event to occur inside, where all the supplies were readied. She eased herself to sit on the rock, to rest a moment before going forward. An even sharper pain surged through her lower body causing her to emit a loud grunting shout until it stopped. She knew she was supposed to count between pains, but she was too frightened to remember how many counts there were as the pain kept coming. Matilda had said it could take half a day or more for the baby to come, so Hope knew she had time to get back to the house. But each time she mustered the energy to stand, another pain would come. She was now squatting on the grass beside the rock. Her screams were getting louder with each new pain, disturbing the livestock. Goats began to panic, bleating loudly, the hogs started squealing, and then Henry's horse began whinnying and stomping his hooves.

Matilda was now up, sipping her coffee. She opened her door and stepped outside to see the sunrise. It was then she noticed the fire on the pit and heard the animals making noises like they never made in the morning. Henry's door was open. Matilda walked over peeked inside to see if Hope was up. Henry was in bed, snoring loudly. She then heard a scream coming from the chicken coop, ran back to her place, and yelled at the doorway, "Boys. Git up n' come running! Hope's in trouble!"

They ran down the path and saw Hope kneeling on the grass, trying to catch her breath. Matilda grabbed Hope's shoulders, settling her on the grass and propping her feet flat on the ground, knees up. She pulled up Hope's shift to check between her legs, then shouted. "Hope's fixin' to have a baby! Run boys!! Thar's a kettle on th' farpit! Stir th' far, add logs to make it blue-blazing hot!! When th' water's a boilin', put rags in n' brang 'em to me when they's scalded! N' brang me a knife!" she screamed. "Oh, n' wake Henry! Tell him his baby's a'comin!"

Matilda was pulling the baby out from between Hope's legs when Henry arrived. "Jake gimme th' knife!" Matilda took the knife, slowly wiped it with one of the hot rags, then cut the cord that connected Hope and the baby. She then tied the short end in a tight knot close to Hope's belly, then laying the baby on Hope's chest, Matilda quickly took the other end of the cord, cut it, and tied it close to the baby's belly, tossing the extra piece aside.

"It's a boy!" Henry exclaimed. "Give him to me!" Matilda handed him the baby. Henry held him up toward the sun. "Another boy. I'm so blessed. I can't believe his eyes is brown n' his hair's so dark, but that'll change when he gits older," he whispered, pulling the baby toward him to stroke the baby's fuzzy head.

"All babies' eyes n' hair change color o'er time," Matilda said, trying to hide the doubt in her voice.

Henry handed the boy back to Hope. "He's gittin' hungry!" Hope held the boy tightly as Matilda and Henry helped her stand, wrapping their arms around her waist to walk her back to the house. They propped her up with the feather-packed pillows on the bed and watched as she began nursing the newborn.

"Jeremiah," whispered Hope. "His name's Jeremiah, a strong servant of God," she said, looking to Henry to seek his agreement. "Jeremiah held God close through terrible times, staying strong to tell his story, setting an example for God's people who lived after him."

"Jeremiah's a good name," agreed Henry. "Let's call him Jeremiah Henry Greer. He'll be a wise man fer sure n' even a good farmer." Henry reached out to touch the newborn. "Jeremiah, me son."

Jeremiah was a good baby, sleeping many hours in his cradle, only crying when he was hungry or needing cleaning. Hope spent most of her time inside, tending to his needs and preparing meals while Matilda, Henry, and the boys spent most days plowing and setting the gardens that would feed them in the fall and winter.

On warmer days, Hope would take Jeremiah down the hill, past the barn, to the rock near the chicken coop and nurse him as she watched the others tend the crops. From the rock, she could see the fields of flax and she took special pleasure in watching the flax grow into a field of blue haze. Jeremiah had been born by this rock and it was now a special place where she would take him whenever they could spend time outside. The boys would run by teasing her, calling it "Hope's Rock". Now, whenever they were headed outside, she would tell Jeremiah gleefully, "We're going to Hope's Rock where you were born. It was a painful time then, but now it's a special place I will always hold dear."

This particular summer the orchard was bursting with apples. Some afternoons, Hope would leave Jeremiah in the kitchen with Matilda and join Henry and the boys in the orchard to help them pull the apples from the trees. Soon there were more apples than they could possibly eat, and Matilda complained. "I made enough applesauce to last til spring. Yer gonna have to let 'em rot or find some other use fer 'em."

This was music to Henry's ears. He took the extra apples and put them in barrels near the firepit, then spent many evenings teaching the boys how to smash the apples in the kettle, then strain the contents into jugs to make cider. There was so much cider in the kettle, he rode to the Watauga settlement to get more jugs.

Fall came quickly and soon the flax was harvested, retted, and rendered into bundles of fibers for weaving. Matilda was planning to weave more clothes for Jeremiah, whom she adored. Jeremiah could now sit on his own, and he soon began crawling. Hope was grateful Henry had laid the wood floors and she took care to keep them scrubbed clean, carefully rubbing every inch to ensure there were no splinters.

Every now and then, Henry would come in, pick Jeremiah up off the floor, raise him above his head, and exclaim, "Me son's hair gits longer n' blacker ever' day! He don't look like any of us!"

As winter closed in, Henry spent more time inside, growing anxious about Jeremiah's appearance. He talked with Matilda asking about the boy's birth and timing. "I married Hope in th' fall, but Jeremiah wuz born in th' spring! Wuz he early? Ain't he a big boy to be born so early?"

Henry's rage grew each day as he watched the boy grow. His muscles ached from the mounting tension. He felt no love for this child -- only resentment. Still, he was conflicted, as he had loved this woman who gave birth in the spring. Yet his mind was totally consumed with Jeremiah's hair and skin color and the possibility that she had deceived him. He would show her he was no fool.

Henry found more and more reasons to ride out in the mornings, citing ideas about trading furs from the bears he had killed when the leaves began to fall from the trees. He had skinned the bears, hung their meat in the smokehouse to cure, then carefully cleaned their hide to prepare the furs for market. As the days grew colder, he would be gone for several nights, returning smelling of whiskey and falling into bed without a word. Other days, he would wake up late in the morning, complaining of a headache, and yell at Hope for no reason at all. At mealtime, his eyes intensely narrowed as he studied the child, looking for signs that it might be his.

Christmas passed without much celebration as the boys, along with Matilda, found it useful to stay in their own home, away from the tension that was building between them whenever Henry was in one of his moods.

Hope did all she could to please Henry, but it was getting harder each day. She was happiest when he was off on another one of his trading missions. On those days, Matilda and the boys would go to Hope's cabin where the boys would sing and play games with Jeremiah while Hope and Matilda cooked a big supper.

Henry had been away for three nights in a row when he returned late one night and started banging on Hope's door, waking everyone. He threw the door open, and screamed, "Whar's that boy?" He slammed the door, lowered the beam to lock it, and turned to Hope, who was now shaking, standing between Henry and the baby. Henry staggered toward them, picked up the chair he had made for Hope just a year earlier, and threw it at them. Hope lunged between the chair and Jeremiah. The chair hit her hard causing a loud crunching noise on her left side, knocking her down. She quickly moved her right arm against the floor to pull herself over to Jeremiah and bring him toward her. Henry shook his fist, shouting angry words Hope had never heard before. "He ain't mine, is he! I married a harlot!" He turned, kicked the door, ripped off the beam, and stormed out.

As soon as he left, Hope scooted toward the table to pull herself up. The pain in the ribs on her left side was unbearable but this was no time to linger. She inched around the table toward the fireplace and picked up a rock and a shard of kindling. She pulled a loose nail from the broken chair, then hammered the nail through the shard at an angle across the door and frame to create a makeshift lock.

That night Henry slept in the barn cuddled close to his jug of cider which was now empty. The next morning he went to Matilda's and demanded he get his bed back. The boys were to get back to sleeping where they slept before Henry got married. He knew not to mess with his mother Matilda and said nothing about making her leave her room.

Matilda wept silently, retreating into her own thoughts. She had seen this before when Henry's father was alive. She had nursed her bruises and hidden them from her son, but she knew Henry had seen and heard the sounds of those terrible nights. As Henry grew older, she would keep her silence pretending not to notice the times her husband dragged her son out the door or shoved him into a wall with a strong anger for which she knew no cause.

After Henry married, she had said nothing when Sarah retreated to the barn to hide her tears after Henry's tirades. With his new bride, she had rightly believed he would be mindful to treat Hope well as long as she was carrying his child, but once the child was born, he had changed.

Matilda recalled the note her mother had left in her Bible warning her that this time would come and that it would be repeated. "Your husband, Henry's father, was known to be an angry man. Sons learn from their fathers' actions til that's how they think they should be. We become their property held by the strings of the past. They are puppetmasters who keep us close, keeping the strings connected, controlling us with their harsh words and brutal actions so we fear them and do their will. They pull the strings tighter while we do nothing because we fear the strings will be cut, taking away the ones we have nurtured and loved from birth." These were a mother's words seared into Matilda's heart, words she held close, words she could not yet share with Hope.

Days passed with Hope staying inside except when she needed to use the privy. She focused on Jeremiah, singing to him, reciting words from the Bible to find comfort.

Then late one night, Henry began pounding on Hope's door, yelling that he was fixin' to take the place apart if she didn't let him in, his gruff voice searing loudly through the night air. He lunged into the door, breaking the makeshift latch, and stormed in. Grabbing her by the arm, he twisted it to him, then threw her on the bed. "Ya's mine n' ya always will be!" he yelled waking Jeremiah who began crying loudly. "I know ya wuz with another'n afore me! That boy's his'n ain't it! I'll show ya what's mine!" Henry shouted, striking her across her breasts. Pulling his tights open with one hand and holding her down, he thrust his hard part into the place that once brought them mutual pleasure. Hope swallowed her will to scream so as not to alarm Jeremiah who was already screeching at the top of his lungs. When he finished, Henry went back to his bed next door.

As soon as he left, Hope began re-arranging the room. She moved Jeremiah's bed to the corner furthest from the fireplace. Then she moved her bed against wall between the fireplace and door. She next placed the table longways between the door and Jeremiah's bed. She prayed to God that this would create a barrier to protect her son.

The next two nights Hope kept the fire blazing to light her new location. She left the door unlatched so there would be no banging to wake her son. Henry found her bed's new location to his suiting, as he no longer had to navigate a path to his muse, especially when he drank too much cider.

Each night after Henry finished, she would stay still, listening for the other cabin door to close. As soon as she heard it close, Hope would pick up her apron and some clean rags, which she now kept at the head of her bed, along with her pockets. She tied the pockets around her waist, checked her pockets for her sling, then tiptoed over to her son's bed to ensure he was sleeping. Then she would quickly scoot out the door, closing it quickly, so as not to wake Jeremiah.

But by this time, Jeremiah had become so accustomed to hearing Henry's rage, he no longer cried, instead finding comfort by escaping into his own imaginary world and pretending to sleep until he was lost in his dreams.

She headed down the well-worn, moonlit path to the river. The river was her retreat, its path becoming a part of her, her bare feet carrying her every inch of the way without thinking. Once she reached the river's edge, she would squat down into the shallow water to rinse herself clean. She then dipped rags into the cold water, wringing them as she walked back inside to treat her bruises, sometimes placing them on her chest and stomach, where they stayed cooling her pain until she fell asleep.

Henry visited Hope whenever he felt the urge, yelling and pushing hard against the door, and even cracking it with his ax even though there was no bar latch to prevent his entry. But even though she did everything she could to ease his entry, she could not stop his rage. He often entered the room, grabbed whatever was within reach and threw it, yelling and threatening to kill Jeremiah. "I can't stand th' sight'a that ugly bastard child!"

He would hold her down, bruising her arms, and sometimes even hitting her in the stomach when he was finished. "Ha! Ya won't be havin' any of me babies if'n I kin help it!" he shouted as he hit her where he had just had his pleasure. "Yer a harlot. But yer my harlot as long as I live!"

On these nights, Hope found only restless sleep, her dreams filled with nightmares, the same nightmares that haunted her since the terrible day she had stopped to escape the heat of the sun. The nightmares were longer now, becoming more vivid, mixed with sounds of Henry's anger, his face gradually fading into the face of the dark-skinned one with the long black hair and ugly scar. That face, the intense dark eyes, would waken her and she would lie awake many hours, terrified in fear of going back to sleep, and even more fearful of seeing him again. Now, during her waking hours, she thought she recognized him in Jeremiah's eyes.

Chapter 8

Maska had become Dragging Canoe's shadow, listening to every word that came from this leader, modeling his moves, even mocking the way he stepped back with his left foot before he lurched forward on his right to throw his tomahawk. Maska would then throw his own tomahawk to the exact same target, then run to fetch the chief's tomahawk and bring it back to the tall, lean one. He listened to Dragging Canoe's every word, asking questions to garner knowledge of the chief warrior's thoughts and plans. Maska also cultivated friendship with Dragging Canoe's brothers, Little Owl and The Badger. He enlisted their advice and spent his alone time comparing the three men, thinking about their strengths and weaknesses, wishing to acquire the best qualities of each warrior.

During the day, whenever he was on his own, Maska would practice his warrior skills, sharpening his abilities with his tomahawk, his knife, and his bow. He nurtured Isaiah and rode his horse hard and fast so that the two became like one animal, moving quickly and deftly down the narrow trails, ducking low limbs, and jumping the felled logs that crossed their path.

After many months, he gained Dragging Canoe's confidence and joined the leader's warriors on the long rides into the white man's settlements. During attacks, he proudly demonstrated his practiced skills riding alongside his hero as they encountered settlers struggling to escape.

Riding fast, and often ahead of his brothers, he would get within inches of a fleeing victim, grab them, pull them up to his side, slice their throat, then drop them to the ground as he rode fast to grab the next one, and another one after that, always staying on his horse, and not stopping until there were no more white men in sight. His name, Maska, the Strong One, became known throughout the village, as stories of his conquests were repeated at campfire gatherings at the Amoyeli Egwa base.

Dragging Canoe was determined to take back the land the white settlers had claimed. His target was vast. He sent his scouts out to many areas west and east, sending them west across the valleys and east into mountains to evaluate potential targets and report back to him with details of each site and its white people. He then spent many nights in the Amoyeli Egwa camp strategizing how to launch simultaneous attacks in multiple areas.

On this night, Dragging Canoe took a puff from his pipe and handed it to Maska. "With this smoke, our prayers go up to the Creator. We pray for peace, but the white man still attacks our people. I pray we do not lose any more lives to the white man's guns. My father Attakullakulla is our Chief of Peace. He says we are brothers of the white man as we are all children of the same Creator. He makes treaties to lease our land and trades our deer hides for copper and brass kettles. But the white man is never satisfied. He rapes our women, kills our children, and then destroys our villages, sparing only our cattle for his own food."

Maska nodded, took a puff, and handed the pipe back to his leader. He looked straight into Dragging Canoe's eyes, pretending to listen, but deep in his own thoughts. *I have learned from this leader but we have lost too much too often. I must follow my own spirit. Tomorrow I go my own way.*

Maska had proved he could work well with large parties of warriors, using his knife skills, but also mastering the power of the musket which was becoming a weapon of choice for many of his brothers. But the musket's fire always broke the silence. A silence he enjoyed. A useful silence that allowed victory.

He was now headed northeast, past the Watauga settlement that had successfully fought Dragging Canoe's multiple attacks. He would leave the State of Franklin to his capable brothers. They could fight the big battles. But alone he would never lose to the white man.

Maska employed solitude to drive his anger. He enjoyed breaking away to find the smaller settlements, and sneaking in under the cover of darkness to burn the white man's homes, forcing the women, men and children to run for their lives. He indulged his passion, hunting them down one-by-one, leaving a trail of slain white men, children, and women behind him. For Maska, this remained revenge for the burning of his home, a revenge which helped to soothe the pain of that night he had fled, never to return to the life and family he cherished -- the night that left him filled with an empty anger that grew greater with each day's rising sun.

He was determined to burn every village in his way, destroy every home, and take the scalp of every white man that dared to challenge his knife. One by one.

Chapter 9

1780

It was now three years since the dogwoods had signaled Jeremiah's birth. Hope was careful to only go out when Henry was in the fields or away with his horse. She had found a loose rock at the foundation footing in the back of the cabin and pulled it out to make a safe place for things she wanted to keep from Henry. Over time, she had loosened several rocks and created extra safe holes for things she needed to hide.

On a few early mornings before the sun rose, Hope went from the river to the chicken coop to gather loose feathers which she then stashed in her safe rock holes. When Jeremiah grew too big for his cradle, she pulled out all the feathers to make him a mattress tucked into the corner furthest from her bed. Jeremiah could still hear Henry's rage whenever he came in, but at least he could cover his head with his blanket and bury his face in the feather mattress to block out the terror. Jeremiah knew his mother was hurt by Henry's visits, but this is all he knew. He had observed these night visits since before he could walk. This was a normal life from Jeremiah's experience and he did not know to question it.

Late one summer day when Henry had ridden down the trail, Hope took flax from her safe hole and braided it to make a sling for Jeremiah. When she gave it to him, she told him the stories of her father and the special times when they went into the woods to practice. "Each time we ventured out, your grandfather would pick a different tree as our target. Sometimes we would come across a rabbit or a squirrel, and he would challenge me to hit the unlucky animal so we could have it for supper."

When Hope and Jeremiah could safely go outside, she taught him in the same way her father had taught her. She showed him how to find the best rocks to use with the sling. On days when Henry was out in the fields, she would sneak Jeremiah to the back corner of the house, so she could keep an eye on Henry's whereabouts. There, she taught Jeremiah how to use the sling. He took great pleasure in shooting at the squirrels that darted around the yard. But since he was only knee high to his mother, the squirrels did not feel threatened. They just scurried higher up the trees when a rock bounced their way.

But Hope also used this time to master her own slinging skills. Whenever Jeremiah grew tired of swinging his sling, Hope would show him what could be his ultimate goal, slinging rock after rock at a large, lumpy round burl high up on a sycamore tree located as far away as she could clearly see. She rarely missed, as in her mind's eye, this distant tree represented Henry. The burl was his head. She sometimes felt guilty for making Henry her target, as it went against everything she had been taught: "Thou Shalt Not Kill." But she also thought of David and Goliath. Henry was her Goliath and surely God understood her pain, her fear, and even the anger she released whenever she whirled a stone into the tree. Over time, the burl looked like it had eyes and ears, as the whirled stones had chipped away pieces of bark leaving dents that marked her repeated success.

With Jeremiah, Hope had become a quiet teacher. He alone made her feel whole and worth living.

Whenever Henry was near, she wished to be invisible. Now, on the nights he sought his pleasure, she made sure there were only embers in the hearth with no fire to light his way. Henry's hands were his only sight and in her own mind, she was now a master of invisibility when he was around. The darkness helped. In these moments, she didn't exist. It was only her body, after all; and she vowed Henry would never control her mind.

Many of God's chosen had fought for their survival, even with God's blessing. And simply surviving became a greater need with each passing day. She had no intention of raising Jeremiah to be a man who lived in fear. With God's help, she found the strength to endure Henry's terror. Still, she had begun thinking of whether she could save Jeremiah from this horror. She worried he would grow up to be like Henry as this was the only father he knew.

"Thy word is a lamp unto my feet, and a light unto my path." she prayed, not knowing if a path would ever be revealed unto her. Henry had carefully created her world, one without knowledge of a path beyond the farm, without knowledge of life beyond what he had shown her. For now, he was in control, having built an invisible fence beyond which she could not escape. She struggled to retain the happy memories of life before the raging fire that drove her away from that happiness and into this place that was dark even when the sun was shining. "A lamp unto my feet, a light unto my path," she prayed again, passionately pleading for guidance, praying constantly just to keep her mind open to the slightest chance her prayers would be answered. But in this moment, she did not feel among God's chosen.

Jared was now sixteen and Jake was fifteen. They had watched as their papa became increasingly vicious, calling Hope his harlot and ranting about that boy who looked just like an Indian child. They made it a point to stay in their bed whenever Henry went next door to release his rage with the verbal and physical assaults they would hear through the walls.

After many beatings for the slightest misstep or overlooked chore, they did all they could to avoid Henry's rage and grew increasingly skilled at anticipating his wishes. They slept in their breeches so they wouldn't need to dress when morning came. Each morning, sunlight pierced through the tiny hole they had poked through the mud wall by their bed to signal dawn's arrival. At the first sign of light, they rolled out of bed and rushed out to begin their chores before he was fully awake. Still, they weren't always successful at anticipating his will, and Henry's vicious temper seemed to intensify for no reason at all.

Matilda also continued to keep her distance from Hope's cabin when Henry was around, only visiting Hope and Jeremiah when Henry was away, taking them extra food and supplies whenever she could. She felt sad for Hope, but could not find the words to admit that Henry's behavior was something she had seen before. Hope was now completely controlled by Henry, having had no contact with anyone other than those in his family. Matilda and the boys lived their lives cautiously, keeping their time with Hope a secret from the man who held the strings of her very being and treated her like his toy, his puppet, controlling her every move.

Hope had been with the Greers almost four years. In her mind's eye, this fragile life was probably typical for other married women her age. Her only reference to marriage was what she had seen in her parents and she had rarely seen them together, except at supper time. Now, each day was filled with fear of if -- or when -- Henry would turn up to lash out at her. But as a mother, she relied on the inner strength God provided her in order to protect her son, Jeremiah. It was the need to provide for

Jeremiah, and fear of the unknown world beyond the farm that kept her from fleeing. Sometimes she would let her mind wander to picture what life was like beyond the fields of flax and corn. But these daydreams would quickly revert to reality knowing that if she took Jeremiah with her, Henry would find them, and bring them back to face an unimaginable wrath. In that case, death would be a blessing.

So, Hope continued to turn to her Bible to maintain her composure, finding familiar words and stories to focus on. During the day, she pressed her mind to recall stories of those who had suffered and survived evil persecutors before Jesus was born. She began sharing these stories and reading the Bible aloud to Jeremiah. As he grew, she would point out different words, spelling them aloud. By the time he was four, she had taught him him to use slices of charcoal to write the letters that spelled his name. He loved to practice his letters and there were marks everywhere -- on the walls and even on the wood floor near his bed. Hope created a game for Jeremiah to see if he could make new words from his name. Each morning as soon as he was awake, he would study his name to find a new word. "Mother, is 'ere' a word?"

"No Jeremiah, try using the 'h'." He loved this new word game, and became obsessed with his letters, soon roughly forming words like 'he, me, him, ham' and writing them wherever he could reach an empty surface.

His favorite Bible verse was one he asked his mother to repeat almost every day. Jeremiah 17:7. "Blessed is the man that trusteth in the Lord. For he shall be as a tree planted by the waters, and that spreadeth out her roots by the river."

"Me wanna be strong like a tree by the river," he said.

And she thought, *Me too. I will be the strong tree for you little one. I have no choice.*

Chapter 10

Hope cherished her early mornings at the river. It was the only time she had completely to herself while Jeremiah slept soundly in his feather bed. Even when Henry hadn't disrupted her space, she would wake, tie her apron and pockets on over her shift, stuff rags in her pockets, grab the wash bucket, and head toward the river. If she didn't need to wash herself, she would still wet the rags, fill the bucket with fresh water, and bring them back inside. After a breakfast of mush and corn cakes, she would take a damp rag and wipe Jeremiah's face even when he didn't need it. This was his sign to wake up and help her by doing his daily chores of taking the plates to the wash bucket to rinse them, then dry them and put them back on the table ready for suppertime.

After rinsing and wringing her rags this morning, she climbed up onto the rock above the swimming hole where she had been rescued by Henry's sons. From here she could see the water moving from the pool as it flowed across the staircase of rocks to create waterfalls that made coves for frolicking trout. She sat down and leaned back to savor God's creations. The morning's light streamed downward to form little stars bouncing off the river. The bouncing light was God's way of showing her He was with her and this was yet another new day. Here, she tightly closed her eyes to cleanse her mind to block out the terrors of Henry and reflect on God's word, count the good things in her life, and give thanks for Jeremiah, God's greatest gift to her. The dark-haired boy was a blessing that loved her completely. She thought of his way with letters and his drive to make new words just for her. He was the reason she stayed on Henry's farm, the reason she didn't dare run. Jeremiah was her sole purpose in life. Her greatest joy. She would endure any pain to protect him and she did her best to give him a happy home. A gentle breeze embraced her and she inhaled the fresh air. Then as she took another breath, the air signalled a change. She sniffed again to confirm a familiar odor. It was the smell of smoke coming from the cabins. *No one should be up stoking the fire,* she thought. And this smoky smell was far heavier than any that had come from there before.

She quickly leaped off the rock and landed in the water at the edge of the slick river bank. Digging her hands into the mud, she pulled herself up then grabbed tree limbs to bring herself up out of the water. Running up the hill, she saw what she feared. Matilda's home was engulfed in flames that were now leaping across the roof onto her own home. Jeremiah was in great danger inside. But she stopped at the edge of the trees at the top of the hill, taking in the sight ahead. Her heart raced as she saw a dark man running out Matilda's door. In his left hand was a large knife dripping blood. In his right hand was Henry's hair. "Oh my God!" She held back a scream as she realized the dark man was holding Henry's scalp. She prayed Jeremiah was still okay. "God help me! Save my son! Give me strength," she prayed as she reached into her pocket and pulled out her sling. In one swift movement, she placed a rock in its cup, swung the string around up over her head and thrust the rock forward. The dark man fell flat on his face.

She rushed past the dark man into her cabin, grabbed Jeremiah from his bed, and holding him tightly in her arms, ran back out, pausing only to pick up the dark man's knife which had bounced across the ground when he fell. She heard Matilda's roof crashing to the ground behind her. No time to look back. She prayed Matilda and the boys survived.

Running down the hill towards the chicken coop, she spotted a cinnamon red horse standing near a big oak tree, no sign of its rider in sight. She ran to the horse, threw Jeremiah up on its back, grabbed the horse's mane, pulled herself up behind her son, then gave the horse a quick kick to urge it forward. The horse responded and began running down the hill with its new masters on board, carrying them away from the terror of Henry Greer, away from the only home she had known since the first fire. Without thinking, she cut the smelly string of scalps that had been tied to the saddle and unconsciously slipped the dark man's knife into the sheath hanging by her right leg.

They rode for hours as the morning light grew brighter as the sun rose above the trees ahead. She had counted at least four other cabins along the way, cabins that were no longer homes, cabins that were burned to the ground, smouldering from the fires that had been set by the dark man. She was saddened by the loss of lives, as she saw not one person along the way. She thought only about what they were leaving and gave little thought to where they were going.

As the day went on, she thanked God for the horse. She was comforted that without time for prayer, God had provided. God had delivered this horse to her, this now familiar animal, this one that stood near the chicken coop waiting to take her to safety. Now, as the sun was setting, she settled into her thoughts, holding Jeremiah close. "We should head east, away from the sun," she whispered to Jeremiah. There, she hoped to find Hawksbill Mountain.

"Go faster, Isaiah! Faster!", she exclaimed, guiding him eastward, without thinking or recognizing what she had called him. Not until the summer sun had set, and she had ridden into an apple orchard, did she feel it was safe to get off the horse and take Jeremiah down to hold him tightly in her arms. She tied the horse to one of the apple trees and placed her hands on its face to where the moonlight shone brightly on its long nose, then stood in front of it to rub its forehead to assure it she was its friend. "I know you need water and I'm sure we'll find some around here somewhere," she said looking into the horse's eyes to reassure him.

As she rubbed its nose, the memories of her youth swirled through her. "You. You. You could not possibly be my long lost friend," she said. "You disappeared four years ago!" She walked a full circle around the horse, coming back to look at him. The horse whinnied, then snorted, shaking its head. To Hope, it was a familiar sound from long ago. "Well, I'm just going to call you Isaiah anyway," she paused, rubbing the wide zig-zagged white blaze running between his eyes and down the bridge of his nose. Then, she began sobbing uncontrollably, looking up to the stars, thanking God, then looking to her son. "Jeremiah, meet Isaiah. Isaiah was my best friend before you came along. And now, we're a family of three."

Hope slept sitting up against the apple tree, holding Jeremiah in her arms, with the dark man's knife by her side. With dawn's light, she saw the long, narrow orchard. "So many trees, enough apples to feed us through winter," she muttered, thinking aloud but quietly so as not to wake Jeremiah. "Their branches arch to form a tunnel. Let's see where it goes."

"Jeremiah, wake up. Let's take a walk and pick some apples." She lifted him into her arms, then set him down on his feet, taking his hand in hers. "Come on Isaiah! All the apples you can eat! I remember you loved apples!" She reached upward with her left hand, grabbed an apple and pushed it to Isaiah's mouth. Isaiah chomped down eagerly, quickly gobbling the entire apple. "There's more!" she said, picking two more, handing one to Isaiah, then taking a big bite out of the other apple. "Here Jeremiah, I know you're hungry." Jeremiah grabbed the rest of the apple and chomped down.

Isaiah followed Hope and Jeremiah as they walked down the trail. Hope wasn't sure if he followed because he knew her or because she was the apple provider. But no matter. She felt a sense of joy and peace walking along with the two most important things in her life. Up ahead she could see the orchard opening into a field. As they got closer to the field, she felt less secure, hesitating to leave the safe net of the apple trees' low branches. She hoisted Jeremiah up on Isaiah's back and led them to the last tree. She climbed up behind Jeremiah so she could see further from a higher level. She nudged Isaiah forward pressing her lower leg against his side, clicking her tongue "tchk, thck" and again "tchk, tchk", while gently rubbing his mane to cue him to move slowly. She made a mental note to shorten the stirrups as the dark man had been taller. She had ridden all this way without using the stirrups, hugging Isaiah's ribs with her knees and ankles.

Hope squinted and held one hand above her eyes to block the blinding sunlight and get a better look at the surrounding land. Then she saw a rock chimney standing like a pillar above the ruins of what had been a fine home. Heading toward it, she repeated to herself, "The Lord is My Shepherd. I shall not want," the words spoken not as much in a prayer to God, but mostly as reassurance to herself that they would be safe. Isaiah suddenly stopped, putting his head down to sniff moist grass, indicating a shallow stream running beneath them. Hope could now see the stream came from a pile of rocks that formed an arc over a doorway. She dismounted to take a closer look at a structure tucked into a hillside thick with high grass. She led them closer, holding Isaiah's reins and opening the door to peer inside.

"Why Jeremiah! It's a root cellar with a spring! A big springhouse," she shouted to her companions. "It's very cool in here. And there's carrots and potatoes! They're covered with root thorns, but I bet they're still good! Oh! And here's some cabbage!" She stepped out to lift Jeremiah down and carried him inside. "This springhouse is bigger than the one back at my homeplace. See! I can stand and touch the ceiling. Why these are cedar beams! And, look! Here's a ledge long enough to sleep on. And plenty of water," she said noting the stone-walled channel in the ground below holding a shallow stream of water that flowed from the spring behind the building. She walked to the side of the room to open a small window to let in air and light. "This looks like a safe place for now. I'm so tired I could sleep all day." She sat Jeremiah down next to the water and knelt to splash water on her face, then scooped water into her cupped hands. She held her cupped hands under Jeremiah's chin so he could drink. "Get down on your knees Jeremiah, and put your hands in the water to form a cup like this." She knelt beside him and scooped water up with her hands showing him how to hold his fingers tightly together to keep the water inside. Jeremiah tried this a couple of times, then he ducked his head down into the water slurping it up from the stream. "That works too!" she giggled, then put her face directly into the water to mimic him. "Much better! And Isaiah is doing it too! Look outside!"

She hugged Jeremiah tightly and pointed to the open doorway where Isaiah was nose down into the water, getting a much-needed drink.

"Isaiah happy!" Jeremiah said clapping his hands together cheerfully then pointing to Isaiah. "Can he come inside?"

Hope took the dark man's knife and scraped each side over and over against the rocks on the spring channel wall to remove the dried blood, *Henry's blood,* she thought, biting her tongue to stop her thoughts from going into the details behind where the knife had gone before. She rubbed it harder against the rocks, dipping it in and out of the water, until it was clean enough to cut the potatoes and carrots into small bites for Jeremiah. She took some carrots and tossed them outside to Isaiah who seemed quite content to finally have food at his feet.

As dusk approached, Hope went outside and used the dark man's knife to cut tall grass to pile on the ledge inside the springhouse, making it softer for sleeping. Thankfully, the cellar door was just wide enough to allow Isaiah to come inside with a little nudging help from Jeremiah and Hope. *He is sometimes like a big puppy,* she thought. She brought him inside with mixed feelings, knowing that outside he would better hear any danger approaching. But for now, she wanted him close and safe from the unknown. She pulled Jeremiah to her chest, hugging him tightly, easing him over to her right side to ease the pain that still lingered through the ribs below her heart. Sleep came quickly. The first sleep they'd had since they had mounted Isaiah to escape the farm that had been her home. She slept soundly knowing there would no longer be an intruder who caused painful bruises. No more would she need to wake at dawn to walk to the river carrying rags to clean herself. She was good at blocking bad memories and on this night she pushed the past four years into the darkness in the back of her mind and dreamed of lying down in green pastures and walking beside still waters with Jeremiah's hand in hers, and Isaiah trailing behind them.

The springhouse proved to be a wonderful shelter, protecting them from the heat of the summer sun. Each day, Hope made it a point to venture out at dawn and out again at twilight. Before each walk, she would take Jeremiah outside to relieve himself near the trees at the end of the orchard, then hurry him back into the springhouse, telling him to think of some new words to share and spell when she returned. She would then tie Isaiah to the wooden door handle, giving him strict instructions to keep Jeremiah inside and to warn them of any danger.

Each time she left the springhouse, she would walk out to survey the land, making it a point to step out to the side just a few feet in a new direction, then walking just far enough to be sure Isaiah was still in sight and within hearing distance. She had started her walks heading east into the sunrise finding fields where corn had once been harvested.

She had walked across the ashes of another large house and found remains of what could be a woman and small child. In the ruins of the farm's other structures she found a large iron pot and some clay bowls and carried them back to the springhouse.

Not far from the apple orchard, she discovered vines of small melons, but she could only carry a few at a time in the skirt of her apron. Melons were new to Jeremiah and when they were gone, he begged her to go out and find more. After several days, there were no more melons in the field, but a few days later, she found a thorny bush of blackberries along a fence not far from where the barn had been. She filled her apron skirt with the berries and brought them back and emptied her apron to fill the iron pot. Soon, Jeremiah had a purple circle around his mouth.

At the end of the first ten days, she had covered half of the area and headed in the direction exactly opposite from where she had started her survey. Looking east, she studied the mountains in the far distance wondering when or even if they should head that way. Some mornings, she saw wild turkeys running away as she approached. In the evenings, she enjoyed watching young wild rabbits hopping high as they played tag with each other. She thought of using her sling to slay a rabbit or turkey for a hearty meal, but she dared not build a fire that could send smoke to be seen from far away. Then, as she had every day for twenty days, she returned to the springhouse at sunset, having surveyed the entire area forming a full circle around them.

Squirrels were scurrying about gathering the acorns that now covered the ground nearby. Soon the leaves would bring bright colors of red and yellow to the mountains beyond. She needed to make a plan. Would it be better to stay in the springhouse with no fire? Or should they risk heading to the mountains to find a better shelter.

Chapter 11

Jared was awakened by Henry's shouting at the dark man running into the cabin. "Get out! ... Out!"

Smoke was filling the room as embers fell in from the roof. He heard his papa struggling with the dark man, then papa emitted a sound he would never forget. His brother Jake pushed Jared up and out the back window. "I'm gonna get granny," Jake shouted as he pushed Jared through. Jared tumbled to the ground below the narrow window frame and waited there expecting his brother and granny to follow. When they didn't come, he ran blindly into the forest, terrified the dark man would find him.

Jared hid in the trees behind the cabin watching as the roof collapsed. He watched as Hope's cabin also burned to the ground. He prayed that everyone had made it out the front as he had not seen them through the flames and heavy smoke.

Now as dusk approached, he inched forward, heading back toward the cabin, hiding behind one tree and then another, trying to get a closer look, afraid to call out, staying out of sight until he rounded the side of the cabin's smouldering ashes to see the dark man face down on the ground near the front stoop. Next to the dark man's outstretched hand was a mess of bloody hair. "Oh my God!" Jared screamed, tripping over the dark man's outstretched arm and landing on his stomach across the kettle on the firepit. "That was papa's hair," he gagged. Bile rushed up into his throat and out his mouth, splattering into the kettle.

He wiped his mouth and looked back. The stoop, along with the chimney, and the rock frame of Matilda's bedroom wall, were all that remained. He turned to walk around the ruins to see if there might be movement. The rubble was up to his knees and the smell from what had been his home was rancid, so overwhelming he could not breathe. Gasping for air, he headed down the hill toward the barn which, amazingly, was still standing.

He ran into the barn. "Jake! Granny! Ya here? Where'd ya go? It's okay, th 'man's dead! Ya kin come out now!" But the silence was deafening. All he heard was his own shouting and his footsteps hitting the dirt floor as he ran, throwing back boards of the gates that been broken by the animals that had panicked and fled. The barn was empty.

He stepped outside and headed to check the chicken coop. Inside the coop, one hen sat on her nest. "Other chickens must've flown away," he mumbled aloud to himself. He walked out of the coop and sat down on Hope's rock, sobbing well into the night.

Jared had slept soundly until he felt a cold wet nudging against his neck. He slapped at it and quickly sat up fearing it was a bear. To his relief, it was a horse. Henry's horse.

He stood up and embraced Henry's horse, holding its cheek against his for a long time. "We could ride away n' see th' country I never seen," he whispered to the horse. "But what if granny n' Jake is near. What if they come back n' we're gone?"

He led the horse back to the barn. "First, let's make us a place to sleep," Jared continued talking to the horse as they entered the barn. "N', ya know! Yer my only friend fer now so I'mma gonna have to give ya a name. Yeah, I know my papa called ya many names. But, I'mma gonna call ya Jesse. Yes, Jesse. Here ya go," he said, gently guiding his friend back into his stall. "We gonna be jest fine -- as long as we's together," Jared placed his hands gently on Jesse's cheeks. "Ya stay here fer now. I'mma gonna find us some food n' I'll find a bucket to fetch ya some water from th' river."

Jared picked the stall door up from the ground and leaned it against the stall's opening to close it off. "Yep. We's gonna be best friends, you n' me," he said as he turned away and walked toward the barn door. Then he heard a loud thump, followed by a shuffling noise behind him and a cold bump against his back.

Startled, he quickly turned around to find himself face-to-face with Jesse. "I see. I see. Okay, come wit' me. Thar's no reason for ya to stay in th' barn as long as thar's light out."

Jared headed toward the river with Jesse following closely behind him.

He dove into the swimming hole, still wearing his nightshirt and breeches, hoping to cleanse himself of soot and its odor. Over and over, he dove deep, holding his breath and staying under water as long as he could, trying to drown out the previous day. When he was too tired to even tread water, he paddled over to the river's edge and collapsed on its muddy bank. Rolling over on his back, he stilled himself, thinking he heard a familiar voice.

"Jared! Help! Jared! Over here! I need yer help! Plllll...ease!"

Jared sat up, looking toward the panicked voice. Downstream he saw the shadow of his brother. "Jake! Is that you?" he called, standing, then running toward the shadow that was kneeling and splashing water on what he now recognized as Matilda, lying face up in Jake's arms. "It's you! I thought ya wuz dead!"

"Help me, Jared! I can't wake 'er up!" shouted Jake, holding her in his left arm and splashing Matilda's face with his right hand.

Jared knelt down next to his granny's still body, then leaned over and placed his ear on her chest to listen for her heartbeat. "I can't hear nothin'! What happened? How'd ya get ' here?"

"When ya left, I ran back to 'er room. She wuz passed out on th' floor at th' edge of 'er wall. It wuz hard to breathe, Jared! Th' smoke wuz so thick. I tried to get 'er up, but she wouldn't move. So, I dragged 'er 'cross th' floor n' outta th' door. I laid 'er on th' ground for a bit so I could get a big drink of air. Then I seen a dark man layin' thar at th' stoop. I didn't know if'n he wuz dead 'r alive, so I grabbed granny n' somehow carried 'er down 'ere to th' river to hide. I thought th' water'd wake er' up. Spent all night splashing 'er n' poundin' on 'er chest," Jake began crying. "I dunno if'n I slept at all, but a couple times I nodded off n' tried agin when I woke up. She's gone, ain't she? She's gone t h'eaven to be wit' our Momma."

"Thar, thar Jake," said Jared, trying in vain to calm his brother, then hugging him for what seemed like most of the day until he calmed down.

Jared stood and pulled Jake up to stand next to him. "Jake, this here's Jesse," he said leading him over to the horse. "I know, I know. It wuz papa's horse, but now it's ours. I named him Jesse. He followed me here. I guess he knew more 'bout what I'd find than I did. Now he kin help us get granny back up th' hill so's we can dig 'er a proper grave."

Together they pulled Matilda up and placed her stomach down across the horse and headed up the hill. "Did ya see papa? Jake asked Jared.

"I seen his bloody scalp near th' dark man's body," Jared answered. "Imma purty sure papa's buried in th' ashes. I don't think we kin git him outta thar, but we'll see."

"Let's bury her next to Momma's grave so's they kin then be closer in heaven."

"Good idea. I'll go to th' barn n' git th' shovels. Ya take granny on up thar n' keep her on Jesse's back til we's ready," Jared said as he headed down the hill to the barn.

Jake walked Jesse over to the side of the house and up the hill to where his mother was buried. When Jared returned with the shovels, they began digging a hole next to their mother's grave. It took them into late afternoon to get the hole deep enough, then they gently took Matilda off the horse.

"Wait! Set 'er down!" said Jared, leaning Matilda's body toward the ground. "She'd want us to have this," he said, nodding toward his younger brother. Jared lifted her arm and slowly removed her wedding ring from her left hand, turned it in between his fingers and held it up to the sun. "I kin see th' writin' inside. "Member? She used to tell us 'bout th' time Grandpa give it to her. She said th' writin' wuz special. It says 'Yer mine fer-ever". Jared held the ring in his palm so Jake could see the writing, then placed it on his pinky finger.

Jake was shocked, but silent, as they lifted her from the ground and carefully placed her into the grave. They stood over the grave for several minutes. "I dunno wut to say Jared," said Jake, staring at the ring on his brother's finger.

"We loved ya more than anyone, Granny," Jared said taking Jake's hand and looking into the grave.

"Amen," said Jake.

They shoveled all the dirt back onto Matilda, covering her face and then her entire body. "We'll have t' find a good rock fer 'er headstone," Jared said. It began to rain. They walked slowly, cooling their spirits as they reflected on the day's events. Then the skies opened wide, releasing buckets of water, pouring torrentially and thoroughly soaking them both before they reached what had once been their home. Jesse soon joined them and stood by their side, his silence providing comfort as they stood staring at the pillows of ashes now soaked within the frame of the rocks that had formed the cabins' foundations.

They soon found themselves staring down at the dark man. "We gotta git rid of 'em," Jared said kicking the dark man in the side. "He took our family from us. He don't deserve no grave," he paused, thinking out loud as he looked around for an answer.

"Let's throw him in th' river!" Jake shouted, bending down to lift up the dark man's feet. Jared took the dark man's arms and together they threw him up onto Jesse's back. The rain was now pounding against their back, a downpour that was long overdue.

Jake led the way, holding Jesse's mane to guide him, while Jared steadied the dark man's body to keep him on the horse as they went down the hill, past the barn, past Hope's rock, past the flax field, past the cornfield, and all the way down trail to the main road. They turned left and followed the road until they crossed a bridge over the river. Below, the river's water was rushing fast downstream, fueled by the hard rain.

"I think this is th' deepest part," said Jared. "Let's git him down."

They pulled the dark man's body to the ground and dragged him to the bridge's edge. "Jared look! He's got an ugly scar on his face. A mean scar!" Jake exclaimed as he reached forward to lift the dark man's arms. Jared grabbed the dark man's feet.

"Wait! Let's keep his moccasins! We ain't got no shoes thanks to th' far he made," Jared said, pulling the moccasins off the dark man's feet and tossing them on the ground behind him.. "Okay! One. Two. Three." At the count of three, they lifted the dark man's body, swung him to the left and then to right, into the river. The brothers watched as the rushing water took him into the waves, pulled him under and into the current, then pushed him back up, as it carried him downstream. They stood on the bridge watching until they saw him no more.

Jared grabbed the dark man's moccasins from the ground, pulled them onto his bare feet, then hopped up onto Jesse's back and stuck his arm out to pull Jake up behind him. Jesse knew the way as he had carried Henry home for many years. Home from his trading for baby chicks, a saw, and supplies. Home from long nights at the tavern -- nights when Henry would pass out on his back, having drunk too much whiskey. Nights when Henry slept for hours still on the horse when they returned to the homeplace. Nights when Jesse bolted and kicked until Henry was abruptly wakened when his whiskey-filled body plopped to the ground.

The brothers dismounted at Hope's rock and led Jesse back into the barn. "Granny's grave. It's missing somethin'," Jake muttered. Jared reacted with a nod, indicating he knew what Jake was thinking. Without a word, they headed back down the path to the river and began searching its banks. "She loved th' river rocks. This one! Look!" Jake shouted. "It's beautiful with soft colors," he said as he knelt down to rub his hand across its surface. "I see blue. N' shades of green. This'un's it!" Together they carried it up the slippery hill and carefully placed it at the head of Matilda's grave. They then picked up their shovels and headed back to the cabin.

"I kin see whar papa's body is," said Jared pointing to the place where Henry's bed once stood. "It stinks so bad, let's jest cover him up wit' enough dirt to stop th' smell."

Ignoring the pouring rain, they proceeded to dig up the wet dirt next to the rock foundation. They took turns shoveling, and at times the dirt was so loose, it was necessary to pack it down hard on their father's body. "It don't hurt him to hit it hard," Jared said as he lifted the shovel high to bring it down with a heavy thump on the mound before him. "I wish it did," muttered Jake.

It took about two dozen shovel loads to cover Henry's body. When done, no words were spoken as they dropped their shovels and headed back to the barn. The rain began to slack off and they slowed down to look back at what had once been their home. "We's gonna have to make th' barn our house fer now," Jake said.

They both stopped suddenly as they approached the oak tree between the path and the barn."What's that?" Jake asked bending down to pick up a mess of what looked like hair laying on the ground. He held up a string of at least ten scalps boasting many different hair colors coated with dried blood. "Ugh! These are from men's heads! Th' dark man musta' dropped them on his way to th' cabins. They's awful smelly!" He dropped the string of hairy scalps to the ground. "Reckon we'll have to either bury or burn these afore some animals git to 'em."

Jared picked up the string of smelly scalps and turned back toward the cabin. "Come on Jake! Let's do it quick. Maybe we can find some hot coals deep in th' ashes where the rain didn't get to 'em n' start a fire in th' pit. We'll want to move th' kettle first," Jared said. "N', reckon we'll have to burn papa's hair too!"

The coals at the pit were soaked and oozing smoke, hardly hot enough to start a fire. They walked over to the side of Hope's chimney, where they saw some coals smouldering in the hearth. "Maybe I kin get o'er thar without burning these moccasins on my feet," said Jared as he cautiously ambled across the ashes until he was facing the hearth.

"Looks like Hope's kettle kept these coals dry. This'll work if we kin get some air under 'em," said Jared, removing the kettle and setting it aside.

Jared walked across the ashes to the site of Henry's demise, picked up the shovels they had dropped earlier and cautiously stepped back across the ashes to Hope's hearth. Using their shovels they scooped up the hot embers and staggered them inside the hearth. Jake tossed the string of scalps onto the smouldering coals. Taking turns, they blew at them until the fire was strong enough to catch the scalps and begin burning them.

"Let's git outta here! I can't stand th' smell no more!" Jake yelled. Needing no further urging, Jared began running back toward the barn, with Jake just steps behind him.

They settled themselves in the straw in Jesse's stall, totally exhausted from the day's work. Leaning back against the wall, Jake sniffed to hold back the tears. "It's jest us now," he said, reaching to pat Jared's leg. "I dunno how we gonna make it. We need food. In th' mornin', we need to hang our breeches n' shirts out to dry. I'mma glad we wore our breeches to bed ever' night. We'll need to look decent if'n we go out to the tradin' post. But I dunno whar tis, do you? And what about Hope -- lil Jeremiah! I don't think they're in thar cabin ashes. We woulda' seen somethin'--like we seen papa. I hope they's ok," Jake rambled on and on listing one worry after another until Jared interrupted him.

"Jake. Hush yer worries," Jared whispered sleepily. "I been thinkin'. Hope went to th' river ever' single mornin'. Maybe she wuzn't in th' cabin when th' fire come. But Jeremiah wuz. Maybe he ran out lookin' fer her when th' fire came. Or maybe she ran real fast n' got him out, too. I dunno. They's down th' riverbank somewhar. I know."

Jake reached into the pocket he kept by tucking part of his shirt into the waist of his breeches. "At least I got me sling," he said, showing it to his brother. "Ever since Hope give me it, I've kept it wit' me. She wuz like me big sister."

"N' lil Jeremiah our brother," Jared replied.

The night seemed noisier than usual as sounds of crickets, frogs, and wolves filled the air. The shrill wind whistled loudly through the barn's front door, through Jesse's stall, and out a wide gap behind them, only to come back around and cut through again and again. Jake snuggled closer to Jared, finding some comfort and warmth from his brother's body, even though their clothes were still wet from the day's rain. They were exhausted from fleeing the fire, lifting Matilda onto Jesse's back, climbing the hill, digging her grave, tossing the dark man onto the horse then lifting him off into the river, shoveling for hours to cover their papa with dirt, and finally, burning the scalps, so their sleep was restless, filled with each other's shivering, shaking, and their own startling dreams.

Nighttime only lasted for minutes before narrow streams of light beamed through the cracks in the stall's log walls, waking Jared. He moved Jake gently to his side, watching enviously as Jake slept on. He decided to head back to the hearth at Hope's cabin to see if any embers were still hot.

He hovered his hand over the embers, relieved to see they were still warm and took one of the shovels they had left behind and stirred the coals and blew on them to get them hotter. They were still warm but he needed something dry to get a real fire started, so he headed back to the barn to fetch some dry straw and sticks.

"Wake up Jake!" Jared yelled. "We need to git th' far goin' agin. Lots to do! Here! Git some of that straw!" They filled their arms with all the dry sticks and straw they could carry and headed back to Hope's hearth. Soon, the fire was blazing.

"It's warmer now n' the sun's comin up. Let's set our shirts out to dry," Jared said unbuttoning his shirt and hanging it on the edge of the mantel.

"Jared! I never! I..." Jake grabbed Jared by the shoulders and turned him around. "Ya got big whelps on yer back n' yer chest! I ne'er seen ya bare chested afore!" Jake let loose of Jared's shoulders and took off his own shirt. "See, looka here!" I got 'em too!" They stared at each other, shocked, but not surprised.

"I hear'd ya screamin' when he whipped ya, but I ne'er went close to whar ya wuz. I always hid, so's he wouldn't whip me too," said Jared.

"Me, too," said Jake frowning as he traced the raised scarred whelps across Jared's chest. "I jest ne'er knew he hurt you as bad as he hurt me. I didn't dare think too much 'bout it. He'd make me go into th' trees n' cut a branch fer his switch, then he would whittle th' switch to make it thin n' sharp so it'd cut like a fine whip. Once his switch wuz sharp, he'd push me into th' woods or deep into th' field to whar no one'd see me. He'd make me take my shirt off so's it wouldn't get stained. N' he'd say, 'If'n ya tell yer brother or he finds out 'bout this whippin', I'll whip ya agin til yer dead!' I dunno what I done to make him anger so bad. He jest wuz."

"I 'member when yer nose got broke," Jared said. "Granny jest gave ya a rag n' said, 'take it to th' river, wet it down n' hold it 'gainst yer nose til supper time.' I wanted t' help ya. It looked like it hurt so bad. When he whipped me, I'd try to think I wuz somewhar's else. I'd shut my eyes n' me mind would go up into th' clouds whar I'd see baby deer dancin' 'cross th' sky. So, then I'd be quiet til he finished. When it wuz o'er I'd go into th' river til th' bleedin' stopped. Then I tried to forget agin til th' next time. I'm glad he's gone Jake. No more screams. No more blood."

Chapter 12

"Get up little one!" Hope shouted as she opened the door to the springhouse letting the light in. "It's a beautiful day. Say goodbye to the springhouse. Maybe we can come back to visit some day."

After days of pacing back and forth and re-tracing her steps towards the mountains, she had made up her mind. She had spent much of the morning gathering what remained of berries, wrapping them in her rags, then packing them along with apples into the buckskin pouch hanging from Isaiah's back. She stepped back into the springhouse. "I've prayed and prayed. We can't stay here and I know the Lord will be with us today and beyond." She gave Jeremiah a big hug. "Drink more of this fine water son. No telling when we'll find another spring." She joined Jeremiah as he knelt down and put his head into the spring, slurping up the water as he had done on their first day. Hope did the same. "We'd best be on our way. Good-bye springhouse!" She grabbed Jeremiah's hand and together they backed out, stepping across the mushy, wet grass to where Isaiah stood.

"Up you go! And here I come!" she said as she climbed up behind Jeremiah. She tugged on the reins and gave Isaiah a light nudge with her feet firmly in the stirrups that now fit perfectly. "Here we go! Let's find a new home!" They headed east across the field following a narrow trail that led away from the springhouse and the farm that had been their home for nearly two months. She glanced back, looking beyond the orchard, thinking of where they had come from, remembering the Greer farm, silently praying that Matilda and the boys were okay. They had been her family even though they couldn't be together as often as she wanted or needed them. "Dear God, be with them. I pray we can be together again some day." With these words, Hope grimaced pushing her thoughts past the pain in her left side, the never-ending pain that was a constant reminder of Henry's wrath.

As they got closer to the mountains, the narrow trail merged with a wide trail that revealed many hoof marks, some quite fresh, indicating this path could be a busy one. "Look down, Jeremiah! See the hoof marks. Many horses have come this way. I think this trail leads up into that mountain, Jeremiah. We have to use our ears to listen for other horses. I saw lots of horse tracks on the trail that led to where we came from, back through the orchard. I hope we're headed away from danger. Headed to find good people who can help us make a new home," she said out loud, looking up into the sky to get God's attention. "Dear Lord, help us find a safe place, please. Please! Guide me to where I can get a shelter built, even if it's smaller than the springhouse. Jeremiah needs a place where he can make some friends. I need a place we can call home. A place where we can plant flax and corn."

Isaiah soon took to the trail without need for guidance from Hope. For the first time this morning, she relaxed, letting Isaiah lead the way along the trail lined with laurel bushes and shaded by arching limbs of oak and hickory trees. They headed up one hill after another, slowly winding higher into the mountains. Hope found her thoughts drifting back to her homeplace, her father's voice echoing in her mind, telling a story with words she knew by heart.

Before I met your mother, I lived in the north, near a place called Philadelphia. That's where your grandparents are. But when I was about twenty-six years of age, my friends and I heard about new land. A land not yet a colony. The Spaniards had discovered many minerals and gems in that land. We heard the Cherokees were there too. But the more we talked, the more we thought about the possibilities. We wanted to be rich and live in fine homes like the ones in the nice part of Philadelphia. My friends and I decided to leave Philadelphia and head toward the mines. We got to a little town called Alder Springs and stayed there for awhile, working in the mines just an hour's ride northwest of the town. We would come back to town every evening, exhausted and dirty. One evening, when walking to the town tavern, I ran into your mother. Literally ran into her!! I had been so tired, I wasn't looking where I was going. That was a blessing, I guess because from that evening on, I made it a point to see her every night. Well, after a time, she and I decided to find some land and make our own place. So, one evening, I used some of my earnings to buy her a horse. I also bought a wagon. The next morning we waited outside the general store til it opened. We bought all the food and supplies we thought we would need to last us several months, packing the wagon full. Then we harnessed our two horses to the wagon and headed northwest.

In her mind, Hope envisioned her parents happily beginning a new life, perched on the bench of their wagon, with two horses leading the way. Patrick O'Connor had told her this story at least a hundred times and each time he told it, he would reach into his pocket and show her a shiny stone. "This is one of the gems I found in the mine. Never told anyone I had it. I've kept it all this time so I'll have something to trade when I get to Hawksbill Mountain. There, I'll build us a fine home," he said. At the time, Hope thought their house was one of the finest in their settlement. She had seen neighbor's houses and knew her home was nicer and bigger than the others. Her father had been especially proud of the green and red flag that hung from a tall post, bearing the O'Connor family crest and marking the edge of their property. She tried to recall the flag's images and wondered if it had survived the fire.

For reasons she did not know, her mother and father had not settled near the mines. They had gone northwest, past Hawksbill Mountain to settle near the Doe River, not far from the Watauga settlement. She had only ridden to the settlement once when her father had treated her to the trip and taken her to the bustling village. Shortly before their own village was attacked, her father had shared stories about Fort Caswell and how it had been attacked by a Cherokee named Dragging Canoe. It was at the time of these stories that Patrick O'Connor had begun putting supplies into the haversacks and hidden them in the cave.

Isaiah began slowing down. Jeremiah was yelling, "I'm thirsty!" Hope realized she had been daydreaming all morning. The sun was almost directly above them, beating heat into the air between the trees. She looked around and behind them. They had come a long way. Just ahead to her left, she saw a shallow brook, its water pouring across rocks stacked atop each other, forming pools of different sizes and depth. High above, two streams of water tumbled from a rock bluff into a wide pool before it fell to the brook below. The waterfall was twice her height and almost as wide as her home had been. She spotted an old trail leading up the hill to the pool of water. "Here's a good place to rest and get some water Jeremiah," she said, turning Isaiah to nudge him slowly up the trail alongside the stream. She slowed him to a brief stop, holding a branch, bending it upward and pushing Jeremiah's head down to pass under it.

"Listen! Shhhhh. Listen," she whispered pulling the reins to bring Isaiah to a halt. "I hear horses! Do you hear horses Jeremiah?" She had never heard a sound like this as she had only been away from the two farms the one time her father took her to the Watauga settlement. But her instincts took over.

"Go Isaiah! Go!" she shouted, giving him a slight kick with her stirrups. "Up the hill. Fast!" Isaiah moved quickly, cutting across the turns and rocks that covered the narrow trail. She guided him up the trail, past the pool of water below the waterfall, leaped down, and grabbed his reins to lead him into the shallow water and on into the middle of the waterfall's arch. Here she stopped, taking Jeremiah down from Isaiah's back. She held him tight and carefully inched forward between two streams of falling water until she could see what was happening below.

She watched with disbelief. It was like something out of a dream. She tried to count, but found herself losing count and starting over. "There must be hundreds of men riding as fast as a horse can go, and horses pulling wagons," she whispered, squeezing Jeremiah so tight he could hardly breathe. She prayed the men couldn't see her, and gratefully thanked the Lord when she realized they were going too fast to look her way.

It was almost dark when the dust of the fast horses settled to where she could see the main trail below. Still holding Jeremiah against her hip, she led Isaiah out of the pool and onto the bank on the other side of the waterfall. "We need to find a safe place for the night," she said, placing Jeremiah up on Isaiah's saddle. She pulled the dark man's knife from its saddle sheath and began cutting branches to clear a path headed away from the pool. "Stay here", she said, tying Isaiah to a tall pine tree. She continued hacking branches ahead of her to make enough space for Isaiah to walk through and sighed with relief when she found a small area of white pine trees that had shed a bed of needles beneath them. She stomped around to pack the needles down, then knelt checking to ensure there were no sharp rocks beneath them. Once satisfied with the newly formed bed, she headed back to Isaiah and lifted Jeremiah from the saddle down into her arms.

"Doesn't it smell nice here? I love the smell of pine," she said as she carried him the short distance from the waterfall. She set Jeremiah on his feet, pausing to make sure he could stand. She led Isaiah to their new camp spot, tied him to a tree, and removed the pouch of apples and berries from his back. "Ahh, here we go," she said as she sat down on the sweet-smelling bed, pulling Jeremiah to her. "There's an apple for each of us and the berries are a little soft, but still good. This will do until morning. Maybe we'll find more food tomorrow."

"Mother, sing!" Jeremiah pleaded. "Sing about the shepherd!"

Hope held Jeremiah in her arms and began to sing, softly. "The Lord is My Shepherd. I shall not want. He maketh me to lie down in green pastures. He leadeth me beside the still waters. He restoreth my soul. Yea though I walk through the valley of the shadow of death, I will fear no evil. For Thou art with me. Thy rod and Thy staff they comfort me. Thou preparest a table before me in the presence of my enemies. Thou anointest my head with oil. My cup runneth over. Surely goodness and mercy shall follow me all the days of my life: and I will dwell. And I will dwell… in the house of the Lord forever. Ahh-ahmen. Ahh-ahmen. Ahh-ahmen. Ahh-a-amen."

Chapter 13

Isaiah's whinnying startled Hope awake. She reached over to calm Jeremiah then sat up with a jolt. Her son was gone.

"Jeremiah! Jeremiah!" she yelled. "Come here!" Hope screamed loudly as if the shrill sound would bring him to her. She looked around growing frantic, not seeing Jeremiah anywhere. The surrounding forest was thick with pine trees too thick for Jeremiah to go far, except for the fact that he was skinny and under three feet tall. *He must've headed through the clearing I cut last night,* she thought, "This way?" She said aloud, shrugging her shoulders, looking skyward praying God would acknowledge the direction as she took Isaiah's reins and guided him back toward the waterfall.

"Jeremiah!" she screamed at the top of her lungs, praying her calls could be heard above the noise of the waterfall. As they got closer to the waterfall, she saw a shadow moving under the falling water. She let go of Isaiah's reins and ran onto the ledge beneath the water's arch. "Jeremiah! Come here!" she shouted running closer to the shadow. "You're soaked! What were you thinking? This ledge is slick! You could've drowned!"

She stepped carefully into the waterfall and lifted Jeremiah onto her hip, the water splashing across her head, and down her shoulders. Stepping sideways, she then cautiously stepped back into the void behind the falling water. They were drenched when they got back to the creek's bank, but in a way it felt good to be washed of the dust that had settled into her hair and skin during their previous day's ride. She twisted her apron and shift to wring out the extra water. "Jeremiah! You gave me such a fright!" she said as she removed Jeremiah's gown, gave it a good wringing and placed it back over his head, pulling its hem to stretch it out to below his knees.

"Let's go see if we can get all dusty again," she said. She lifted Jeremiah to the saddle, grabbed Isaiah's reins and led them back through the pool under the misty arch of the waterfall, across to the other bank and onto the narrow trail beside it. She stopped to look down at the road below. She still could not hear because of water pounding across the brook's brown and gray rocks so she guided Isaiah to slowly descend the hill until they were about halfway to the road. She stopped to listen again. The brook was quieter now and she heard no galloping sounds from the road. When they reached the road, she mounted Isaiah and nudged him to stay close to the left side of the road and move slowly under the canopy of tree limbs arching above. She pulled the reins tightly back enough for Isaiah to sense that moving slowly was the best way forward.

Between each step, she cocked her right ear and then her left upward to listen for any sounds coming their way.

"I'm hungry," Jeremiah shouted.

"Quiet son," Hope answered, clasping her hands across his mouth. "We need to move like a turtle, without a sound. Listen to the birds singing. Hear them?"

Jeremiah nodded.

"I wonder what they're saying. Try to listen and when we stop again, I want you to tell me what they sang."

Jeremiah thought this was a fun idea and he looked up into the trees and angled his head to hear the birds' voices.

They moved slowly along the road only stepping into the woods once to let three riders pass by. The sun was now high above them and Hope thought *I'm hungry too, Jeremiah. Dear God, how long must we go on like this?* She prayed, closing her eyes so God could comprehend the intensity of her pleas.

When she opened her eyes, she saw the arching tree limbs were growing farther apart.

She prayed again, whispering. "Dear God. Keep us safe for we near a strange space where we cannot hide."

As they moved closer to the clearing, she saw narrow trails shooting out from the main road. "Look! The trail has changed into many little trails. I wonder where they go," she told Jeremiah.

She counted four narrow trails leading away from the road. As they passed each trail, she felt torn, wondering whether she should turn into one. Would they see families tending to their crops or perhaps find a chicken coop housing hens with fresh eggs, or would there be another springhouse filled with cabbage and potatoes, or even a barn with hay for Isaiah. Would they find angry men like Henry, or a kind woman like Matilda? In her nineteen years, she had only known two homes. She could not imagine how other people lived.

Fearing the unknown, she stayed on course, pushing Isaiah into a gallop, guiding him faster down the main trail which took them through another tunnel of arching branches shadowing what lay ahead. Suddenly, the sounds of birds were interrupted as they crossed a long wooden bridge over a wide shallow stream. The sound of Isaiah's hooves hitting the planks on the wood shook the air with a loud pounding noise that echoed across the open land and bounced off the trees nearby. Hope ducked her head down behind Jeremiah's back, as if to hide from anyone who may have heard Isaiah's hooves beating to signal their arrival. She then turned her head back and forth quickly, ready to respond to the unknown if it came rushing out of the woods.

After the bridge, the wide trail grew quieter and she sat up, looking behind her, relieved that no other riders approached. Up ahead, she saw a large building next to a river. This river was deeper than the one they had just crossed, even deeper than the waters that had been her retreat for the past four years. Next to the building was a large wheel made of stone and wood. The wheel kept turning, moving water from a large pond above it to the river below. She nudged Isaiah to slow him down and pulled the reins to move him closer to the wheel so she could watch it more closely. The wheel's turning never stopped, its continuous movement catching Hope's imagination. She scooted Jeremiah up and turned him sideways toward the water to show him this beautiful site. "Jeremiah, look. Can you see the circle of wood moving the water between the stones? And look, there's ducks on the water above the wheel!"

"And we can still hear the birds!" Jeremiah said gleefully. "I know some songs they were singing on the way here, wanna hear me?" Jeremiah began making chirping sounds in a rhythm that mimicked birds he had heard.

"Did you hear one like this?" Hope said, making her own song of chirping sounds. Then Hope stayed quiet to listen and relish this rare moment, one where they were immersed in each other, their surroundings, and their songs, taking turns sharing their individual tunes, then chirping together. As they rode, she hugged him tightly, her eyes sharpened toward the sight before them.

She was reminded of a time she had shared with her father. A time when they were on horseback on the way to the Watauga settlement. She had seen a moving wheel like this, attached to a stone building next to a river. But that building had been one of many new things she had seen long ago on a short day's journey with her father and she regretted she had not paid enough attention to his words, or appreciated that special day until now, much too late. The memories of yesterday would not bring her father back today.

Her thoughts focused on the large building and she studied it while still listening to Jeremiah's songs. Next to the turning wheel, the large stone building stood on stones stacked to make a wall twice her height. Above the stone walls were walls made of logs with windows set about two horses' lengths apart. There was a big barn to the side of the building opposite from the falling water. She turned Isaiah toward the building to take a closer look. As they got closer to the front of the stone building, she heard a loud clanging noise coming from the barn. "What's that big noise? It's scaring the birds away!" shouted Jeremiah.

As they came closer to the middle of the tall stone and wood building she saw a broad stone stoop in front of a very wide door, slightly ajar. To the left and front of the stoop stood two short posts holding a long log hanging next to a wooden tub of water.

"Well Isaiah," she whispered, guiding him toward the log. "Looks like this is a good place for you to rest and get some water." Dismounting, she tied Isaiah's reins to the log, and felt in her pocket to see if her sling was still there. She breathed a sigh of relief as she felt the sling's flax ropes. She then bent down to pick up a rock and slipped it in next to the sling in her pocket.

Now I have to make a big decision. Leave Jeremiah here on Isaiah, or take him to the unknown inside, she thought prayerfully. Just as she turned to pull Jeremiah off the horse, the clanging stopped. She heard a man's deep voice coming from where the noise had been. "Kin I help ye?"

Startled, she lifted Jeremiah into her arms, and turned to see a man walking toward her. He was grinning, his opened mouth revealing a missing tooth. A long, soft white beard flowed below his grin. He wore a white moustache between his grin and a wide nose set in the middle of a parched, wrinkled face. He looked to be a bit taller than she, though he had a rounded belly pushing tight against his shirt, which was partially covered by his faded blue jerkin. She realized she was staring, frozen in place, not sure if she should answer or throw Jeremiah back on Isaiah's back, put her foot in the stirrups, mount, and gallop away. She kept one hand in her pocket, tightly gripping her sling. Stay or run, she pondered.

Recognizing the man was watching her with some puzzlement, she suddenly realized she was only wearing her shift and apron. Looking down, she saw her worn and dirty shift, the fabric thinning, thin enough to show the parts of her body that her short gown would normally cover. In the past few days, she had only thought about Jeremiah and Isaiah, forgetting herself and how she must look. She quickly pulled Jeremiah to her chest, wrapping his legs around her waist so his small body completely covered her front parts.

The man stepped forward slowly, keeping his hands in his pockets, aiming not to startle her. His warm blue eyes twinkled brightly as he smiled. And, unlike Henry, his voice was kind with no strain of evil behind his words. "Looks like you'ns rode a long ways Missy. N' yer horse could use some new shoes," the man said moving closer, bending over to take a better look at Isaiah's hooves. "Horses' hooves are like fingernails. They don't feel pain there, but they need tendin' to so's they can run better." The man looked up at Hope, smiling and gesturing toward the big door. "Come on in. I was jest about to grab a bite to eat afore I finished working on my neighbor's plow. Bet yer young'n would enjoy some of my biscuits n' blackberry jam. Best biscuits in the country cuz I make the flour right here," he said.

The fear left her, as the old man's gentle voice gave her comfort. "Thank you, I'm sure he would like that," she said thinking hopefully that he would also have enough biscuits and jam to share with her. She followed him to the building, holding Jeremiah tightly to her chest to cover herself.

"I'm Mitchell, Thomas Mitchell," the man said holding the door open for Hope to walk in. "It's a lil cold in here cuz of th' grist mill and river. Lemme see if I can find ya somethin to keep yerself warm." He disappeared into a doorway off to the right and quickly returned to hand her a thin quilt and small blanket. "Here's another blanket fer th' little one. You'ns sure need some more clothes. Fer sure. Oh, forgive my manners. Folks 'round here call me Mitch. This here's my quarters. I work jest 'bout all th' time, between forgin' tools and horse's shoes, and keepin' th' grist mill goin' I oftimes work dawn til dark then on til daylight as folks always need their corn n' grain ground up so's theys can eat good. So, I sleep here when I can," he said pointing to a small bed in a corner not far from the door.

"Thank you Mr. Mitch," she said quickly setting Jeremiah down so she could wrap the quilt around her shoulders. Thankfully, it was long and thin enough that she could loop both ends and tie them at the front, making a temporary shawl to hide her embarrassment. She gave Jeremiah a quick hug as she bundled him up in the blanket.

"O'er here," said Mitch leading them through a maze of barrels to the center of the room where an iron cast stove stood surrounded by bulging sacks, lanterns of all sizes, and four stools. In the middle of the stools was a short, small table topped with a square piece of worn leather marked with light and dark brown squares. On top of the squares were dark and light wooden circles.

"Here's a seat fer ya little one." Mitch pulled over a large sack of grain and patted the top of it, signaling Jeremiah to sit on it. "Yep, that's 'bout perfect. Here, let me move th' checkers so's you'n's will have a place for yer biscuits. Have a seat Missy and I'll brang ya some grub."

Hope didn't sit down right away. She stood, turning around slowly, breathlessly taking in her surroundings. Shafts of sunlight from the high windows warmed the room to reveal more tools and barrels than she had ever seen. She couldn't believe her eyes. On a shelf she saw tin plates, bowls, pitchers, and iron skillets. Gourds and jugs were scattered about and hung on winged posts throughout the large room. Brooms, axes, knives, nails, and more sacks that looked like they held flour or cornmeal. Churns for butter. And even clothes -- breeches, shifts, petticoats, and more -- were hanging in random order on long pegs across the wall.

"Sit o'er here by th' table Missy," Mitch gestured with a tray of biscuits and a bowl piled high with blackberry jam. Hope sat in the chair closest to the table as Mitch set the tray in front of her and handed her a knife. She didn't know how hungry she was until she saw the food in front of her. Taking the knife, she opened a biscuit, spread it with jam, then handed it to Jeremiah. Jeremiah grabbed the biscuit and shoved it into his mouth, his cheeks puffing out as they filled with the goodness. He licked his lips and held out his hand beckoning for more. Mitch stepped away and returned quickly with two cups and a pitcher of water.

"Now, tell me. Where'd ya come from Missy?" Mitch asked, as he sat down in the chair across from Hope.

Hope took another bite of biscuit, not sure where to begin. She realized she didn't know where she came from. "I'm not sure exactly. It was northwest of here. Henry Greer was my husband. Did you know of him?"

Mitch shook his head left to right several times, looked down at the floor, then looked back at Hope.

"Well, I grew up not far from Fort Caswell and the Watauga settlement if you know where that is. We had a nice home, with a loft and a wood plank floor. My mother had a loom like that one," Hope said pointing to a loom in the corner. "Then, a few years ago, the Cherokee came and burned my homeplace. It happened late one evening before supper. My father pushed me out the door. I found my horse, got on him, and we raced away. I didn't know where I was going, except I realized I was going east when the sun came up and I was near the river. I think it was the Doe River, the same river that ran by our home. Father always said the Doe went to the east ..." she stopped and took another bite, not knowing if she could ... not wanting to remember most of her story. She slowly chewed her food, then swallowed to bury most of the past few years beneath her thoughts. "Anyways, I ended up at the Greers' place. That's where I married Henry," she tightened her lips thinking. "Then Jeremiah was born," she paused again. "A dark man took Henry's scalp and burned our cabins. That was just a few days back. God gave us a horse, my horse, and I escaped carrying Jeremiah. And yesterday I saw many men riding on horses going this way and now... now we're here." She looked up at the windows, avoiding Mitch's gaze. "I just, I just...."

Mitch said nothing, knowing there was much more to her story. He stood, and gently took her cup from her hands. "Let me git ya some more water," he said walking over to scoop up some water from the barrel near the counter. Walking back to her, and handing her the cup, he said, "Ya have quite a story, Missy. Ya don't have to tell it all today," he sat back in his chair.

"But fer now, this here place is pretty safe, if ya need to rest fer a bit. I've seen just about ever' kind of person walk through that door. Soldiers, Injuns, farmers. I'm the miller and th' blacksmith -- both. Plus, I keep supplies folks 'round here need. I trade fer most things they brang. They know's it, too. Sometimes they brang deer skins, sometimes they brang clothes the women have made or chillen's outgrowed. So, they ain't gonna do me no harm. That is, 'cept fer one fella who kept comin' here 'bout ever' week. Then ever' few days. Turns out he had a hankerin' fer my wife. She wuz younger n' so wuz he. So, one day, she just left and rode off with him. Now I jest keep busy, 'specially since I have to do her chores as well as mine!" Mitch exclaimed, then looked over at Jeremiah, realizing he was getting a bit too loud.

Jeremiah's face was covered with jam. Mitch walked back over to the counter, took a rag, dipped it into the barrel of water, and brought it back to Hope so she could wipe his face.

"That's the short of it," Mitch continued. "Now, I reckon we have to see 'bout you two. Thar's a bed up in the loft whar my wife slept til she left. It's purty nice and separate from whar I keep the flour and grain. She was quite feisty and liked the nicer things. You'll see. The bed's high so's thar ain't too many mice that gets in thar. As I got older, she seemed to get younger so's we rarely shared a bed. Or shared much anythin' fer that matter. Anyways, that's another reason why my bed's down here o'er near the door.

"So. Here. Take this pitcher of water. Thar's a washin' bowl up thar if ya want to rinse yer face. You'ns can go up n' look around to see if ya want to stay th' night. I've got to tend to my books, tryin' to keep my records straight as I ne'er know who's comin' or when. Sometimes they don't pay me or trade me anythin' til they got somethin' to bring me. I'll put some rice on to boil. Ya ever had rice?' he asked. "They's just started growing rice south of here, n' some farmers been tradin' it fer muskets n' gunpowder, what with the war n' all. Where ya come from, don't sound like ya had any neighbors or visitors much. So reckon ya don't know much 'bout the war do ya? Anyways, rice is really good with beef stew, especially when I put the beef n' rice in th' same pot n' let th' juices mix in. I'mma gittin' to be a purty good cook, if I say so meself."

"Mr. Mitch, I don't know how to thank you," Hope said, taking the pitcher of water. "Bless you. That's all I can say as I don't have enough words to explain how we got here. I prayed and prayed for God to light the way, to give me a path and He did, all the way to here."

"I'm glad for the company," Mitch said. "And don't worry, soon's I get th' rice and stew goin' and catch up on my books, I'll take that fine horse of yours to my barn and make sure he gets plenty of grain and water. I bet he's worn through as much as the two of you. Maybe I'll fit him some new shoes in th' mornin'."

With Jeremiah on her hip and the pitcher in hand, Hope climbed the stairs up to the mill's loft. It was a lot warmer and drier here, well above the water that moved under the first floor below. She walked past sacks filled with grain and flour, to the back of the room and opened a door off to the right. The room was as long as the building, filled with sunlight streaming in from windows at each end. At the far right side of the room, she saw a bed standing on four knee-high legs with posts that came up from the legs to about her height. She walked over to feel the mattress that sat between two stained boards at each end. The mattress was fat and fluffy, stuffed with tufts of cotton and covered with a linen blanket. Two linen-covered pillows, also stuffed with cotton, leaned against the tall board at the head of the mattress and a quilt lay folded halfway toward the other end.

Next to the bed was a table with a large blue and white porcelain bowl on the top shelf. She set the pitcher to its side. At the foot of the bed was a large cedar chest and next to the chest was a rocking chair. "We really are blessed, Jeremiah," she said. She plopped him down on the bed, so soft and thick, his body sunk deep into the cushy white linen. He rolled over and over, and sensing the softness, he began giggling uncontrollably. "Shh, be quiet or he won't let us stay," Hope whispered, holding her finger to his lips to suppress his giggles. She then plopped backwards onto the mattress with her arms outstretched. "Ahh, this feels good."

"Missy! Can ya hear me? Suppa's ready," yelled Mitch, standing at the foot of the stairs. "Don't ya worry. Young Jeremiah's with me. He actually climbed down the stairs all by hisself and he's been a very helpful young lad. You'll see. He even set the table fer me."

Hope sat up, startled, wondering how long she had slept. She surveyed the room again, still stunned and amazed to be in an actual bed, inside a very nice room. She stepped over to the porcelain bowl, filled it with water, splashed her face, wrapped herself in the thin quilt Mitch had given her earlier, then headed downstairs to the main floor below.

"While ya wuz sleepin' I thought 'bout yer story. Ya know I hear'd of Fort Caswell, Missy. There's been a lot of talk on all the fightin' there," Mitch said, gesturing to guide Hope over to the long, narrow wooden table at the back of the mill. Jeremiah was sitting on a long bench near the wall, completely enthralled with a small round piece of wood, carved to a point that allowed him to twirl it around, spinning it in circles on the table top. "Oh, I think Jeremiah likes his toy top, don't you Missy?" Hope grinned, her heart filled with a burst of joy at seeing her son playing without a care for anything but his new toy.

Mitch continued talking as he spooned the stew and rice into the pewter bowls on the table. "Anyways, jest yesterday the place wuz jammed with men from west of here. Some of 'em said they'd gathered at the waters of Sycamore Shoals near Fort Caswell. They's headed south to fight the British. Said the British wuz tryin' to take North Carolina into their territory. Thar wuz hundreds of 'em ridin' down the road headed that way. Not all of 'em came inside, mind ya, but my place was packed fer hours as whenever some of 'em left, more of 'em come in. They said they had slaughtered some of thar cattle as herdin' them slowed them down. They had too much beef to handle so they traded some of it, along with some deer and rabbit skins. Traded fer all th' gunpowder I had, Missy. Jest pray for 'em when ye pray. We need to end this war. Too many have died already."

Hope listened, amazed at the story, especially the part about Sycamore Shoals. "I really like the rice, Mr. Mitch. I never ate it before," said Hope, pausing so as not to talk with her mouth full as her mother had taught her. "Yesterday, we hid in the woods and watched hundreds of men riding down the trail on horseback. I had never seen so many men on horses --- all my life I've lived with just two families. I only left our home once when I went to the Watauga settlement with my father. So, it was quite a sight to see. I knew the men at Fort Caswell had fought many battles with the Indians cause my father told me. But I didn't know they were fighting the British too."

"Well, he must've been a very good father. I can tell ya come from a fine family. Ya speak with proper words, like ya had some schoolin', Missy. Any chance ya can read? I can't read or write good -- jest use my marks to tell who folks are. I have my own way of keepin' up with 'em now that my wife's gone. She used to keep the books as she could read and write and even do some numbers. Now, I'm doin' the best I can."

"My father taught me how to read by reading the Bible to me. He came from up north. Pennsylvania. Where he had good schooling. When he read me a verse, he made me read it back to him and tell him all the letters. That's how I learned and that's how I'm teaching Jeremiah," Hope responded. "And, Mr. Mitch, my name is Anna Hope O'Connor. You can call me Hope, if you will. Hope O'Connor."

And, for now and for the future, Mitch resolved not to mention the name "Greer", as it was clear the young woman no longer wanted her husband's name.

Once Mitch learned Hope could read and write, he immediately asked if she would be willing to stay and help out for a few days. In return, he offered her pick of the shifts, aprons, stays, and petticoats hanging on the mill's walls. She had gone around the room and picked one of each, along with a new gown for Jeremiah. As soon as she got to the loft, she removed her old shift and pulled on a new one. She felt a flush of emotion, lightly sliding her fingers across the clean fabric.

The next morning, giggling woke Hope as Jeremiah rolled up and down his side of the bed. That was the most wonderful sound Hope had heard since she could remember. And watching him, she took a moment to savor this vision of her son, safe, without a care in the world, and wearing his own clean gown. She sat up and stepped onto the floor, then whirled around and around, relishing the smooth, wooden floor beneath her feet. She turned again and again, until a flash of light and motion bounced out from the wall, the shock bringing her to a sudden halt. She was stunned to see her own reflection. "Oh, what is this?" she blurted. "It's a mirror! A real looking glass! Jeremiah, come here and look!" She pulled him up to her chest, and carried him, turning so Jeremiah could see their image framed on the wall.

"Mommy! Mommy! Who are they?" a terrified Jeremiah screamed.

"Why, Jeremiah, that is you. And that is me holding you! It's a looking glass! It's like looking into still water where you can see yourself staring down. It's a reflection. I haven't seen a looking glass since the one on the wall near my mother's bed! We used to look in it together when I had a new petticoat or apron. Now, you can see yourself. And I can...oh my!" Hope said, setting Jeremiah down, then moving forward to take a closer look at herself. She realized she had not given thought to her appearance since the first few months after Jeremiah was born. Now she felt embarrassed as she thought how she must have looked when Mr. Mitch first saw her.

"Oh my! I haven't seen myself in almost five years! My face is entirely freckled and my hair! My hair! It's a matted mess! I can't let anyone see me like this! I'll have to do something to look more presentable for Mister Mitch and his customers. He wants me to start helping him today."

She stood in front of the mirror and watched herself as she put on the new petticoat, leather stay, and apron. She picked up the pockets that she had thrown aside when she put on the shift the prior evening. The pockets were worn and dirty, but she did not feel right without them, especially since they held her trusty sling. Turning around to check her reflection, she still felt unsuitable for meeting Mr. Mitch's customers. Her matted hair fell nearly to her knees. She tried to untangle it with her fingers, but it was an impossible task.

"Jeremiah, go downstairs and ask Mr. Mitch if he has any scissors. Don't you try to carry them up here. Just bring them over to the stairs and I'll step down to get them." She walked Jeremiah over to the stairs and watched him as he tentatively backed down just as he had the previous evening while she was nappng. "I'll stay right here. I just don't want him to see me with my hair like this."

She stood by the stairs and listened as Jeremiah ran around the mill's first floor yelling, "Mr. Mitch, Mr. Mitch. You have scissors? Mommy wants scissors."

Momentarily, she saw Jeremiah at the foot of the stairs. She stepped down, took the scissors back up to stand in front of the mirror, and proceeded to cut her hair to half its length. She then twisted it and pulled it back through the hair at the top of her head as she had done many times over the past few years. *Maybe Mr. Mitch has a hair pin that someone's traded,* she thought as she carefully stepped down the stairs to begin her first day of work at the mill.

She stepped down the stairs and Jeremiah followed her into the large room. The sound of water rushing under the floor brought comfort to Hope as they walked through the maze of sacks, barrels, and tools, looking for Mitch. "O'er here," Mitch yelled, waving his arms. He waved them over to the long table on which sat two bowls of porridge.

"You'ns need a good breakfast cuz it's gonna be a busy day. I can feel it in th' air," said Mitch. "Miss Hope, you jest follow me around, watch, n' listen when I talk to our customers. I can't tell ya what to 'spect as ever' day is differ'nt. This mornin' Imma gonna check on yer horse n' see if I kin take off his worn shoes. He won't be needin' shoes whilst he's in the pasture n' I'll tend to his hooves so's they kin heal a bit whilst he's here. I bet Jeremiah can help me, can't ya son? I'm gonna teach him how to use the bellows."

Jeremiah nodded his head up and down eagerly, then spooned more porridge into his mouth.

"Folks come when'er they need somethin'. Sometimes I'm in th' barn firin' a piece of iron n' they want me to stop so's to feed thar corn into th' mill. I did have a young fellar helpin' me, but he's gone off to fight th' British. So, folks jest have to be patient til I kin get to 'em. Yer gonna be a big help. I know it. Specially since you kin write down what I did and what they give me fer it, or if'n they can't pay," Mitch said as he walked over to the counter, brought back a large black book, and handed it to Hope. "Here, why don't ya read this whilst I'm lookin' after yer horse. He won't be needing them worn shoes whilst he's in my pasture. N' he's got lots of pasture to roam, fer sure. Why I got so much pasture and land along this river, I can't hardly tell where it begins and ends."

"N' another thing," Mitch said reaching into his pocket. "I made ya this," he continued, opening his hand to reveal a sparkling ring. "Yer gonna be causin' lots of talk 'round here 'bout where ya came from n' why yer boy ain't got no papa here 'bouts. I sanded the high spots so it'll shine when ya hold it to th' light. Ye can determine if ye wants to wear it."

Hope was taken aback by his gesture, but she took the ring from his outstretched hand. "Why Mitch! It's beautiful! Henry never offered me a ring, but Granny Matilda had one and she never took it off, even though her husband had been dead and buried for many years," she smiled as she slipped it onto the finger of her left hand. "I will wear it until I see no need."

Chapter 14

Jake and Jared made the barn their home, spending every night cuddled in the straw bed near Jesse's stall. Late one evening, they were nodding off to sleep when Jared shook Jake's shoulder to wake him.

"Ya hear that?" Jared said. "Listen, shhh. It might be a turkey."

"Or a bear," Jake said.

"Be quiet. I think it's th' chickens!" Jared said. "We'll see in th' mornin'. I ain't goin' out thar in case it really is a bear or a wolf."

The next morning they ran out to the chicken coop to see three chickens scratching around the pen and pecking at what remained of the feed Matilda had left them the day before her last. "Maybe we'll get some eggs tomorrow or th' next day," shouted Jared. "Let's go find 'em some feed!"

They scoured the fields and filled their arms with corn that had not been harvested before the dark man came. They shucked and scraped some of the corn straight into the pen to feed the chickens and left the rest of the corn still in its husks in a burlap sack in the barn. In the orchard, they found trees full of apples and filled another sack to feed Jesse. "We'll not be making cider with these apples. But we kin cut 'em up n' cook 'em like granny done," Jake said.

The next morning they used their shovels to carefully dig through the ashes in both cabins. "I'mma gonna scrape 'round our bed. I left my belt ax on th' floor aside it, 'n it might still be good if'n th' handle's not burned up. The handle's made of a deer's thigh bone n' they don't burn too easy," Jared shouted.

Several hours later, they had made a pile of their findings in the big tub outside. A knife, pewter bowl and plate, along with some badly burned gourds that might be useful for storing whatever seeds they could find. Jared also found the belt ax, handle intact, and wiped it against his breeches to remove the ash.

The small kettle at Hope's hearth worked well for steaming the remaining corn until it was soft enough to nibble off the cob. And a smooth, flat rock inside the hearth was perfect for frying eggs the hens gave them. But they only went back to Hope's for the hearth where they kept the fire. They never lingered there, only going back to check the food in the kettle, or heat the rock for the eggs. Lingering brought too may memories of Hope, Granny, and Jeremiah.

On rainy days they went to the barn for supper. But when weather allowed, they took their meals sitting on Hope's rock. The wide, long rock gave them comfort. With the exception of the barn, firepit, and chicken coop, it was the only place that had stayed the same as before … before there was just the two of them, the chickens, and Jesse.

One evening as they sat on the rock eating the last of the corn, Jared asked, "Did ya see that bear hide on th' ground at th' back of th' barn?" He shoveled up a spoonful from the bowl that sat between them. "Th' frame must've fallen from th' animals kickin' durin' th' fire."

"I 'member brainin' th' hide not long ago, but I ne'er saw it agin."

"I think it's still good," Jared handed Jake the spoon. "Here. Finish this corn so's we kin take a better look afore it gits dark."

Jake sunk his teeth into the last corn cob and threw it into the chicken pen when he finished. They headed into the barn. "See, here 'tis," Jared said, leading Jake to the far back corner of the barn. The bear hide was still stretched out on the willow frame. "Let's take it outside n' see if it's got any bugs in it."

They picked up each side of the frame, carried it out the front of the barn and laid it down near Hope's rock. "I 'member this bear," Jake said. "It made a good stew. Granny used its fat to cook it. Once I even seen 'er stick 'er fingers in th' fat n' rub it in 'er hair."

"And on 'er face," Jared chuckled.

"Papa was mean, but he sure wuz a good bear hunter. If'n he wuzn't, I dunno whut he'd been trading with."

Jake examined the bear fur, brushing it with his fingers to check for bugs. "I sho' wish his musket hadn't burned. If'n we coulda fixed it, we could hunt bears ourselves. But he ne'er would let me shoot it anyways. I think he let me shoot it nigh to maybe four times, 'n I ne'er could hit anythin'. So's that's why he said I couldn't far it no more."

"Well, this here bear skin has to be worth takin' to th' Fort to see whut we kin git fer it. Maybe we kin at least trade fer a musket, n' maybe even a buckskin shirt 'r two," Jared said excitedly. "Let's get Jesse ready n' we'll go first thang in th' mornin'."

Jake was so excited he barely slept. As soon as the sun peaked through the cracks in the stall's log walls, he leaped up, grabbed Jesse's reins and led him down to the river for fresh water. He left Jesse by the river and ran back up to the barn.

"C'mon Jared, let's go!" he said, pulling Jared up from his sleep, noting the bear skin underneath him.

"This here bear sho' made good sleepin'," Jared mumbled, scrambling to put the dark man's moccasins on his feet.

"Well, pick it up n' brang it wit' ya. Time t' go!"

Jake helped Jared drag the bear skin out to Hope's rock where they dropped it, then raced his older brother down to the shallow part of the river where they splashed their faces with water, then scooped handfuls to drink. They led Jesse back to the rock, threw the skin across his back, and mounted, with Jared sitting behind Jake. Jake gave Jesse a nudge and off they went, down the hill and onto the trail, then across the bridge where they had tossed the dark man into the river. This was a familiar trail for Jesse, so Jake let him take the lead.

The sun rose high in the sky and began moving westward as they rode down the winding trail along the river. As daylight turned to dusk, the trail grew busier with more and more men riding past them, headed in the same direction.

"Let's follow these men! They must be headed to th' tradin' place n' thar prolly ain't much tradin' after it gits dark," Jake yelled, turning his head back a bit to be sure Jared heard him. He nudged Jesse to follow the other horses. But there was no need for nudging as the horse was simply following the path Henry had taken for the past many years.

The river by the trail was now very shallow, unlike the deep rushing water where they had tossed the dark man's body. All along the river, men were dismounting from their horses and forming small campsites, sitting on logs and smoking their pipes while talking excitedly. Jake guided Jesse back over toward the field where several men were standing with their horses getting supplies for their campsite. "Good evenin'," Jake said tentatively, reaching back to pat Jared on the leg indicating he should dismount. The boys dismounted and stood close together so as to not show themselves too much out of embarrassment from their lack of buckskin, haversacks, and the many other belongings that these strangers held.

"Evenin' boys," a stranger said. "Yer here to join th' muster?"

"Yep," answered Jake, making a mental note to ask Jared what a muster was. "We brought a bear skin to trade fer buckskins n' a musket."

"I see," said the stranger, assessing the scene in front of him and noting the two young men wore nothing but their long shirts and breeches, one with moccasins and the other barefoot.

"Well, we're one n' th' same here at Sycamore Shoals," the stranger said. "We Patriots aim to ride together 'til we find Major Ferguson n' his men. Some of us might die, some could even git crippled, but we's gonna kill or capture ever' one of his men, n' then we'll be free -- finally free."

"Dat yer only horse?" said another stranger who had been listening to the conversation.

"'Fraid so," said Jake. "He's a good 'un tho'. Strong as an ox," he said, then thinking he had never really seen an ox, he had only heard his papa say the words.

"We's from the Sullivan County Regiment," said the stranger. "But men n' women come from all o'er fer this mission. Women is brangin' supplies n' a Mary Patton's providin' much-needed gunpowder. I'm sure we kin find ya another horse, muskets, n' maybe even a buckskin. That is, if'n you'n's will come with us," he paused to give the brothers a chance to answer. Seeing them nod, he continued, "And..." he paused looking at Jake's bare feet.

"I'mma gonna make it a point to find ya some moccasins, young fella!"

A sealed cloak of darkness pushed light fog in from the river. Jared decided he should take Jesse for some water and to find a patch of grass for grazing. "Ya stay here n' listen to thar plans. I'll be o'er yonder by th' river," Jared whispered to Jake. Jake watched as his older brother led Jesse away into the fog. He studied hard trying to remember Jared's path, marking the different trees Jared passed until he could no longer see him. This was the first time Jake had been on his own among men and he stood his straightest, holding his shoulders back, but kept fidgeting with his arms, not certain where to place his hands in order to look confident and unafraid. He shuffled his feet back and forth to gain a proper stance. He placed one hand against his right hip and glanced around casually, realizing the men were intensely engaged in their own conversation, one which did not include him. He turned his head and leaned his ear upward to listen to the other voices, voices that were just as intense and excited as the men from the Sullivan County Militia, then stepped to the side and back a few steps to appear ready to move on to his next destination. Finally, he turned to view the activity he had heard behind him.

The high-pitched voices came from three young girls walking in his direction. They were walking slowly and chatting excitedly, not mindful of their surroundings and seeming to have no particular destination or path defined. A tall, heavy-set girl was leading a horse. A rather striking, short and thin brown-haired girl, was carrying two burlap sacks which looked to weigh more than the young girl herself. The other had her forearm held upward at her shoulder, her hand holding a rope strung with tin cups and a skillet slung across her back. They were looking this way and that, not paying attention to their feet or the ground beneath them. "Ouch!" exclaimed the girl in the middle. Jake ran forward and caught her just as she fell, her foot caught in a tree root growing inconveniently above the ground. The weight of the burlap sacks brought her down with such force she flew into Jake's arms, pushing him backwards onto the ground, her nose landing hard against his forehead.

"My foot! My foot!" she screamed, clearly in pain. Jake carefully put his hands under her hips and lifted her up to view her foot. It was stuck between two branches of the thick root. He slowly scooted over and out from under her, gently laid her back on the ground, then quickly crawled over and held her foot with one hand while he lifted the root and pushed it forward ever so slightly.

Her two friends stood watching, stunned, their mouths wide open. "You! Put yer hands under her shoulders n' th' other'n hold her upper legs carefully jes' above th' ground," Jake ordered the two girls who scurried to respond without a word. "When I say go, slowly move her towards me," he said as he held her foot tightly to keep it from twisting. "Go!" Together they moved the brown-haired girl toward him while Jake held the root away from her foot. Her friends helped the brown-haired girl turn and slowly sit upright so she was facing Jake. She leaned forward to rub her ankle.

"Do it hurt much?" Jake said eagerly. He realized he needn't have asked as he watched the tears stream down her face. "Do you'ns live near here?" he asked the three.

"We've been walking to here since mornin'," the tall heavy-set girl answered. "We took turns ridin' th' horse, but decided to walk him when we seen so many people. We brung th' horse n' provisions to help ready th' men for thar journey. We thought we'd be able to just leave 'em here, but we ain't found anyone to tell us where to take 'em."

"Well, I come here with my brother Jared 'n he's gone down to th' river wit' our horse," Jake said. "Let's see if'n we kin find him n' maybe build a far."

Without asking, he took the brown-haired girl in his arms and lifted her onto the horse. "Follow me," he said, wrapping the reins around his wrist so he could carry each of the heavy burlap bags as he led the way.

The two girls followed quietly as Jake guided the horse carrying the brown-haired girl toward the river where he had last seen Jared. Darkness fell quickly revealing bright rays of moonlight peaking through leaves and bouncing across the mist to light a path in between the many campsites that had popped up in nearly every direction. When they got to the riverbank, Jake began calling, "Jared ... Jesse ... tchk tchk," then pausing, listening for a familiar voice among the strange ones. He continued calling, staying as close to the riverbank as he could.

"What's in them bags anyways?" he asked the two girls walking beside him.

"One's got corn meal and th' other'ns got taters, I think," said the heavy-set girl.

"Those potatoes are heavy!" The girls and Jake looked up toward the voice to see the brown-haired girl leaning over their way. "Where are we going?" she asked.

"And I'm getting hungry," whined the girl who had said nothing until now.

"I ain't found my brother, so's we' un's jest gonna have t' make our own place I reckon," Jake said. He led them on along the riverbank until he found what looked like a good spot. "Here!" he stopped, dropping the bags to the ground. "We got a big tree to lean against n' some small ones nearby where we kin tie yer horse, after'n we git it some water from th' river." He lifted the brown-haired girl down from the horse and set her down where she could lean against the tree. "One of you'n's take th' horse n' th' other'n see if'n ya kin find some wood for a far," he ordered in as nice a voice as he could offer, being that he was tired, flustered, and uncertain of how he was going to manage three girls without his brother's help. "I'mma gonna go o'er thar 'n see ifn' that fella will let me have some hot sticks from his far, so's we kin start our own."

Soon they were settled next to the big tree with a small fire in front of them. The heavy set girl had taken five of the potatoes from the sack and tucked them between two rocks under the fire. "We coulda ate 'em raw, but they's better roasted a bit," she said as she walked away from the fire. "I'll be right back." Moments later, she returned holding tin cups filled with water from the river. "Glad we brought these here provisions," she chuckled.

Jake took a cup and handed it to the brown-haired girl. "Is yer foot still hurtin'?" he asked.

"Not so much now. I think it's just bruised a bit," she answered. She held the cup with both hands and sipped her water. "I guess we can stay here until we find your brother."

After their potato supper, the three girls formed a circle, seated back-to-back and told each other stories that generated giggles and an occasional loud burst of laughter. Jake sat leaning against the tree watching and listening, only getting up once to fetch more firewood to ensure their fire was strong enough to last through the night. After placing more wood on the fire, he stood silently, poking it with a stick, thinking of what he should do next. The girls seemed not to notice him, so without a word, he went back to the tree and assumed his prior position. He rubbed two fingers across the bony ridge of his once-broken nose, pondering his situation. There were men and campfires scattered as far as he could see. But, they soon faded from his mind, as the scene immediately before him was most compelling.

He had never heard such chatter. In fact, he had never seen any women other than his mother, granny, and Hope. How was a young man to manage himself with these girls? His papa was his only reference. So, that meant women were there to serve him and give him pleasure. He vaguely recalled papa playing his fiddle to entertain Hope. After they married and she gave him a son, yelling and hitting became the best way to ensure she did his bidding. Granny and mother were always quiet around him. They never giggled like this. But this was not the farm. In less than a day his world had changed completely. It was larger than he could ever have envisioned.

He vowed never to go back. This moment was one he wanted to keep forever. Heaven must be like this. The water rushing along the shallow shoals made music behind him. Campfires sparkled in the distance as he watched and listened to the three girls he had only known for the best part of a day. Their mere presence made him smile and he felt a new gladness inside, especially when he looked at the brown-haired girl.

"Headin' out!"

"Patriots! Put out yer fars, n' gather yer supplies!" commanded a voice across the field. That voice was joined by many others shouting orders, some even cheering, as they began to gather in a long line formed ten to twenty across, some on horses, some walking. All headed to the east.

Jake stood up, startled, then saddened, then excited as he realized he was among hundreds of men, young and old, who were joining together for a single purpose. He didn't know the purpose, maybe they were searching for a muster, whatever that was. But there was no doubt that he was going with them. He looked over to see the three girls standing together, their burlap sacks, tin cups, and skillet were on the ground in front of them. The brown-haired girl held the reins of their horse.

"We came to share provisions n' a horse for th' mission. Everyone from all around supports what yer plannin'. And we girls can't thank ya enough for helpin' us, n' 'specially helpin' Melissa when she fell," said the tall, heavy-set girl. "So, here's yer horse n' supplies. We hope ya find yer brother."

Jake stood, staring at the three girls. He had no words as he stepped forward to take the reins from the brown-haired girl. For the first time, he could see the color of her eyes. They were a deep brown, almost black, so dark, and penetratingly beautiful it felt like she could see into his soul. As she handed him the reins, their hands touched, and she gave him a look that brought him confidence and simultaneously took his breath away. He slowly bent down to pick up the two sacks and twisted the tops to close them and tie them together then secure them behind the horse's saddle. The quiet girl handed him the string of tin cups and skillet and he placed them across the horse's back where the two sacks connected. He turned to take a final look at the girls, trying not to be conspicuous in avoiding the brown-haired girl's eyes. Nervously, he placed one hand across his chest and nodded his head indicating his thanks. He turned, stepped up into the stirrups, and mounted the horse. With one swift kick, he was on his way, falling into line with the other men. He felt the edge of his shirt where it was rolled up and tucked into his breeches. The sling was still there. He turned his head back to get one more look at the girls and raised his hand in a quick wave. "Melissa," he whispered aloud. Just the sound of her name stirred his senses in an unfamiliar way.

With some hesitation, he guided the horse to fall in with strangers who rode with their friends. This was another unfamiliar situation for him. When Jared had headed to the river, conversation with the men from the Sullivan County Regiment had failed him. He was surrounded by men well-prepared for battle. It seemed every man had a weapon. Some had more than one musket, some with bayonets attached. All he had was a sling. He longed to find Jared, praying that he had been able to trade the bear skin for a musket. *At least Jared has his tomahawk which promises to be a better weapon than a sling*, he thought.

The riders appeared to be in groups of all sizes, some on horseback, some driving herds of cattle. Each group had a leader, he observed. He lined his horse up to ride on the outside of one group, getting closer to a young man who appeared to be about his age. He was riding alongside the man when he heard music. It sounded a bit like whistling. It was definitely not a fiddle. The tune floated across the air offering a cheerful beat as the men marched ahead. The only music he had heard before was that of his papa playing tunes after supper in the days before Jeremiah was born. He mustered up enough nerve to ask the fellow riding alongside him, "Wut's that music I'mma hearin'?"

"It's a fife," the young man said. "I like it. It's inspiring. I'm sure he'll stop playing once ever' one of us gits on th' main road, tho'. We can't make a lot of noise if'n we're gonna sneak up on Captain Ferguson n' his men. That's fer sure."

Jake nodded, taking in the young man's words. The night before he had heard enough from the men of the Sullivan County Regiment to know this was a serious mission. "We ain't huntin' bears ya know," a man had said when discussing their plans.

"I'm Charlie. Charlie Edwards," said the young man. "Wut's yer name?"

"Jake. Jake Greer."

"I come here with Colonel Shelby n' th' Sullivan County Regiment from the Holston settlement. I seen ye last evenin' but ya disappeared after a bit. So, where ya from?"

"My older brother Jared n' me come from jest up th' road apiece. We had a farm up thar on th' Doe River. But a dark man come one mornin' n' burned our place to th' ground."

"So that's why ya ain't got no shoes?"

Jake looked down at his bare feet placed firmly on the stirrups. He had forgotten he had no shoes.

"They say thar's o'er 1,000 men with us today. Maybe one of 'em has some extra moccasins," Charlie continued. "My mama packed my haversack. She wuz cryin' but tryin' to keep me from seein' her tears. I don't even know wut's in it. If'n she put some extra stockings, I'll give em to ya. They say it gits right cool at night in 'em mountains."

With Jesse's reins in hand, Jared had walked throughout the camps trying to find a taker with supplies to trade for the bear skin. Late in the evening, he came across a group of men who had set up a small supply unit. At that point, he was disheartened and willing to trade for anything he could get. The men took a close look at the bear skin then huddled to discuss its value. Jared watched with a prayer in his heart hoping for much-needed supplies. The huddled men took turns looking back at Jared, then searched through their supplies to see what they could spare. Jared expressed his gratitude feeling lucky to have anything at all. He left their encampment with a musket, a gunpowder horn, and a buckskin jacket.

The next morning was one of much scurrying and excited chatter as Jared wandered the camp in search of Jake. He watched as each group gathered their equipment and left to follow the many men before them. With no sign of Jake and realizing he would soon be left alone, Jared mounted Jesse and fell in with the last of the militia.

Jesse took to the road without missing a beat as they were headed back along the familiar trail Henry had taken so many times before. They rode uphill on a winding trail that soon followed the Doe River. As daylight faded, Jared saw men dismounting and forming camps far ahead. Suddenly, Jesse pulled his head against the reins and turned up a narrow path. Jared recognized this as the trail at the edge of their farm. Sadness and the trauma of the days before rushed through his mind so intensely they blocked any memories of the good times he had enjoyed with his granny, Hope, and Jeremiah. Fighting tears, Jared jerked the reins and cornered Jesse back onto the main road to follow the last of the men riding into the new encampment. As he got closer, he decided to ride past the last group to see if he could find his younger brother.

The men were camped on both sides of the road, some near the river, some near a large overhanging boulder where they were quickly moving their gunpowder and other supplies. Drops of rain were now streaming across Jared's face, blurring his vision. He rode slowly, shaking his head to toss the water away from his eyes. He was past most of the men, when he heard a familiar voice shouting. "Young man! I been lookin' fer ya. O'er here. I found ya some moccasins!"

Just beyond the large boulder, he saw the man from the Holston settlement waving some moccasins high in the air. Running in the man's direction was a barefoot, blonde-haired boy with a crooked nose. Without Jared's nudging,

Jesse headed in the boy's direction. The boy grabbed the moccasins then turned, bumping straight into Jared and his horse. "Did ya see we jest passed th' farm?" Jared shouted, quickly dismounting to give his brother a big slap on the shoulder. Jake stepped back a bit, hardly believing his eyes and ears.

"Jared! Jared! Whar wuz ye? I thought I lost ya -- n' Jesse too!" Jake grabbed his brother by both shoulders and locked his eyes onto Jared's to make a point. "Jared. I have a friend. I ne'er had a friend afore -- 'cept'n ye, me own brother. Name's Charlie! N' do ya know wut's a muster? Charlie told me. It's friends gatherin' together to go fight th' enemy. Jest like we saw at Sycamore Shoals n' now here at th' Shelvin' Rock! N' we's gonna fight a man called Ferguson -- n' his army! We' un's might even die! Charlie knows ever' thang." Jake paused, then continued, "N' I got a new horse. It ain't got no name yet. But first ya gotta meet Charlie!"

Jake took Jared's hand to lead him toward Colonel Shelby's encampment. Jesse followed closely behind. "Oh n' I got me some moccasins!" Jake suddenly stopped, lowering his voice. "Here! Forgot I had 'em!" He leaned onto Jared to balance himself. "Mmm. Me feet's swelled. Reckon they'll fit better after a time." As soon as he settled into his moccasins, Jake regained his pace, pulling his brother through another maze of men to find his new friend. "Thar he is! That's Charlie!" Jake shouted, grabbing Jared's hand and pulling him into a huddle of serious voices. "Charlie! This here's me brother Jared!"

An alarmed Charlie excused himself and gently escorted the two brothers away from the conversation. "Jared! We wuz worried 'bout ya. Grateful to see ya found us. C'mon n' I'll show ya whar yer brother n' me made camp. Then I'll have to git back to th' meetin' afore they miss me."

After Charlie ran back to the huddle, Jake cleared a space for his brother's gear to the right side of his own, making sure that Charlie's place to his left remained secure. He didn't want to miss a word of Charlie's stories about life back at the Holston settlement and silently prayed his friend would quickly return from his meetin'.

"What a day!" Jared said as he settled in.

"And a night!" Jake exclaimed, anxious to tell his brother all about the girls, wondering if he should share his feelings about a girl named Melissa.

Jared, Jake, and Charlie spent much of the night catching up on the previous evening's events and discussing the militia's plans going forward. It was on this evening that Charlie learned of Jake and Jared's upbringing where their days were spent in the field or doing other chores. He was shocked to hear of their father's greed, especially in the ways of hunting. In Charlie's world, every son had learned to hunt and fire his musket as soon as they were strong enough to hold a gun. Henry Greer had only one musket, and his attempts to teach his sons to shoot had ended as soon as each son had failed to fire with accuracy. No matter that it was the first time. The first time had been the last and Henry had kept his musket to himself, leaving his sons with no knowledge of how to handle a firearm. Charlie surmised he would soon be teaching Jared how to use the musket he had traded for the bear skin. Jake only had a sling for a weapon, but allowed he could also use the tomahawk Jared kept tucked into the back of his breeches.

The riders stayed with the group they had initially joined when they had traveled to Sycamore Shoals. Identified as a company, tying them to their region of origin, they stuck closely to the leaders that had brought them to the muster. Jared, Jake, and Charlie were now solid members of Colonel Shelby's company of Patriots.

They departed the site known as Shelving Rock and pressed on as the rain turned to snow. They climbed steep hills, through a gap between two mountains, and through a meadow called "Bald of the Yellow". By the time they reached the meadow, the snow was shoe mouth deep. They continued along Roaring Creek then joined the group's encampment near the base of the mountain. As the men dismounted, the company leaders gathered to discuss the next day's plans. Charlie had made a habit of lingering close to the leaders' huddles and soon learned that each company leader was planning to test his militia's firing skills. *This will require some preparation and improvising,* thought Charlie as he eased himself away from the leaders to find Jake and Jared.

The leaders had their men line up and fire their long guns, one-by-one. Charlie placed himself near the end of their company's line, and set Jared to his left, with Jake in between. He gave Jake his ramrod, balls, and horn of gunpowder and had Jared do the same. Wearing Jared's buckskin and Charlie's saddlebag, Jake now held most of their ammunition. When it came his turn, Charlie fired, then handed his musket to Jake, who immediately re-armed it. Jared fired, then Jake handed Charlie his re-armed musket, as Charlie re-positioned himself to Jared's left and fired again. They repeated the same steps after Jared fired. The commander watched, seemingly impressed with their teamwork, as the men on down the line demonstrated their firing skills.

When their line disassembled, Charlie, Jake, and Jared went back to the campsite where they had originated their plan. Charlie took Jake aside and placed his hands on his friend's shoulders. Staring straight into Jake's eyes, he said, "Yer gonna be in charge of makin' wadings and keepin' us armed and ready when we go into battle. But I want ya to know one more thing Jake. Ye've come to be my best friend on this mission, 'n I trust ye with all I have. So, if'n I get shot in th' battle, yer to grab my musket, and keep fightin' -- ya hear?"

The next day, they followed a well-worn trail up to the crest of another mountain. There, the trail split, taxing the commanders with a difficult decision. Would they choose between trails, or split up. Not knowing their enemy's exact location or which direction their enemy might take, the commanders determined they would split the militia into two groups with the goal of reuniting when the trails again merged.

Charlie led the way as they followed Colonels Shelby and Sevier along the Toe River upstream to Heffner Gap then descended to North Cove where they camped along Honeycutt Creek. Along the way, they stopped at a grist mill to trade for additional supplies in preparation for upcoming battles. From the grist mill, they proceeded for another two days until they reunited with the rest of the militia at Quaker Meadows.

For the next seven days, the Patriots continued south, depending on spies and scouts to report their enemy's location, often requiring the militia to turn back several miles to reach their location. Finally, after thirteen days of traveling in soaking rain, through muddy terrain, and across flooding rivers, they reached the foot of Kings Mountain. Their enemy was confidently entrenched at the top of the mountain, threatening Charlie, Jake, and Jared who, along with their company, began preparing for battle from the woods below. At that point, they realized they would not be able to carry out Charlie's plan for re-loading. Since Jake had no gun, he assisted as Charlie and Jared took the time they had to prepare their gunpowder, wads, and balls, and stuff them into their pouches. Two of the companies charged up the mountain slopes, but were driven back by the enemy's fire. Finally, half of the militia's companies reached the other side of the mountain, in effect, successfully surrounding their enemy's loft.

At their leader's command, Charlie, Jake, and Jared dismounted and began moving through the trees and up the hill toward their target. Shots rang through the trees as Charlie and Jared fired their long guns. Jake pulled Jared's tomahawk from his brother's belt, prepared to protect his friend and brother if anyone came close. The Patriots continued uphill as their enemies moved closer. They continued firing and reloading as they ran. The entire mountain and surrounding woods were ablaze with sparks and smoke from the firing muskets. Jake stopped to get a clear sighting as he watched Charlie and Jared move toward the enemy, firing, re-loading, and firing again. Suddenly, Charlie fell, tumbling back toward Jake. Jake ran to him, hoping to pick up his musket, but it had been knocked out of Charlie's hand as he hit the ground and rolled down the hill. A soldier was running down the hill bayonet ready to pierce Charlie before he could regain his balance. Without hesitation, Jake threw the tomahawk and hit the soldier squarely between his eyes. The soldier fell forward on top of Charlie. Jake ran over and jerked the soldier off his friend. "Charlie, Charlie. Talk to me," Jake said as he pulled Charlie into his arms. Charlie's blood splurted onto Jake's buckskin jacket and onto his leg.

"Take my shoes n' take care of me horse," Charlie muttered. And those were the last words of Jake's first friend.

Chapter 15

The nightmares continued, with flaring colors of deep purple and stark reds flashing through Hope's mind, as her body jerked abruptly to break away from its attacker.

"Mother! Mother! Wake Up!" Jeremiah was on his knees beside her pushing his hands against her ribs, trying to wake her. "Okay. It's okay," his young voice pleaded. "Please don't cry. Don't cry!"

She woke and rolled over, pulled Jeremiah close to her heart and held him tightly until she could transition from the terror in her mind to the little child next to her. Back to the sweet comfort of his innocence. Back to now and the day ahead.

She said nothing as she released his hug and rolled over to step out of bed. Standing, she stepped over to the mirror. Her face was swollen and sticky from the tears. The swelling was an all too familiar sight. She leaned over the porcelain bowl and splashed her face again and again with cold water, holding the water in cupped hands against her face to wash away the redness in her eyes. She let the coldness of the water sink into her mind, through her soul, to absorb it into her very being. This morning ritual helped her move her thoughts into the present to become the young woman she must be to make it through the day.

"Jeremiah, get dressed and go downstairs. You can warm the leftover biscuits on the wood stove and spread them with jam for your breakfast. I'll see you later at supper."

She now assumed her daily persona. Cool. Distant. But polite and pretentious, strong in spirit. Stronger from the days and nightmares past. She now headed downstairs, her outer shell set firmly to guard against potential threats.

Hope had worked in the grist mill daylight to dark for the past few weeks, greeting neighbors who came to have their corn ground into meal and their wheat into flour. When they entered, she would greet them, learn of their need, determine their method of payment, pick up the quill, dip it into the ink well, then enter the date and transaction into the account book. She would then send them on to Mitch who was still dividing time between handling the mill and managing his blacksmith duties. In the few hours when there were no customers, Hope took inventory and re-organized the mill's wares and provisions to make them more visible and appealing to folks who had the funds to shop for necessary supplies.

Word soon spread about the battle of Kings Mountain and the brave men who had journeyed from Sycamore Shoals to defeat Captain Ferguson and push the British out of the Carolinas. Hope was intrigued with the stories, and she and Mitch would share the tales they heard over supper each evening. Jeremiah would sit quietly, eating his supper, intently listening to every word.

Weeks after the battle, a few men arrived at Mitch's mill, boasting of their success at Kings Mountain, their horses in great need of re-shoeing. More and more men came with each passing day. It was at that point that Mitch realized he needed more than Hope's record-keeping skills. The increased demand for his blacksmith services soon affected his ability to keep up with the demands at the grist mill. One evening after supper, he took Hope up to the milling wheels and showed her how to run corn through to make meal. The next evening he taught her how to adjust the stones and run the wheat through to make flour. She learned how to open and adjust the gates to control the amount of water rushing through to run the wheels. When it became clear that Hope didn't have the strength to adjust the stones herself, she suggested that they set different days for grinding wheat and corn. In this way, Mitch could help her move the stones after supper on just two evenings a week to prepare for grinding the next day's victuals. Hope even made a sign that she placed at the mill's entrance: "Corn - Monday, Tuesday, Wednesday. Wheat - Thursday, Friday, Saturday". Soon the locals learned the system and she found this to be quite manageable.

Each morning, Mitch took Jeremiah out to the blacksmith shop and enlisted his help in moving the coal and using the bellows to fan the flames of the forge. Jeremiah was a curious boy and it seemed he was constantly asking questions of Mitch. "Why" was his most-used word. Mitch enjoyed the company, and while Jeremiah was not quite four years old, he was tall and stocky for his age, his shoulders reaching well above Mitch's waist. Pumping the bellows had created visible muscles in Jeremiah's upper arms and he took great pride in flexing his arms to show visitors how strong he was.

Hope now spent much of her time at the milling wheels, as the early winter months were the busiest. During this time she learned the names of each man and woman who brought their grain and corn to the mill. To Hope, these strangers would never be real friends, but acquaintances. She listened to their conversations with one another. They became her teachers, though they did not know this was their purpose. When she was writing in their accounts, she asked about their farms, their families, their ancestors, and inquired of how they spent their days and evenings. Whenever they responded with curiosity about her life, she quickly turned their queries into a new question about their own.

So, while Hope built a mental library of the community and its people, they knew nothing of her. Her years with Henry and days of learning to be invisible had instilled a protective shell that prevented her from speaking of herself. During her waking hours, she dared not open her mind to reach into the past.

But the neighbors did observe her keen intelligence. She was one of only a few who could both read and write. They were fascinated with her ability to count and quickly factor their debts. Never mind her stunning green eyes and ginger hair. It was her quick mind that she was known for. So, even as they brought deer hides, bear skins, and outgrown clothing to trade, they also began to bring her books. Books that had been passed down through generations by their ancestors from Ireland, Scotland, and England -- places where books were treasured, even by those who could not read.

Soon they were asking her if she had read this book or the other. And, before long she was spending her evenings with an oil lamp by her bed, a book in her hands, reading late into the night until she fell asleep. Sometimes, when Jeremiah hadn't fallen asleep straight after supper, she would read aloud, sharing the tales by Shakespeare, Cervantes, and Milton. When she discovered Defoe's stories of Robinson Crusoe, she set aside Sunday afternoons to read the adventures to Jeremiah. It wasn't long before Jeremiah was repeating the tales of pirates and cannibals to Mitch. And those who stopped by the blacksmith's shop, lingered, captivated by the young boy's imagination. Jeremiah was so heartened by the interest of those who lingered, he began inviting each one to come listen to his mother on Sunday afternoons.

Henceforth, Sunday afternoons became storytelling at the blacksmith shop. Neighbors brought Sunday dinner leftovers to share and stools to sit on while they listened, enthralled by the young ginger-haired woman and her stories.

But, unfortunately, the neighborly Sunday readings were short-lived. Soon, the trees began to paint the surrounding mountains with brilliant colors of red and orange, but it seemed only moments later that the multi-colored leaves left their branches to cover the ground, only shifting as more and more horses galloped through them. What was once a thriving community became a land filled with strangers, as men returning from Kings Mountain set up campsites along the river while they waited for their horses to be re-shoed. Women who lost their husbands in the war found themselves hauling the wheat and corn from their farms to the grist mill and leaving it there only to return for their flour and meal days later.

Stories of war and bloodshed brought sadness and apprehension to the community -- yet it remained free of bloodshed -- and the strings of fear remained loosely suspended above their daily lives.

Mitch was overwhelmed with one request after another. In order to keep track of who was next in line, he sent each person back to the mill to put their name on a list. With each new customer, Hope began a new entry in her books. While she had detailed information on those who had established homes in the community, the records were thin when it came to the returning militia. She realized they had little to offer in terms of payment and even less to record when it came to their homeplace or plans for the future. She was amazed that so many had no intention of returning to the settlements they had left behind, but she also recognized that some were battle-scarred, unable to speak of their past or their plans. She could identify with those whose spirits were bruised by sad memories.

However, many were carefree, boastful, and flirtatious -- each one with a different approach. That is until they got close enough. To her, each one was a threat, though she made every effort to disguise her fear. She would acknowledge their approach with a nod, her right fist clinched but ready to grab the dark man's knife within easy reach under the counter. As she nodded hello, she placed her left palm firmly down, and tapped the counter, to make certain they saw her wedding ring. When they stared inquisitively, she responded, "He should be home any day now." The new customers never saw her out among the wares as she made it a point to stay close to the dark man's knife when unfamiliar faces entered.

As winter set in, many of the soldiers began negotiating with Mitch to acquire plots of his land to build their own cabins. Mitch took pride in the vast acreage of his land, but he also took pity on the men who had seen battle but had no home. He sold large tracts of land in multiple acres so as to keep the number of his neighbors low. By spring, five cabins anchored the land along the river. And with spring came courting between the soldiers and the widows who had their own farms along the trails Hope and Jeremiah had passed when they first found the grist mill. Familiar crops of corn, wheat, and flax along with fields of rice and peas were beginning to pop up all around. Tobacco fields also emerged as farmers began to diversify and develop options for trading with their neighbors.

The grist mill and blacksmith shop remained the geographical center and heart of this new settlement, and what was once only two buildings with some nearby farms, soon came to be known as Mitchborough.

Chapter 16

Together, Jared and Jake carried Charlie's body to where they had stationed their horses at the bottom of the hill. They placed Charlie's body across the back of his horse, took Jesse's reins, along with the reins of the horse Jake had ridden from Sycamore Shoals, and quietly walked to the field where the injured were being cared for.

The next morning, Jared and Jake joined their fellow militiamen in digging shallow graves to bury the dead. They placed Charlie's body next to others from the Holston settlement and stood in silent prayer, grateful that they had befriended such a brave young man.

There had been little time for celebration of their victory over Ferguson's Loyalist army. Shortly after the dead were buried, the Patriots were commanded to stay with their companies in order to take the British prisoners to trial. Jake and Jared re-joined their regiment to assist in accompanying the prisoners. They traveled for several days until they finally arrived at a plantation owned by a man named Biggerstaff. After trials, and the hanging of nine prisoners, Jake, Jared, and the rest of Shelby's regiment spent several more weeks corralling the remaining British prisoners, with some escaping and others being delivered for trial and imprisonment.

Finally, Colonel Shelby released his unit to return to their homes. Throughout the weeks of traveling with their regiment, Jake and Jared had kept Charlie's horse alongside carrying the extra supplies, guns, and clothing they had retrieved from the prisoners who had fallen ill and been left behind along the way. Now, with Charlie's horse still in tow, they proceeded to head west, re-tracing the same trails that had brought them to Kings Mountain. They rode through Quaker Meadows, past a grist mill, past Heffner Gap and over the mountain. This evening, they set camp near the spring at the base of the Big Yellow Mountain.

"It's gittin' colder," said Jake as he threw some branches onto the fire.

"Yep, not many leaves on th' trees. I saw th' colors changin' them last few days with th' prisoners," Jared said. "Thar's still some grass fer th' horses tho', but we best git goin' early in th' mornin'."

"I think I'mma gonna ride Charlie's horse th' rest of th' way," Jake muttered. "N' thar's somethin' I been meanin' to tell ya. Th' horse I been ridin' belongs to th' girls I met at Sycamore Shoals."

"I know," replied Jared, with a note of irritation in his voice. "Ya already told me 'bout them girls."

"Well, I aim' to take 'em thar horse, if'n I kin find 'em. I reckon Sycamore Shoals is 'bout two days ride from here -- at th' most. So, in th' mornin' if'n yer willin', I wanna split up our souvenirs n' supplies so's th' girls' horse will be in good shape fer returnin'. It's a bit worn fer th' journey, but perhaps we kin return it wit' an extra one of th' prisoners' muskets as I'mma gonna keep Charlie's fer me own."

Jake took the reins of the girls' horse, then mounted Charlie's horse which now carried Jake's share of supplies. It made him sad to be riding the horse of a friend, the only friend he had ever known except for his brother. Charlie had taught him how to shoot a musket and had left him his shoes. But more than that, Charlie had shared stories of growing up in the Holston settlement. Stories that included gatherings of people, Sundays at church, how he had traded goats for boots, the importance of changing a horse's shoes, and even stories of the girl he was courting with the hope of making her his wife. Charlie had given Jake insight into a world that had been hidden from Jake and his brother. It was a puzzlement to him -- why his papa had never taken them to the Watauga settlement or taken the time to teach him how to use a musket. He guessed his papa had wanted his sons to be protected from the outside world. But he constantly questioned why.

Now the brown-haired girl named Melissa occupied most of his thoughts. He was both excited and afraid. What would he do if he found her? Give her the horse and leave? Where would he go then? Too many questions. No answers.

Jake and Jared continued to re-trace the path they had taken on the way to Kings Mountain. They were now headed back down the winding trail toward the camp that was called Shelving Rock. As they grew closer to the campsite, they recognized the river, the river of their youth, the river that ran along the farm that had been their only world.

Jesse stirred and slowed down as they traveled past the Shelving Rock, across the bridge where they had thrown the dark man into the river and approached the trail that led to the farm. Jared pulled the reins to bring Jesse to a halt. "Stop! Jake!" he shouted to his brother riding ahead of them. "Come back! I want to check on th' farm! Go wit' me! Please!"

Jake heard the shouting, but was too far away to understand the words. He slowed Charlie's horse and looked back to see Jared sitting on Jesse, frantically waving to get his attention. He nudged Charlie's horse, jerked the reins of the girls' horse, and turned both horses to head back to his brother.

"Wut ye doin'? It's almost sunset! We need to git goin'."

"Ya don't even know where ya is, do ye?" pleaded Jared. "Jesse knows! This here trail goes up to our farm!" Jared pleaded, fighting back tears that were breaking through the emotions pounding in his head. "It's our farm now! OUR farm!"

"I only came down that trail two times in my life! Once to throw th' dark man into th' river then th' other'n when we headed out to trade th' bear skin. So, how'd I know it wuz our trail?"

"Jesse knew," Jared replied sullenly.

"Ya's wantin' to go up thar?" Jake inquired loudly, the emotion now heating up, making his face warm, his heart racing and his palms so sweaty, he took to wiping them on his breeches to make them dry.

"Yer face is gittin' red," Jared exclaimed. "Git down off that horse n' splash some water on it!"

"Ya's wantin' to go up thar?" Jake repeated, taking the horse's reins and holding them tighter. "Up THAR?"

"I been thinkin' 'bout it e'er since we passed here th' first time. We camped at that Shelving Rock just a short ways from here. It's my home, it's all I ever knowed. You too!" Jared gestured, throwing his arms out and up above his head to show his feelings.

"Too much sorrow thar, let's git on. We gotta git to Sycamore Shoals afore dark."

"So ye ain't goin' home wit' me?" Jared pleaded.

"I can't go back thar. N' it ain't home. I'mma gonna go find a happy place," Jake said, shaking his head back and forth sideways over and over. "Come on!"

Jared closed his eyes to gather his thoughts, then opened them as he gave Jesse a knee nudge. "Bye brother! Come see me when ya can't stand that happy place no more!"

Jake watched, stunned, as Jared rode Jesse up the trail, through the trees toward the farm. He watched until he saw only the trail of darkness in the trees' shadows, a trail now hollow, just like his heart which at this moment seemed to be still.

Jake slowly turned Charlie's horse to head back down the road toward Sycamore Shoals, still loosely holding the reins of the horse that belonged to the girls. Fighting back tears, he didn't look back. He swore to make this day a new beginning. *No, it's not th' end of livin'. It's just th' end of us as brothers -- as we knew it,* he thought. *I'll make a new life. A life like th' one Charlie had. A life with people gathering, Sundays at church, tradin' at a general store, takin' care of Charlie's horse, n', just maybe, I'll share that life with Melissa, th' brown-haired girl. Just maybe.*

It was dark when Jake arrived at Sycamore Shoals. Clouds floated slowly across the sky, allowing only a spotty, thin light from the sky's half moon. Mindful that the girls had ridden and walked for hours before reaching Sycamore Shoals, he decided the Shoals was not to be his destination anyway. As he rode on past the Shoals, along the river, he felt forlorn and lost. The girls' horse snorted, indicating it had found familiar ground. Doubting his decision to make this journey, he let the horses lead the way, as he had no idea where he was going and at this point he didn't care. Drifting in and out of sleep, his body slumped forward, his head resting on the neck of Charlie's horse.

Dawn peeked through the clouds to bring the sun's rays to light the beginning of a new day. Jake sat up, realizing his horse was moving very slowly, grazing on tall grass next to a well-worn trail that marked a path across the ridge. Just ahead he saw a small building, unlike any structure he had seen on his journey to and from Kings Mountain. It was constructed of logs with a single high window at one end. The door was large and thick. As he looked around and down the hill from the ridge, he saw houses scattered across the meadow below, many situated near a river that flowed as far as he could see.

As Jake dismounted, his legs trembled to adjust his tired muscles as his feet hit the ground. He caught himself holding onto the saddle horn just in time to stand. It had been well over a day since he had mounted Charlie's horse near the Yellow Mountain and his body felt the strain. He stretched to touch the ground then reached to the sky before he walked around the back of the building to relieve himself.

When he came back around to the front of the building, he paused, captivated by the spectacular colors of red, yellow and orange rising across the river in the valley below the ridge. He sat down on the low stoop at the building's door to embrace the stillness and the beauty in front of him. It was the first time he realized complete solitude, knowing his brother was far away - far from the nearness he had known all his life.

As the sun rose over the distant mountains, he heard voices from down the trail. He ran, quickly grabbed the horses, and led them into the trees away from the building. He watched as people arrived, some walking and some on horseback, joyfully gathering and greeting each other with loud and gleeful chatter, then entering the building. After the last person entered, the door closed and there was a long silence. He contemplated what caused such noisy folks to quickly go quiet. Then the noise returned, this time louder, as there was singing. All the sounds were together as if with one voice, ringing rhythmically with different tones. The sounds reminded him of the forest at night. The singing was followed by more silence. Suddenly he heard a single booming voice shouting, then a fist pounding on wood as it continued on and on, sounding not unlike his papa when the anger got the best of him. The booming voice made him sad and he wished it to stop. Finally, after what seemed a day of punishment, the booming voice stopped. There was more singing, but only for a short time, as the door flew open releasing the flocks of people, this time speaking with less glee, perhaps reflecting on the words of the loud, booming voice.

He watched as each person departed, hoping for a glimpse of Melissa. But she was not among them. The gatherers went down the trail in different directions until he could see them no more. The door was left wide open revealing long, narrow rows of split log benches and a tall, thin table at the far end. The shadow of a man stood behind the table, his profile highlighted by the sun's light beaming in from the high window behind him. The shadow moved slowly, gathering what looked like papers. Then it moved forward, toward the door. One last man, tall and lanky, holding a tall black hat and wearing a long black coat. The man turned, stepped onto the stoop, stopped to latch the door, then headed toward the last horse grazing near the building. Jake struggled with his thoughts. This could be his only chance to ask if a Melissa was near. It was also his best chance to learn of a place for food and shelter.

Jake took the reins of his horses and led them out of the woods toward the tall, lanky man.

"Ayy!" said the man loudly. "I thought ever' one had gone already. I don't know ye, do I?" he continued, surveying Jake up and down as he moved toward him.

"No sir. I'm not from these parts," Jake replied. "I wuz here when we mustered fer to fight Captain

Ferguson's men. But now…now I come back to return a horse."

"When's th' last time ya had a good meal son?"

Jake thought a moment. "Well, sir. Twas my granny's supper afore a dark man burned our home," he reflected and paused a beat to hold back the tears.

"Come with me, then. Yer's skin n' bones already n' thar's always lots of food at th' parsonage after church ever' Sunday. It's just a short ride from here."

Jake mounted Charlie's horse and held tight to the reins of the horse he hoped he would return to Melissa on this very day. He rode alongside the tall, lanky man for what seemed a blink of the eye before they arrived at the parsonage. He recognized many faces from the earlier gathering as they moved about placing large platters of food on a long table set on the grass outside.

"I'm Pastor Tilden, by th' way," said the lanky man as they dismounted. "This here's my church family n' ever' one's welcome to these here vittles. Thar's a kettle of warm water n' some soap off near th' privvy, if ye wanna freshen up a bit. I'll settle yer horses o'er near th' creek so's they kin git some water."

The warm water brought back more memories of granny and the little things he had never appreciated before. A large chunk of soap lay on a rock beside the kettle. The last time he had seen soap had been when they unpacked a small chunk for Hope's bath the day she had married papa -- the morning he and Jared had picked flowers to float in her bath water. This soap was a privilege and he tried to use it sparingly as he lathered his hands, then rubbed them across the soft fuzz on his face, realizing he had not shaved since the morning of the big battle. Recent days flashed through his mind. The daily shaves expected by Colonel Shelby -- the razor shared with Charlie and his brother. The teasing he received over the facial fuzz he insisted on shaving even though it wasn't necessary. *I'm wearing Charlie's shoes...* He splashed his face again and again, catching his memories in the warm water, then rinsing them away. Over and over. Lost in his movements and unable to stop, he finally stuck his head full down into the water and shook it to bury his grief. He wondered if he could drown himself here and now so as to be with Charlie and his granny. *What would Charlie do? Breathe.* Jake stood, shook the water from his head and placed his hands behind his back to straighten up, shoulders back, head held high. Through Charlie's spirit, Jake gained the courage to face the strangers gathered beside the long table.

"Welcome friend," said the pastor, motioning Jake to stand beside him. "Let us pray n' give thanks to th' Lord fer them among us n' fer them that gave thar lives so we kin stand here n' enjoy th' meal afore us."

Jake tried to remember granny's words about how to eat without offending those around him. During the journey to Kings Mountain, little thought had been given to how one should consume the rare morsels they found at camp. He decided to take a bite, then nod at a stranger, then take another bite, repeating this plan, not noticing he was still eating when everyone else had finished. They didn't seem to mind, as they smiled and watched this thin, frail young man before them. Looking at him, they wondered and whispered whether his nose had been broken in battle, but those who knew better could tell it had been broken years ago. He was a stranger, but certainly not the first one to return hungry. And not the first to arrive wearing eyes darkened with shock and sadness despite their victory at Kings Mountain. In a way, they had all returned as strangers in need of patience and prayer.

The pastor's wife took pity upon Jake and offered him room and board. "Ye fought to save our land, so ye owes us nothin' fer givin' ye a roof o'er yer head til ye find yer own place," she said.

"Thank you ma'am. It's been a long time since I slept in a real bed."

Charlie fell into his arms again and again, covering Jake with blood. Jake dove deep into the river to rinse the blood, but was unable to rise to the surface as the dark man's body formed a solid block of mud above him. Jake pounded the mud roof with his fists, unable to breathe, as his own body sank deep into the vast dark red liquid. A bright light struck a hole into the muddy surface far above him. Struggling to breathe, he followed the light, pulling his arms forward then down through the thick, dark liquid, kicking with all his might to push up toward the light. As he got closer to the light, he fought to wake from this nightmare, to wake from the sleep that had evaded him most of the previous nights. At last! He gasped and opened his eyes. He sat up on the edge of the cot, took deep breaths, and thanked the Lord he was actually alive, then asked himself if he wanted to be.

But as he stood, thoughts of Melissa returned to his mind. *That's why I'm here. That's why I'm alive.* He stepped down to the warm quarters and into a welcoming smell of burning embers, bread, and other familiar odors that reminded him of his granny's cooking.

"Ye wuz purty tired I reckon. Why it's almost dinnertime! But I've made ye a breakfast of salt pork, eggs, gravy, n' biscuits! I knows ye must be hungry as a bear!" grinned the pastor's wife. "Sit here n' I'll brang it to ye. Here's some coffee to git ya started."

Jake resisted the urge to give her a hug and settled into the chair at the end of the table just as a large platter of food was placed before him. His belly urged him to dive in head first, but he refused, willing himself to use the knife and fork to attack his food. He was so busy devouring the tender pork and gravy-smothered biscuits that he didn't notice the pastor seating himself in the chair to his right.

"Mornin' son! Or shall I say, good afternoon? I gather ye slept good?"

Jake nodded, not wanting to recall the night's visions of blood and drowning in dark red waters.

"Well, I'm wonderin' what brangs ye to these here parts son. Ye got family here?"

Jake swallowed his food quickly so as to answer. "I'mma tryin' to return a horse t'wuz give to me when we wuz at Sycamore Shoals. I dunno thar names, but one. Her name's Melissa. She's got dark brown hair n' eyes. They gave me some food, too. If'n I hadn't had their horse, I'd prolly had to walk to Kings Mountain, or rode on my brother's horse, but he wuzn't 'round when th' troops took leave n' I had ta' follow. So's this horse wuz a life-saver in a ways."

"I see," said the pastor, mulling over Jake's words. "Well, I guess if ya'd seen 'em at yesterday's gatherin', ya would've returned it then. So's we'z gonna have ta make us a plan," the pastor paused to ponder a moment. "Horses kin be like family 'round here, so's I'm sure someone woulda recognized it if they's seen it."

Jake stopped eating, his eyes growing wide with anticipation as he listened.

"We's jest gonna have t' ride our horses, brangin' th' gifted one with us, to farms out beyond this here settlement, beyond whar my parishioners live. We'll head east back toward Sycamore Shoals soon's yer ready, but we'll have to be back here afore suppertime, or we be facin' reckonin' from me Missus. I learned a long time ago, that bein' late fer supper kin make her madder than a hornet - n' ye knows how mean hornets kin be, don't ya son."

"That's th' Watauga, if'n ye don't know it," shouted the pastor as they rode the trail along the ridge. "Th' Injuns named it Watauga. It means 'th' land beyond'. So's that's whar we's headed. To th' land beyond," he chuckled. "Th' river goes oe'er to Sycamore Shoals. It makes a bend jest afore th' shoals. So's if'n we follow this trail along th' river, we'll go by all th' farms whar yer horse'd be from."

They rode along the ridge, then to a new trail along the river, then up every trail leading to a farm. From farm to farm, the air was filled with the rich smell of burning oak, birch, and maple, sending tall waves of smoke rising from the chimneys. Jake was impressed and somewhat overwhelmed by the pastor's bravery in approaching total strangers and asking them if they knew the owner of the horse.

It's th' hat, Jake thought, as he watched the pastor ride tall up to each house, brush his long coat tails to straighten them as he dismounted, and slowly remove his black stove pipe hat to express his apologies and make introductions. They had visited at least seven farms and the sun was beginning to settle toward the western horizon.

On leaving the last farm, the pastor slowed his horse to a walk. "We's gonna have to turn back soon so's we kin make suppertime. We'll try one more farm, then be headin' back."

Riding the path along the next farm, Jake saw several people in a field, pulling turnips. Then his heart skipped a beat. *Could it be one of the girls from Sycamore Shoals?* Without a thought, he gave his horse a kick, and rode straight into the field and dismounted, his feet landing atop the turnip greens. The tall, heavy-set girl stood quickly, placed her hands on her hips and shouted, "Wut d'ya think yer doin'?"

Jake's shyness returned causing his face to turn beet red. "I…I…uh…"

"I know you. Ye's that boy from Sycamore Shoals! The one who helped Melissa and set our campfar!" she exclaimed. "And, ain't that th' horse we give ya?"

Jake nodded and finally spoke. "Yep. This here's th' horse. I come to return it ifn' it's yor'n."

"We thought we'd never see ya agin. Looks like ye got skinnier, but it's good to see ya jest th' same," she said. "Th' horse ain't ours. It belongs to th' farm up th' road. It's th' Warners' horse. They's gonna be glad to see it cuz they weren't so happy wif thar daughter when she got home without it. Now git on outta here n' take it to 'em. Maybe they'll even give ya some grub fer brangin' it back."

Pastor Tilden rode with Jake to the fence that marked the trail to the next farm. "This here's whar I gotta leave ya son. My Missus is prolly pacin' roun' th' table by now. Ye go on up thar n' give back thar horse. They's prolly gonna have a lot of questions and I's sure they'll be grateful as they hardly expected to see it agin. Ya knows ye have room n' board at th' parsonage if ye need it. Jest follow th' same way back and ye'll find us."

Jake watched as the pastor turned his horse and headed back the way they'd come. When he could no longer see the pastor's stovepipe hat bouncing beyond the hills, Jake nudged his horse slowly toward what he hoped would be the last farm he'd visit today.

The split-rail fence wrapped around what looked to be the largest farm he'd seen. Not like any he had seen on the seven farms they had visited. It was more like the pastor's parsonage. No logs were visible. Nicely cut planed and white-washed boards covered two stories of the home. It had more windows than any he had ever seen. He dismounted and tied the reins of both horses to the railing in front of the large covered porch. *Now's a time of reckonin'*, he thought nervously as he stepped up to the wooden door.

The door flew wide open as he approached. In the frame stood a tall, husky, round-faced man wearing a heavy, well-groomed beard of silver. "How can I help you young man?"

"Evenin' sir, I ... I believe I may have ya-yer horse out here," stammered Jake, stretching his arm outward to show the horse.

"Why, I'll be," the silver-bearded man stepped out on the landing, his voice ringing loud with a strong British tone, reminding Jake of the men at Kings Mountain. "Why that's Chester! It sure is! My daughter is rumored to have given him to a young man at the Patriots' mustering a few months back," he said, pausing to assess the young man before him. "Would you be that boy?"

"Yessir! It's me! This horse was a blessin' at the time, as my brother n' I had only Jesse ... that's our horse from th' homeplace...I'd had to walk to Kings Mountain ifn' it wasn't fer yer horse. Sir, I didn't ask fer th' horse, th' girls jest give him to me afore I knowed it. But I kept him good. 'N I think ye'll find him in purty good shape, 'cept for 'bout 100 days of ridin'."

"I did hear about how a boy saved my daughter from a frightening fall," the man pondered, rubbing his beard. "Well, don't just stand there. Come on in! We're about to sit for supper and the least we can do is feed you."

Jake tucked his head down a bit, almost to a bow, as he stepped inside the large room. It was well-lit with crystal lanterns on fine tables and a desk next to another doorway. Five large chairs sat in a semi-circle facing the fireplace. To his left was a staircase, set in planks of cedar, leading up to the next level.

"Who's there?" shouted a female voice from the top of the staircase. Jake recognized the voice as the one that had echoed like a softly cooing bird in his mind over the past few months. He looked up to see Melissa, her dark brown hair hanging loosely across the shoulders of her white gown. She held a lantern up with her right hand, the light framing her softly, as she seemingly floated down the stairs toward him. "Oh! It's you!" she exclaimed and turned to run back upstairs.

"I'm certain she'll be down for supper," said the silver-bearded man. "She's always hungry! So much, you'd would think she was a boy," he chuckled. "My dear, would you bring me a damp rag?" he shouted toward the room beyond the desk. "We have a guest for supper, and he probably wants to clean up a bit."

Jake took the rag from the strikingly beautiful, but rather robust woman. She had long, dark brown hair like Melissa's, but it was braided to the back. "Thank you ma'am," he said, wiping his face and hands with the rag and handing it back to her, embarrassed that it was painted in dust from the day's ride.

"Come on in to the dining room and have a seat," said the woman as she led him through the door into a room with hand-carved chairs placed on both sides of a long, wide, darkly-stained table. The wall above the fireplace was painted with a colorful scene of sheep grazing near a field of glorious flowers. Hanging above the table was a circle of iron holding many candles that cast a bright light on the feast before him. The pewter plates sat on squares of finely-embroidered lace. Jake had no words to share his thoughts as he took in the impressive scene before him.

His loss of words was salvaged by Melissa, who entered the room and sat down across from him. She had changed from her gown and now wore a pale blue gingham dress, trimmed with light blue lace along elbow-length sleeves and a ribboned bodice that revealed her soft, honey-toned skin. He smiled and looked down at his plate, hoping his face hadn't reddened from the blood rushing to his face flushed from the sight of her.

After supper, Melissa pushed back her chair and politely excused them both, saying. "It's a warm evening. We're going to get some fresh air. We'll be just outside on the porch," she said in a confident manner that was more of a statement than a request for permission. She picked up the lantern from the desk, wrapped her shoulders in a shawl, and led Jake out to the porch swing. Before sitting, she hung the lantern on a large hook on the clapboard wall near the swing. The lantern created just a glimmer of light above her head highlighting golden strands among the long curls of dark hair that followed the creamy skin along her neck and shoulders. Sensing Jake's timidity, Melissa proceeded with what was a one-sided conversation, telling him about the long walk she and the girls took from Sycamore Shoals, and the stern words her parents had used when they had learned their horse was gone. She went on to tell him about her family, and how her father now owned the sawmill he inherited from her grandfather who had just passed. "Grandfather's family was from Hertfordshire, England. He came here from Virginia and was one of the first to settle along the Watauga River. Being first meant he could claim hundreds of acres here. He built our sawmill with the help of his slaves. But we only have two slaves right now, Emma and Joseph. They have two children. I really miss grandfather," she said, pausing to catch her breath.

Jake was mesmerized, hearing her voice, but not every word. His imagination took his thoughts to the shapes below the lace of her bodice, then back up to the movement of her plump lips. He had seen Henry and

Hope kissing in the early stages of their marriage, so he thought this might be the right time to give it a try. Taking advantage of the pause in Melissa's voice, he leaned over and placed his mouth on her lips just as his papa had done with Hope. Melissa did not resist. But the kiss was quick as Jake backed off, pushing Melissa's shoulders to move her away from him. Having never kissed a girl before, he had had no warning of the passion that surged through his body when they touched. He felt incredibly warm and there was hardening beneath his breeches. He couldn't sit right and he couldn't stand.

Melissa stood, and without a word leaned to kiss him lightly on the forehead, then went inside, slowly closing the door, leaving him alone under the lantern's light.

Charlie's horse readjusted its footing patiently while Jake moved him close to the steps so he could pull himself up to raise his leg over the saddle. Immersed in his emotions, he hardly realized the journey back along the trail and it seemed only seconds before he found himself back at the parsonage.

In the next few days, Jake accompanied Pastor Tilden on his visits to check on parishioners who had not graced the church with their presence the previous Sunday. Jake watched as the Pastor prayed with those who were sick, spoke comforting words to those attending a graveside service for their mother, and berated those who had missed Sunday service. When the time seemed right, he told the Pastor about returning the horse, and described the details of the evening at Melissa's, including the fine furnishings and proper language spoken by the girl and her family. He expressed his concern about returning for no good reason except to see the girl. The Pastor quickly recognized Jake's insecurity, fear, and lack of enough confidence. So, the next morning, he took Jake to meet another parishioner. This time, it was a simple introduction.

"Jake, this here's my friend Doc Taylor. He's been lookin' for someone to help with his practice. Someone who'll do whatever's needed, be it scrubbin' th' floor or cleanin' his instruments. We think yer just th' one fer th' job, if'n ye'll have it."

From that moment, Jake found a purpose. He adapted well, listening intently to every instruction, and swiftly became the doctor's valued apprentice. The Doc took a strong liking to Jake, recognizing the young boy had great potential. Over the next few weeks, Jake not only did what he was told, he closely observed the patients and the doctor, learning their way of life. It was a way of life he had never been exposed to due to his isolation on the farm and his papa's controlling manner. Each evening when they were preparing for the next day, the Doc encouraged Jake to talk about his upbringing. It only took a few days for the Doc to sense Jake's need for education in the ways of folks who interacted in the community. When he learned of Jake's interest in the Warner girl, knowing she was from a family of high status, Doc took it upon himself to coach Jake in the manners and words of a proper gentleman. With the Doc's guidance and encouragement, Jake became more confident and soon realized he would not only need to behave like a gentleman, he would need to look like one. Jake expressed his concern to the Doc, seeking his advice as to how to dress and behave if and when he got the courage to visit the Warner home again. Hoping to buy a proper coat like the Pastor's, Jake asked the Doc to hold his wages until he had the funds to make such a purchase.

Once Jake accrued two months' earnings, Doc took Jake aside and handed him a purse full of coins. "This should be enough to get you some proper clothes and here's the address of the local merchant. He's well-informed and stocked with the best fashions available in these parts."

Elated, Jake embraced the Doc to express his gratitude. Doc continued, "Get on outta here. He's expecting you this afternoon, but you're to report back to work in the mornin'. Just 'cuz you're gonna have nicer clothes doesn't mean you're to stop working for me. You're just getting started here and I aim to make you the best doctor's assistant around. See you tomorrow!" Jake was to never know the Doc had secretly promised the merchant he would make up any shortage of funds, thus ensuring Jake got everything he needed.

The next Sunday, Jake shaved cautiously, put on his new linen shirt, pulled up his white silk stockings, stepped into the kneed breeches, and buttoned them at the side. After adding his lace-trimmed waistcoat, he proudly placed his arms into the tight sleeves of his kelly green dress coat. The coat wasn't as long as the Pastor's, but Jake thought his to be more becoming to his own stature and was particularly proud of the way the front sloped to the back to form two narrow coat-tails. He carefully wrapped the white linen cravat around his neck and stepped into his new leather shoes. He was finally ready to begin courting Melissa.

By this time, Jake was a familiar face at Pastor Tilden's church, but on this particular Sunday, he was treated with new respect and favored with many compliments from the parishioners. He sat impatiently listening to the shouting and stood for the singing, all the time wishing for it to end. As soon as the service concluded, he politely excused himself, walked briskly out the door, mounted his horse and galloped away. Now, as he traveled east toward Melissa's home, his head was crammed full of emotions. His elation from the parishioners' praise conflicted with sheer fear as he struggled to find the words to ask her father's permission to court her.

When he arrived at the Warners' farm, he took a deep breath, dismounted, stepped up to the door, and knocked meekly so as not to seem eager or anxious. He waited for what seemed an eternity before he made another effort, this time knocking loudly four times. The door opened wide. Jake blurted his rehearsed words, "Mr. Warner, hello. I hope ya remember me. I'm th' one who brought back th' horse some weeks back," Jake said as he reached to shake Mr. Warner's hand firmly, as Doc Taylor had taught him.

"Son, of course I remember you. It's not every young man who would be thoughtful enough to return the gift of a horse. And I was even more impressed that you traveled here straight from the battlefield to do so. Come inside and have a seat by the fire."

Jake carefully tucked the tails of his coat beneath him as he sat, clearing his throat. As soon as Jake sat down, Melissa tiptoed to the base of the stair railing and slowly sat on the steps to listen, careful not to stir or be noticed by Jake or her father.

"Sir, I wanna thank ya agin for th' delicious supper you'n's give me when I wuz here."

"It was our pleasure son. Now, may I inquire. What brings you here on this beautiful Sunday afternoon?"

"Sir, since I come here, I was fortunate to acquire employment with Doc Taylor. I been staying at the parsonage, but I soon hope to have a place of my own," Jake said, trying to use proper words as the Doc had taught him.

"I heard you were working for Doc Taylor. Our sawmill attracts folks from Shelby's Fort all the way west to Fort Patrick Henry. So, not much happens around the

Watauga without my learning about it. I hear you are doing a fine job there."

"Yessir. Doc Taylor has been a great teacher and I aim to keep workin' there. But ya asked why I come here. Sir, I've come to ask your permission to court your daughter."

Melissa clinched her hands tightly on the railing and held her breath, waiting for her father's answer.

"Jake. You seem to be of good character. Folks from Pastor Tilden's church speak well of you, too. I knew you weren't here just to return our horse. It was clear you had taken a liking to my daughter. You're both young, but I don't see any harm in your visiting her every Sunday. You can come for dinner after church and visit for an hour or two until we get to know you better. Then we'll see where we go from there," Mr. Warner paused and turned toward the steps. "Melissa, I know you're listening! Come on down here so you and Jake can visit. I know you have a lot to talk about."

Melissa shyly entered the room and sat in the chair across from Jake.

Standing, Mr. Warner spoke, "Pardon me while I go check on the Missus to let her know we have a guest for supper, that is, if you'd like to stay for supper Jake?"

Jake stood trying to restrain his excitement. "Yes sir. I'd be honored to dine with you and your family this evenin'."

Every Sunday thereafter Jake appeared at the Warners' home, having squirmed through Pastor Tilden's church service, then riding as fast as he could to meet the young girl who had caught his fancy at Sycamore Shoals. The Warners soon invited him to join them for suppers as well as dinners and he spent a very special afternoon and evening at Christmas where he met other relatives who came according to family tradition.

On Easter Sunday, Jake was invited to join the family at their own church. He arrived early, just as the first attendees began to gather. These churchgoers seemed not very different from those who gathered at Pastor Tilden's services. As he stood near the entrance, he greeted several familiar folks who were also Doc Taylor's patients. Melissa and her parents arrived just as the church doors were closing, so they sat near the back of the room. Jake had prepared himself to remain calm amidst the expected shouting that was customary in Pastor Tilden's services. But much to his surprise, this pastor was calm, speaking distinctly in a soothing voice. And the singing was more serious and less spirited. "What did you think of the service?" Melissa asked as they were departing.

Jake chose his words carefully as he knew her parents were listening. "Well, it's a peaceful gathering, for sure."

"Methodists are different from Baptists, Jake." Melissa said, holding back a giggle. "We're much more civilized."

Jake wisely smiled without speaking.

After Easter, Jake joined the Warners at the peaceful church for every Sunday service. He found the sermons a bit boring, but sitting next to Melissa erased his interest in the livelier option. And besides, the Warners' church was closer to the boarding house where, for the past year, he had rented a room within walking distance of Doc Taylor's office.

Walking to the office was his favorite time of day. On this late summer day, however, he headed in a different direction as he had to make a short stop before heading to the clinic. Today, he had abandoned his coat and wore only his waistcoat, as the hot sun was already generating beads of sweat across his brow. *Thank goodness, I can buy a new waistcoat today. After all, if I'm to be married on Sunday, I must wear clothes of comfort, clothes that don't turn one's body into a sticky, smelly place no girl dare touch,* he thought as he entered the merchant's building.

"Welcome. I can't wait to show ya what I found! When ya told me ye wuz gittin' married this month, I knew ye would need a coat of thinner cloth. I have your new waistcoat and formal coat right here. They's made of cassimer, the latest in fashion, straight from Charleston. Here. Try 'em on." After the fitting, the merchant gracefully accepted Jake's payment, this time knowing Doc Taylor's additional funds would not be needed, and proud that the Warners' new son-in-law would be properly attired when he joined their family.

The Methodist Church was packed for the wedding that Sunday. Packed with patrons of the Warners' sawmill, parishioners from Pastor Tilden's church, patients from Doc Taylor's office, and even a few of Jake's fellow Patriots who had known him from the journey to King's Mountain. Jake stood proudly in his new attire, beaming with delight as he repeated the words the Methodist minister spoke and listened to Melissa repeating the promises that made her his 'until death do they part'. The minister concluded the ceremony with a powerful prayer asking God to hold them together as one and bless them with a life without anger, without sadness, and without doubt in each other's faithfulness and trust.

The Warners' home was filled with guests, so many that the reception overflowed to the front lawn where refreshments, including fine wines and whiskeys, were also being served. The newlyweds mingled among the guests for an acceptable amount of time, then eagerly headed across the field to their new home. The former Miss Warner was now a gleeful Mrs. Greer and her husband Jake was now a young man with new responsibilities. Responsibilities that included not only being a good husband, but also the responsibility of living up to the expectations of one who just married into the community's most respected family. He lifted his bride up into his arms and carried her across the threshold of their new home, a whitewashed clapboard structure gifted by her father, much like the Warner's, only respectfully smaller.

Nearly three years ago, Jake and his brother Jared, had used strength garnered from shock and fear to toss a dark stranger into the river. Now Jake was a young man whose heart was nearly bursting with happiness. Happiness that filled every inch of his being. Happiness. An emotion he had not known until this very moment.

Chapter 17

1781

When Jared returned to the Greer farm, he found things nearly the same as he and Jake had left them. That is, except for the chicken coop. Now it was only a coop, without the chickens. It saddened Jared to see it empty, but he was not surprised. His papa had shot many a wolf and bear over the years, and without anyone to protect them, the chickens were bound to be victims of his absence. This was also a warning, he thought. Without the help of family members to keep a watchful eye, he knew he could easily become a critter's next prey. Tonight would be one without supper, tucked in next to Jesse, with the stall door pulled shut. At least he had his musket and he knew how to shoot it. He quickly loaded it with one round of powder and rammed the ball down the barrel before he set it to his side.

Jared spent the next day gathering stones from both chimneys to build a fireplace where the door had stood at the front end of barn. With each stone he carried a memory from its old home to his new one. Matilda cooking her incredible turkey stew. Henry playing his fiddle. His mother's peaceful passing. Hope teaching him how to hurl the sling. Beautiful blue flax in the summer. Racing Jake to the fields so they got there before their papa could be angry. Seeing Jeremiah in Hope's arms for the first time. Tossing the dark man into the river. Digging Charlie's grave at Kings Mountain. Watching his brother ride away. With each stone he placed the memories one by one to withstand the flames he would watch through tear-filled eyes each evening. Finally he had burned enough memories to let them go, or at least hide them deep within the ashes that had hardened around his heart.

He left just enough space between the fireplace and side wall to squeeze through. The next day he cut logs and bound them together to make two doors to stand against each side of the opening. It took all his strength to move the doors to close his side of the fireplace whenever he left or entered. But after weeks of sleeping on the ground while traveling to and from Kings Mountain, this roughly-constructed barn was now a place of comfort.

In his absence, wildlife had grown accustomed to roaming the grounds especially when twilight sealed their shadows, so Jared didn't have to step far outside to find options for his next meal. Many winter days were spent skinning and cleaning the wolves he killed. Once he had skinned a wolf, he would stretch its coat and hang it against the wall, just as he and Jake had done with the skin of bears killed by their papa. Soon, he not only had plenty of food, he had several fur blankets, making a warm fur bed over the straw in the stall. He even hung a pelt across Jesse's back for extra warmth.

As spring approached, Jared turned his focus to the garden, and the graves of Matilda and his mother, clearing the ground that covered them and planting seeds of wildflowers.

Now that it was warmer, he took his meals outside on Hope's rock, just as he and Jake had done. Sometimes he reclined against the rock, spending hours turning his left hand toward the sunlight to flash shards of sunlight off his granny's ring, his thoughts twisting time into reflections of her stories, how his papa had once been her baby, born of a relationship he dared not imagine. His mind rang with boastful voices along the trail to Kings Mountain crowing about intimacy with wives and wild girls. And visions of Hope, whose very presence had stirred sudden rushing sensations through his own body even though she belonged to his papa, a joyful beginning that had turned dark after Jeremiah's birth. Conversations with his brother dissecting curiosities about how holding a girl could turn into met expectations. Wondering if Jake had found the girl Melissa and taken her for his own.

Chapter 18

1787

This Sunday morning, Hope sat reading in her rocking chair on the grist mill's wide stone stoop. It was now the tenth year that she counted the dogwoods in full bloom since Jeremiah's birth. She reflected on his early years and thanked the Lord for the blessing that was Mitch. Keeping his journal of transactions had also given her perspective on her own life. She had turned back the pages and reconstructed her early years, remembering Christmases and birthdays. Today was her 26th birthday. The only person who knew of this day would be her father and she longed to hear his voice. She wondered if he would be proud of the woman she had become. Or would he recognize her hardened strength, a strength derived from pushing back against the dark memories, a strength that came from the days and nights when she blocked out the terror of Henry's passion. She was no longer the lively, sweet little girl her father had known. The laughter of her youth had churned through pain and tears, until it was hardened into hurt, hurt that shattered into emotionless grains scattered into the wind leaving only an empty heart.

Jeremiah had been her reason for living. He had needed her to survive. But in this moment, she recognized his growing independence. He had taken over much of the blacksmith's duties, maintaining the fire, and pounding the iron to soften it with his anvil. Mitch was grateful for

Jeremiah's skills, for his business had more than doubled with the growth of the settlement.

And Hope was especially grateful for the pasture that was now Isaiah's paradise. Mitch was known not only for his blacksmith skills, but also for his exceptional knowledge of horses. The pasture's horses were his children and he took pride in ensuring their well-being and enlisting Jeremiah's assistance in their care. *The Lord has blessed us -- and Isaiah -- with this haven.*

On this day of rest, Jeremiah took Isaiah for a ride to explore the farms that had matured around them. As Jeremiah rode across the farms, neighbors waved and shouted his name, recognizing him as a favorite member of the community, filling his head with pride and a sense in his own mind that he was much wiser than his ten years.

At supper that evening, Hope listened intently as Jeremiah described each farm, naming its owner, and relating a conversation he had when he had been stopped by a neighbor. "Mother, there are great lands beyond what we can see, beyond the valley and over the mountains. I talked to Mr. Carroll, you know, the man with the fuzzy red eyebrows? He told me that if you ride past the mines and up one of the trails, you can see over the mountains, ridge after ridge. He said there is even one mountain the Cherokee call "Attocoa" which means Table Rock. It sits atop a mountain, wide and flat like a table! He said it is just a half day's ride from here. I'm going to ride up there when I get older. From there I bet I could see the whole world!"

Hope had heard talk of the mines and wondered if they were the same mines her father had worked when he met her mother. Now the mention of Table Rock sparked a vague memory, recalling another of her father's tales. He had talked about the mountain ranges he and her mother had seen as they rode northwest from Alder Springs. Perhaps this is where he saw Hawksbill Mountain.

Table Rock and the mountains consumed her thoughts over the next few weeks. She had not ventured away from Mr. Mitch's property since that day she arrived tired, frail, and hardly dressed seven years ago. She recalled her father's stories and tried to focus on the details of his journey. Had he mentioned a mountain called Table Rock?

It would take all the courage she could muster, but she made a mental note to ride Isaiah over to Mr. Carroll's farm in the near future. After all, could a ride to the Carrolls' be more frightening than fleeing from the farm that had been controlled by Henry's rage?

A few weeks later, Mr. Carroll was surprised to see the beautiful woman from the grist mill ride up to his place in the field. He was particularly surprised as this young woman had quite a reputation -- a reputation of being rudely aloof and of few words.

Hope decided to stay on her horse and speak from there until she felt it was safe to dismount. "Mr. Carroll. We haven't seen you at the mill for some time, so I thought I would ride out to check on you," Hope stated, her voice reflecting confidence from all the times she had rehearsed her words. "My son, Jeremiah, told me about your conversation. He's still young and it's entirely possible he stretched the truth a bit. So I wanted to see you in person to learn more about what he said. Is it true that there is a mountain called Table Rock? One that looks like a table on a tall hill? How far is it? And, are there mines near there?"

Mr. Carroll leaned on his shovel as he listened, then placed it on the ground. "Missus O'Connor. I am surprised to see you. You must be thirsty. Why don't you come inside. I'm sure the Missus will be happy to make us some tea or we could at least give you a cup of water from the well. It's high time we got better acquainted."

While sitting at the Carroll table and listening to the conversations between the man and his wife, Hope recognized that they didn't speak in the same manner as the local folks. This in itself gave her a comfort level, allowing her to let go of her usual protective temperament. "I sincerely appreciate your inviting me in for a cup of tea. I've lived and worked at the mill for almost seven years and this is the first time I have ventured off Mr. Mitch's property. I admit I have been rather cautious when it came to getting better acquainted with our neighbors."

"Missus O'Connor, we're pleased to have you in our home. Why, just listening to you is a pleasure. You don't speak like most folks in these parts. It seems you have a bit of an accent. As a matter of fact, your way of speaking sounds very similar to ours," Mr. Carroll paused. "And your name is definitely Irish. Is your family, by any means, of Irish descent?"

Sitting in this kitchen filled with familiar smells and hearing Mr. Carroll's voice made Hope feel at ease. It was as if her father was speaking, especially as Mr. Carroll's thick red eyebrows moved up and down and his green eyes twinkled when he talked.

"Yes Sir. My father was Patrick O'Connor. His family was from Ireland. He was very proud of his education, and especially mindful of speaking properly. We were separated when the Cherokee attacked our settlement. I fled on my horse, Isaiah, and I haven't seen my father since. I miss him so. And a big part of me believes he is still alive. Now that Jeremiah is older, I aim to take some time for myself to see if I can find him. At least I will have tried, and that will give me some comfort." As she continued all the thoughts and questions that had filled her mind over the past few weeks, and even years, came spilling forward one after another.

She persuaded Mr. Carroll to draw her a map. It was rough, he said, because he had only traveled that way once a long time ago. He had never been to the mines, but knew they were southeast of Mitchborough. The mountain called Table Rock was northwest. There was no settlement that he knew of, unless folks had settled there in the past ten years. But again, it was somewhere between Alder Springs and the Watauga settlement. Few land grants had been awarded, but it was possible that settlers had taken acres of land for their own.

"It would be a brave man who would settle near the mountains at Table Rock at the risk of being threatened by the Cherokee or even the British who retreated from Kings Mountain," said Mr. Carroll, his eyebrows furrowed. He moved his forefingers back and forth rubbing his chin, contemplating the intentions of the young woman before him. "But from what you told of your father, he sounds like an Irishman just stubborn enough to do it. Let me see what I can learn from the neighbors. For now, it's getting late and I want you to get home before dark. I know one thing and that is that it's a journey you shouldn't make on your own. I'll come to the mill when I think of a way for you to go safely. That is, unless you're as stubborn as your father."

As she rode back to the mill, Hope began to form a plan. This was her time. Her time for resolution.

Hope spent the next days and evenings perfecting her plan. She began setting aside supplies she would need for her journey. She could be gone anywhere from one day to a week, or even longer. Her thoughts turned from concern to anxiety over leaving Jeremiah. Should she tell him she would be leaving? Or, was it best to simply go without a word. She was confident that Mitch would look after him, no matter what. If Patrick O'Connor was alive, he had made a journey almost as difficult as her own. If so, he would not be the same father she knew when she was the center of his life. She knew she was no longer the daughter he had known. So, was it worth the effort? Would she bring him more sadness than joy? Still, she needed answers.

These lingering questions and frail answers stayed with her throughout the day, and into the evening, stretching late into the night, disturbing her sleep as she tossed and turned, waking and nodding off. And waking again. She prayed for guidance and waited for answers. And waited. Then she made a firm decision. With or without the Lord's guidance, if she didn't hear from Mr. Carroll by the time the sun set tomorrow, she would have to make the trip on her own.

Ever since Mitch built Jeremiah his own bed in the far corner of her room, Hope was accustomed to his waking on his own and even making his own breakfast before she headed down to begin her day. Once he started his day, Jeremiah always stuck with Mitch and rarely came back upstairs. Today was different. "Mother! Mother! It's Mr. Carroll!" Jeremiah screamed, shaking her with both hands to wake her. "He's here to see you! Come on! Wake up! Now!"

When she came downstairs, she saw Jeremiah run past Mr. Carroll en route to the barn. Mr. Carroll was standing at the door. When he saw Hope, he stepped forward, took her by the arm, and guided her to the far corner of the mill so no one could hear him. He whispered almost frantically. "Hope, just last evening I learned the Carsons are heading to Watauga to see their daughter and grandson. Mr. Carson fought with Colonel Avery in the final battle with the Cherokee. They drove out the

Cherokee and some of their fellow fighters settled not far from Table Rock Mountain. He says it's still not safe for anyone to travel that way alone but he knows someone you can stay with and who will even show you the way and introduce you to them," Mr. Carroll caught his breath. "But they're leaving in the morning so you have to come with me now. They live about an hour west of my homeplace so it will take us at least half a day to get to them and the Missus insisted I get back home before dark."

"Oh Mr. Carroll!" Hope said trying to keep her voice down. "I've hardly slept since I last saw you. My mind has been racing trying to sort out the way. I must go. And I am already packed. Meet me at the pasture barn below the bridge. That's where my horse is."

She ran up the stairs, grabbed her haversack, tied it over her shoulder, and slipped down the narrow path at the side of the mill opposite from the blacksmith shop. For just seconds, she stood at the corner and watched to make sure Jeremiah and Mitch were occupied with their morning's projects. Then she ran quickly to the pasture. In moments, she saddled and mounted Isaiah, her haversack still hanging over her shoulder. Mr. Carroll waved her to his side, gave his horse a brief kick and signaled Hope to do the same. Hope didn't look back. She was now only focused on what lay ahead.

On the way, they stopped by the Carrolls' cottage where the Missus served them a quick dinner as they told her their plans. The trail west was not well-traveled, so it took them over two hours to reach the Carson homestead. Mr. Carroll wasted no time in introducing Hope to the couple and promptly left them to get acquainted.

The Carsons were not the friendliest couple Hope had ever encountered. But, as their journey began, she decided to reach out in an attempt to make conversation. "You say you're going to see your daughter? In Watauga?"

"Yep!" Mr. Carson replied. "She's married to a preacher thar."

"I was in Watauga once. With my father. We saw a grist mill there. It was near the Doe River, I believe."

"Yep. We pass a grist mill on the way into th' settlement where my daughter lives. Caroline's her name."

The trail narrowed forcing Mr. Carson to ride ahead with Mrs. Carson falling in behind him. Hope found herself shouting her comments into the air. "Caroline. That's a pretty name." She heard a faint "Yep!" ahead as the distance grew greater between them.

This suited Hope just fine as she wasn't much for small talk herself. She let Isaiah take the lead following the Carsons' horses along the rocky trail. The trail twisted up and around steep hills that reminded her of the path she and Jeremiah had taken after she felled the dark man with her sling. It felt strange to be riding alone, without little Jeremiah sitting between her arms. But she also felt liberated.

When they reached the top of the ridge, the Carsons took a sharp turn along a narrow path that led to a large cabin set atop a ridge overlooking the mountains. As she got closer, she was taken by the incredible view. At least five mountain ranges stood before her, each rising higher than the other, green and lush with trees reaching above the other in competition for sunlight. Below, the mountains swept upward on either side of a rushing river carving a canyon between a sea of gently rolling hills for as far as she could see. To the east, the mountains were more barren, with huge rocks jutting out over a gorge.

Then she saw it. The Table Rock stood large, looming outward with a flat surface that angled slightly downward. West of the table was a larger rock, with a sharp profile; and a slanted ledge that stood out sharply like a beak from its summit. It looked like the head of an eagle aiming for its prey. No! It couldn't be, but as she stood staring at its profile, she realized a different view. She turned her head sideways and squinted her eyes. Was it possible? Could it be the head of a hawk? Was this the Hawksbill her father had spoken of many years ago?

Her intense thoughts were suddenly interrupted with loud shouting. "Hey! Missus O'Connor. We're here. This is where we leave ye. Come on. I'll introduce ye to th' owner," Mr. Carson shouted loudly from his horse in an effort to announce their presence without having to dismount.

A tall man answered the door. His stunning appearance shocked Hope as she had expected to be greeted by an elderly couple. His long coal black hair streaked with random strands of grey hung loosely tangled against his broad shoulders indicating he was not expecting guests on this day. He brushed his hair back with his large, battle-scarred hands, as if to repair his dishevelled appearance. "Why if it isn't the Carsons. Good afternoon. What brings you to these parts? And who is the beautiful young woman sitting atop that cinnamon horse?" The way he said 'cinnamon' made her heart flutter. As he spoke, his distinctive British accent took her breath away, completely seizing her attention, erasing any thoughts of a hawk's bill.

Mr. Carson spoke, "This is Missus O'Connor from Mitchborough. We apologize for not sending ye notice of our arrival. This visit was not planned until this morning. Is yer Missus here?"

"Mr. Carson, it's been a long time since your last visit. But as you may recall, I'm a solitary man and as yet I have no Missus. But do come in. I'll make some tea."

"Forgive us. We need to continue our journey westward as we aim to be at Watauga by dark," Mr. Carson began turning his horse to ride out the narrow path. "We'll try to stop by on our way back when we have more time!" And, with that, the aloof couple rode away, leaving Hope speechless, still seated on her horse.

"Please Missus. Do step down and join me on the porch. I promise I am a true gentleman, properly raised by my Mum, and I will behave accordingly. While you are settling into one of my rockers, I will do what I said. I will be right back with a cup of tea."

Hope dismounted and chose a rocking chair that faced the mountains and the gorge below. Her mind was racing again, confused with multiple thoughts. Was this Hawksbill Mountain? Was this a safe place? Could she trust this handsome man with the distinguished accent? Could she push back against the memories of Henry and the dark man -- enough to survive just one night and perhaps a day -- with an owner who may have answers she desperately needs?

"Here you go," he said, handing her a cup not of tin or clay. This was a cup of fine porcelain with a thin handle that curved up to the rim. Hope held it tightly with both hands and took a sip, giving her pause and time to take in her surroundings and assess the man before her. She noticed his hair was now pulled back and tied with a black ribbon. He had also changed into a clean white shirt and black breeches.

His steel blue eyes focused intently on hers as he pulled a chair to face her. He made a conscious decision not to mention the apparent wedding ring on her left hand. "I apologize as I have not properly introduced myself. My name is Spenser. William Spenser. I met Mr. Carson about eight years ago when my cousin Waightstill Avery convinced me to come to America to help in his law practice. But shortly after I arrived, he was called to lead the Jones County Regiment and I found myself fighting alongside him for the country's independence. Many members of our family died in the war but Waightstill and

I, along with Mr. Carson, survived. After the war, Waightstill acquired hundreds of acres all over these parts. I was so awestruck by these magnificent mountains, I did not wish to leave. So, he kindly granted me several acres along this ridge; and, as you can see, I was compelled to stay and make it my home."

"I see," said Hope, still tightly clasping her cup, holding it just below her chin. Lost for words, she smiled and listened to William Spenser, as listening was of great pleasure at this moment. His voice was both strong and gentle. And his face reflected a life that had experienced much of the outdoors, both in battle and in hunting.

"You can call me Will, if you wish." His easy smile stretched wide forming long, curved dimples on either side of his lips. Clusters of tiny fine lines framed the outer corners of his eyes. A face of sun-kissed kindness. The face of a man who had laughed often. "It is clear that you have had a long day already. And I assume you will be hungry before long. So, if you will excuse me, I will go inside to see what I might prepare for our supper. Please feel free to come inside when you are comfortable doing so."

Hope stayed outside, gently rocking to and fro, embracing the view and sorting her thoughts until the light vanished behind the mountains. Walking around to the entrance, she was overcome by the warm light throughout the front room. Inside, there were stacks of books piled against the walls on both sides of the fireplace and across the room. This was the first time she had seen so many books in one place. She couldn't resist picking up one after another to see if she recognized any of the titles or authors.

"Do you read, Missus? And, by the way, would it be an intrusion if I asked your name again?"

"I'm sorry. I have been so rude. It's just that this entire day has been a bit much for me. Yes, I do read. And my name is Hope O'Connor."

"Well, Missus O'Connor. I have prepared what I trust will be a suitable supper," he said as he gestured toward the table and pulled out a chair. "And, I've also had a lot of time to think about your arrival and how we might handle your stay. After supper, you can consider the entire cabin your private quarters as I will make my bed on the porch. You may even bolt the door from the inside and I will see you in the morning at a time you deem suitable."

~

The sound of an ax splitting wood. High winds whistling upward, bending the trees outside. The cabin was darker and a bit cooler this morning as she had not tended the fire. After lifting the heavy wooden bolt, Hope paused. She pulled her fingers through her hair and re-twisted it high on her head. She had not thought of her appearance until this moment. She had slept in the clothes she had worn on the ride up here. *Well, it is too late now*, she thought.

"Good morning Missus O'Connor." Will shouted from the woodpile across the way.

Oh that voice. That smile, she thought, not realizing her smile was just as grand, her emotions responding uncontrollably until she caught herself and reset her face to focus on her goal. She sat down on the front stoop waiting for him to come her way. As he approached, she said, "Well, it's time I told you why I came all this way. I'm looking for my father, Patrick O'Connor. We lived near Fort Caswell when there were many Indian attacks. They burned our home. I took Isaiah, my horse, and fled, just as my father had instructed. I never saw my father again. But I believed he survived. Before I was born, he had come this way from working in the mines near Alder Springs. He spoke of a mountain that jutted high in an arch above the others. He said it looked like the beak of a bird. He called it Hawksbill," she swallowed, choking back tears. "I think I saw it yesterday. Over there. If he is alive, he would be near Hawksbill."

Will pulled a chair from the porch and sat down in front of her. "I have not heard it called Hawksbill. But that huge mountain face does stand above them all. And it does have somewhat of a beak. I can see that." Looking at his face, Hope could see he was thinking quickly, trying to make a plan. His expression turned serious and he was looking westward toward the mountain in question, even though it wasn't currently in his view.

"Well, several of the men Waightstill and I fought with have settled on lands near here. And I believe we were fighting for this land about the same time your father would have come this way. I am happy to ride with you to show you the mountain from a different angle and it will be my pleasure to escort you to places where we can inquire about an Irishman who may have settled here," he paused and looked at Hope enlisting a response.

She stood, brushed her skirt with both hands, indicating she was ready to go.

"I'll pack us some food and supplies. And…" Will turned to watch Hope walking steadfastly toward Isaiah. "I'll even bring us some leftover biscuits to eat on the way."

This man makes really good biscuits, Hope thought, as she took her last bite and steered Isaiah's stride alongside her new friend's horse. "Thank you for this kindness. I'm certain you had other plans for this day." she said in an effort to make conversation. Conversation was something she had consciously avoided for several years, with the exception of suppertime with Mitch and Jeremiah.

"Well, I have cut and split all the wood I need for winter and my small garden is cleared and ready for planting next spring. Actually, this will be my first winter when I shall sit by the fire and read. As you could see, I have collected many books. My cousin Waightstill has a huge library and he brings me books every time he comes through this way. I've read maybe half of them and am looking forward to escaping into worlds and adventures of many new characters, that is, after we find your father."

"What books have you read? What are your favorites?" Hope asked.

The next few hours were filled with conversation. Conversation like Hope had never enjoyed. Conversation into which Hope escaped, forgetting the past, immersing herself in the sheer pleasure of sharing stories, especially the words that rang from the voice of a well-educated man. His manner of speaking reminded her of her father, though her father's Irish brogue was much livelier. She also enjoyed the quiet moments when the narrow trails forced her to follow behind him. She studied his every move, the strong back that stayed upright even as he navigated the twists and turns of the steep path leading down toward the gorge. This was a proud and confident man without arrogance, nor did he seem to harbor the bruised demeanor she had observed in so many who had seen battle.

As they guided their horses down the treacherous trail, her thoughts turned to her father. This kind man is leading me to places he has never seen to find a man who may no longer exist. Doubt and fear twisted through her mind, replacing the happy feelings she had enjoyed just moments earlier. *What have I done? I've left my son without a mother. I have no reason to believe father is alive. Only the memory of his words and his dreams of a place called Hawksbill Mountain. I have followed an illusion, just like Don Quixote. I am a roaming fool lost in the storms of my mind. And now, I've convinced this handsome man to be my Sancho, chasing windmills.*

Will led the way down freshly carved trails winding through the forest into clearings and small settlements that had been established by soldiers returning from the Revolution. Fighters who had grown fond of this private yet rugged valley surrounded by tall rocky peaks and rushing waters. These settlements were isolated, tended by those whose battle scars were far deeper than those inflicted by swords and muskets. The wounds of their mind had bruised their souls with horrific memories repeatedly pushing good thoughts aside, making solitude and independence preferable over life among the interdependent sorts who thrived on social gatherings.

But Will was not one to give up easily. He identified with these sole survivors, having chosen solitude himself. He had listened to Hope's stories and developed a vivid description not only of her father's appearance, but also of his mannerisms. Hope maintained a respectful distance and quietly observed Will's respectful approach to each new encounter. He took his time to acknowledge each individual with sincere empathy and patiently listened to their stories before stating the reason for his visit. In many ways, he was grateful for this opportunity to become acquainted with those who lived not far from his own home and left each Patriot feeling pleased to have encountered a kindred spirit. Yet none had heard of an older Irishman by the name of O'Connor.

"These men are still fighting," Will told Hope as they mounted their horses. "Fighting for their own survival. They have not ventured beyond the land they first claimed. So, it is clear they would not have seen or heard of your father, unless he had come to them. I'm sorry to disappoint, but it is time we looked beyond these scattered dwellings. We need a new plan, or perhaps we must face the facts before us. That is… That is, this could possibly," he hesitated, then continued, "Possibly be a lost mission."

Hope listened, then gave Isaiah a swift kick to ride ahead. She pushed Isaiah into a fast gallop through the trees, across a shallow stream and onto a dry, dirt trail, her thoughts concentrating on the reasoning behind Will's disheartening words. Suddenly, a sharp, crisp wind whipped trail dust up and into her eyes causing her to scream in pain. Will caught up in time to see her dismounting and running back to the stream to wash the dust from her eyes. As her eyes cleared, an exhausted Hope headed away from the horses, seeking privacy and a moment to reflect on this seemingly lost mission. Will fought back the urge to run to her side, determining it was best to let her be. He led the horses across the field and left them in the shadow of a tall cliff he hoped would provide a shield against the stinging winds. Mindful of Hope's need for privacy, he pitched two tents side by side, aiming to keep each one a respectful distance from the other. Then taking his ax, he went into the forest to find wood for the night's fire.

Hope brushed her fingers through her hair to clear the dust that had mangled into mud when she had splashed her face. The sky was now a gleaming golden tone, as the clouds formed shapes of birds and bears dancing across the sky in the wind. She turned and headed back toward the cliff to cut the breeze to her back. "Where is Hawksbill Mountain?" she asked herself aloud, turning slowly in circles to seek the arching rock among the shadows of the surrounding mountains. Then she glimpsed a single piece of cloth, twisting in the wind, on a hill in the far distance. She squinted her eyes, startled by the site of this movement, totally out-of-place high above the trees. The glaring rays of the setting sun streamed sharply, blocking her vision. Shadows quickly replaced the tree lines until only curves of the mountains remained, marking the day's end. She ran back toward the cliff to tell Will what she had seen.

As soon as breaking light erased the shadows and again revealed the sharpness of the tree lines, Hope ran ahead and across the stream, shouting back at Will to follow. She retraced her steps as best she could, again turning slowly and squinting to find the piece of cloth twisting among the trees. Curiosity compelled her while doubt crept through every move. As Will approached, she shrugged her shoulders. "I guess I only saw a small cloud. I'm so sorry for your troubles. I've been a Don Quixote chasing my mind's wishes and now I'm chasing clouds of my imagination and wasting your time. And mine. It's time for me to recognize my father is dead and go back to Mitchborough, and my son."

"Well, Missus O'Connor. We have two options. We can re-trace the trails we've already ridden, or we can head back up around that bend. If there's a twisting cloth atop that mountain, we'll surely see it along the way. And..." Will paused trying to choose his words carefully. "Perhaps along the way, you can tell me about your son."

At this moment, Hope realized that she had inadvertently mentioned her son, but decided this was not the time as she had consciously avoided thinking of Jeremiah.

They left camp at first light and by the time the sun was holding its own directly above them, they had reached the summit above the cliff. "This is a good place to stop and cross to the edge to see if we can see that small cloud again," Will stated, stepping down and over to help Hope from her horse.

They agreed to walk in opposite directions in order to quickly cover the entire scope of the immense view. Will counted over five mountain ranges knowing there were even more peaks beyond what he could see. They had traveled a long distance from his cabin and he found himself searching for a glimpse of his own home. He re-focused to take in the entire scene, looking for that mysterious twisting cloth. Then, behind the last range, he saw a profile of what could be the bill of a hawk. *This view must be the opposite side of what we saw from my cabin,* he thought, noting that this view was much more distinctive than the first. Excited, he cupped his hands over his mouth and called to Hope to come his way, signaling her to stand by his side as he pointed toward the tall curved peak. The view took Hope's breath away and tears streamed down her cheeks releasing the emotions of the moment. Watching her take in the site, Will was so overcome that he unconsciously placed his arm around her waist to comfort her, then quickly pulled it back when he realized what he had done. To his relief, she did not seem to notice.

He stepped back to distance himself from his lack of judgment, wiped his eyes, and turned to walk back toward the horses. *This young woman is stirring feelings within me. Feelings I never had. Yet there is a wedding ring. And now a son. I know every book she has read, but little of her life, except that she ran from a raging fire and now seeks her father,* Will thought. *A father she has not seen for eleven years. A father who is most assuredly dead. And now. And now. I watch her cry with the belief that he is nearby, all because of a mountain peak that is shaped like a hawk's beak! This is beyond a waste of time. And I am not a Sancho. I am a well-educated man -- and one who surely must come to his senses and trust his own mind.*

Will watched patiently as Hope lingered for what seemed an eternity. She stayed near the bluff's edge, holding her palm above her eyes and turning slowly, obviously looking for any promising signs of yesterday's vision. Finally, unable to take her eyes from the mountain she had longed to see for so long, she began stepping backwards toward him. He took the reins, slowly walked to her side and stood quietly until she was ready to move on.

Chapter 19

Patrick O'Connor's thoughts were filled with memories. Memories of meeting his wife, Elizabeth. Their journey from Alder Springs to the Watauga settlement, memories of his daughter's birth. She had been a miracle, he knew. He had been in his mid-40's and Elizabeth a few years younger. They had given up on the possibility of children until she had realized the weight gain and ceasing cycles were not the signs of aging but actually signs of a new life within her. Their prayers had been answered. Their daughter was a gift from God, and they had called her 'Hope', Anna Hope.

Sitting on the stoop of his mountain home, Patrick rubbed the thick, lumpy scars along his right arm, the arm he had used to pull his wife from the flames. The scars still held the searing pain of that day, the day he lost not only his wife, but also his daughter. In the past few days, his heart had ached with sorrow and he imagined Hope alone and wandering, searching just as he was with prayers streaming upward pleading to God for answers. Today, as with yesterday and the day before, he succumbed to overpowering thoughts, re-tracing every step of the past with the fervent desire to find the future he longed for. His efforts were even more compelling now, and urgent, as he knew he was losing control of his mind. He had feared this all his adult life. He had seen his grandfather become increasingly forgetful and letters from his mother had confirmed that his father had died at their home in Ireland without knowing who she was. So, he repeated each memory to himself, so as not to forget. His only reason for living was to see his daughter one more time. He prayed that he could hold onto her long enough to tell her his story. He closed his eyes and again turned his thoughts back to recall that horrible night in July, 1776.

> The joy of riding alongside my daughter died with news of nearby attacks. We rode fast to tell your mother. As soon as I heard the torches hitting the roof, I knew there was little time to act. This moment was one I had feared yet planned for. I pushed her out the door.

The memory now replayed vividly in his mind.

> After sending my only child away, I rushed back inside to find Elizabeth. The doorway crashed behind me. She was screaming. The flames embraced her. I picked her up and pushed her out a window and dove out behind her. I rolled her over and over in the wet grass to quench the flames. But it was too late. As she lay dying in my arms, I was torn, unmindful of the searing pain caused by the burns on my arms and legs, knowing my wife would not survive. I wished for the courage to leave her be, so I could follow my daughter and ensure her safety. Once my wife took her last breath, I ran to the cave and saw Hope had already taken the haversack. Stunned and heartbroken, I fell to the ground and sat sobbing, my face buried in my hands. The next morning, I was still dazed. I went back and found a rain-soaked Elizabeth on the ground where I had left her. Now I've lost everything and everyone I loved. Life itself blurred. I heard the loud sound of my shovel packing the ground above her freshly-dug grave. Now my feet are shuffling through wet grass. I went back to the cave, collected my own

haversack, and also Elizabeth's. I headed down the trail along the split rail fence that had been my labor of love many years ago. I see flashes of my little girl, sitting on the fence, smiling. Then I'm watching her ride the horse she named Isaiah. The sun was now peeking through the clouds. I glanced up, squinting, "Was she already in heaven?" I asked myself. "No. No" I told myself. "I will find her. Please God, help me find her," I prayed to the sky. Then I saw the flag bearing my family crest hanging from the post at the edge of our property. I slowly pulled the ropes to bring it down, removed it from its strap, and tucked it into the waist of my breeches. I took one last look back at the smoke still rising from my home and walked away not knowing where I would go. The smell of Elizabeth's ashes clung to my clothes and followed me everywhere I went.

Solitude became my new home. I wandered aimlessly for weeks, trying to find Isaiah's tracks, turning to one stranger and then another to ask if they had seen a freckled, ginger-haired girl about fifteen years of age. I had no plan, no purpose, except to find my daughter. At first, I walked without thinking of my destination. But, as my mind cleared, I realized I was retracing the path my bride and I had followed from the mining town years ago. I began to recall the stories I had shared with my daughter. And after days of wandering, I began to recognize the mountain landmarks that had been the center of my shared memories. When I saw the the high flat surface that was Table Rock, I sensed I was finally home. This was the place I had spoken of in so many of the stories I had shared. I stopped and turned to survey the sights that had been seared in my memory long ago. And there to the west of the Table Rock, just as I had remembered, was the vivid rock carving an arch to form what I had remembered. A hawks' beak. I had named it

Hawksbill Mountain. I made camp there, on a crest above the apple orchards. I remembered the gem and pulled it from my pocket. I couldn't believe it was still there. I clasped it tightly in my fist, laid back with my arms behind my head and looked up at the stars. "This is home. This is where I'll hang the family crest, high on the tallest pole I can find." With my father's Irish resolve, I formed a plan.

The trek to Alder Springs passed quickly, as I now had a purpose. I was on familiar territory, though the small mining town I had known in my youth had grown into a bustling center of commerce and government and it was now called Morgansborough. There, I found a trader who valued my gem at a price far higher than I had ever expected. With my newfound fortune, I went to the county office and inquired of the land where I had made camp just two days earlier, then I tracked down a surveyor familiar with the land I had described. The landowner held deed on over 100,000 acres and was pleased to accept my exceptionally generous offer, eagerly signing a warrant for the 1280 acres I desired.

From the same landowner, I also purchased two slave families who would provide me with the labor and servants required for my planned homestead. I didn't take kindly to owning humans but this purchase was a necessity. My property was so remote, I had to acquire reliable help, whatever the cost. Next, I purchased two large wagons, oxen and horses, along with the materials needed to begin building my new home. With the materials and slaves in tow, I led the way back to this large crest of land overlooking Hawksbill Mountain.

As we began preparing my homestead, I insisted my servants sleep in the main room of my house until their own homes were completed. I told them "You will be much stronger if you have proper comfort when you're resting." I treated my slaves like family as, in fact, they were my only connection to humanity. In return, they grew to honor me more as a father, not as a master, for their previous owner had been a cruel overlord. Discipline was never a consideration or need. Together, we worked dawn to dusk until all three substantial homes were established. When the last door bolt was installed, we spent a day searching for the tallest tree on the property, cut it down and trimmed it to make a post, then led the oxen as they pulled it to the sight where I had originally set camp. We carefully attached a rope and set the post firmly in the ground. We took the tattered flag I had tucked into my breeches over a year ago and raised it to a pinnacle from which it could be seen from miles around.

My determination was matched by my growing enthusiasm and strong belief that one day my daughter would find me. I spent my days walking across my land with the expectation that Hope would come riding toward me at any moment.

But as time passed, disappointment gradually replaced anticipation. Depression was reinforced by self-imposed isolation. Even though I had my servants, I insisted they leave me alone. Now, ten years later, the two families have settled into their designated routines and I only interact with the cook and housekeeper to acknowledge their presence, and even then only when it is absolutely necessary. Otherwise, my servants go about their duties and leave me be. Their instructions hold only one exception. At any sound of approaching horses, they are to drop everything and run to identify the riders. Only one rider is to be allowed to enter my property and be escorted to my home.

That would be a woman rider with ginger-colored hair.

And that was his story. Patrick raised his head, opened his eyes, and looked to the sky, thanking God that he had recalled almost every detail and vowed to repeat this story to himself again momentarily.

He looked out to the mountains and smiled to see his family crest twisting in the wind high above the trees. It was now torn and tattered, but shades of green and red still marked its image. *Now, back to my story,* he thought, placing his elbows on his knees and his face in his hands to concentrate.

... A sweltering, humid day turned into a foggy,
evening of drizzling rain ...
The joy of riding alongside my daughter died with
news of nearby attacks ...

"Sir! Sir!" Approaching voices shouting loudly, disrupting his concentration. Patrick struggled to hold onto his train of thought. *Voices*?

"What is it?" He said, standing up to see what could possibly be causing such commotion. Three young black boys were running toward him. Behind them followed a vaguely familiar site. A red dun Spanish mustang with a female rider. She had ginger-colored hair.

I'm dreaming, he thought as he took hold of one of the white columns to steady himself. *My mind has truly left me.*

"Father! Father!" Hope shouted as she quickly slid down from Isaiah's back.

"Is that horse called Isaiah?" Patrick queried. "And who are you to come here riding my daughter's horse?" he shouted emphatically.

"It's me, Anna Hope, your daughter!"

Patrick stepped slowly down the steps, then stumbled back as Hope's rushing hug nearly tackled him.

"Oh, I can't believe it! I've searched for you so long! But we followed your flag." Hope clasped his face with both hands. "Oh, and here's my friend, Captain William Spenser. He helped me find you!"

Will dismounted his horse and stepped forward to shake Patrick's hand. "It's a great honor, sir," said Patrick.

"Are you her husband?" Patrick inquired.

"Just a friend, sir," responded Will.

"Then go!" Patrick shouted. "This girl says she is my daughter. If this is true, and you are not her husband, you have no business here! Get off my property!"

Will nodded and bowed slightly, then backed slowly to his horse. As he mounted his horse, he took once last, long look at the young woman he had known for just a few days. With a kick to his horse, he said, "Be well Missus O'Connor."

Hope felt a twinge of sadness as she watched Will ride beyond the twisting flag until he disappeared in a trail of dust.

Loud sobbing sounds took her breath away. She turned and embraced her father, pressing her face into his chest, and wept.

Patrick wrapped his arms around her and held her tightly. Hope didn't mind the excruciating pain that resurfaced when his arms squeezed her left side. "My little one. I'll never let you go away ever ever."

"Come with us," a gentle voice spoke. Hope peered up to see a large, black woman gesturing from the porch to invite her into the house. One of the teen-age boys took Patrick's hand and led him inside. Hope watched as another black boy entered and helped guide Patrick to place him in a large cushioned rocking chair. The black woman fluffed a pillow and placed it behind Patrick's head.

"Are you Miss Hope?" the black woman asked.

"Yes, I am his daughter. I have come a long way. It has been over ten years...." Hope fought back the tears, but they came rushing back down her cheeks.

"I know'd ye wuz soon's I laid eyes on ye. Ya's all he's talked about ever since we know'd him. He know'd you'd find him. He watched fer ya ever' day," said the woman. "He is a kind soul. But I fear he's come to be quite forgetful," she whispered, taking Hope's hand. "Come with me, sweet child. I'll fix ya some tea."

Hope was torn between staying near her father or following the woman. But through her tears, she could see that her father was nodding off to sleep, unaware of her presence. "Don't ya fret none. Me boys 'll keep an eye on him while he sleeps so's to make sure he don't fall out of his chair." Hope followed the woman, turning back briefly to see the boys sit down on the floor on either side of Patrick's chair.

"Me name's Phoebe. My husband n' I, our two sons, been with Master O'Connor for over nine years. He bought us and another family from our master in Morgansborough. Since we's been here, your father has treated us like his own family. But, I have to tell ya, his memory's goin'. Some days he's the same man who brung us here. Other days he sits alone, repeating th' same story o'er n' o'er agin. I's sure ya'll hear it tomorrow. Or maybe the next day."

The next morning Hope found her father seated on the front stoop, exactly where he had been when she arrived. She sat down beside him and patiently waited until he glanced her way.

With a startled look, he exclaimed, "Is that you? Hope? When did you get here?"

Patrick repeated his questions nearly every day. "When did you get here?" "Do I have a grandson? Or granddaughter?" Hope struggled with whether to tell him the truth and decided against it. She vowed to keep the past ten years to herself and swore to stay with her father until he died. It saddened her that he would never know her son, his grandson, but she also realized that the father she had known was no longer here.

Nearly every day she listened to him tell his story, beginning with *"... The joy of riding alongside my daughter died with news of the attacks. We rode fast to tell her mother..."* and ending with the command to "watch for a girl with ginger-colored hair." The story was always the same, with the exception of a few words that had the same meanings. In the beginning, she listened intently, but as days passed, she found her thoughts drifting. She wondered if her father had traversed the same trails, trails that paralleled the Doe River, trails that crossed the path to Henry Greer's farm, or the same trail she had followed when riding Isaiah to flee from the horror of Henry's anger and the dark man's fire. Had he walked past the grist mill when he went to sell his gem in Morgansborough? Her thoughts followed the trail to Mitch's mill, Isaiah's pasture, and back wandering toward Hawksbill Mountain, the Table Rock, and she imagined herself seated in the rocking chair where she had admired the large distinctive rocks jutting out over the gorge.

When Patrick wasn't telling his story, Hope passed the time reading her father passages from his Bible. She read aloud with a strong Irish brogue, imitating the way he had read to her when she was a child. At first she believed the familiar tone and verses would stimulate his mind and provoke new memories, or even bring him into the present. This effort seemed promising until one reading when he abruptly interrupted, shouting "Stop! Stop now!" He placed his arms on her shoulders to look directly into her eyes, and pleaded, "My life is too big to hold in my mind anymore so I'm letting some of it go. I'll tell you as much as I can remember and you can hold it in your own mind as long as you need to." Then, as if nothing had been said, he proceeded to tell of "*...The joy of riding alongside my daughter died with news of the attacks. We rode fast to tell her mother...*"

On most days, he wandered away from the house as he had in the years before she arrived. At first Hope followed, then in the ensuing days, she walked alongside him as he repeated his journey across the usual paths, searching for his daughter, not realizing that the ginger-haired girl was holding his hand. They walked across fields of wildflowers kissing the wind, shuffled through fallen leaves of red and gold, and traversed frozen fields while snowflakes gracefully danced around them. During their walks together, Hope found herself lifting her shawl to her cheeks to wipe away the tears, tears that came without warning, tears that welled up from her heart to release the grief, the sadness, the loss that came with death. She had spent each day since the fire praying that her father was alive. Now, though he resembled a healthy man walking beside her, she knew his mind was quickly dying. The life she held onto was merely a shell holding a beating heart without a future.

As the dogwoods began to bloom, Hope recalled the birth of her only son eleven years ago and wondered if she would ever see him again. But now, a year after finding her father, she knew she must not think of the day her son cried forth in life, she must cling to each moment of the present and hold onto a life that was fading, distancing itself from its very being and drifting into its own infinity.

Chapter 20

1788

Hope looked away from the grave and stared down at the rushing river in the gorge below Hawksbill Mountain. She could not bear to watch Phoebe's husband and sons shovel the dirt onto her father's resting place. The clanging shovels reminded her of her father's repeated words *"I could hear the loud sound of my shovel packing the ground above her freshly-dug grave."* Now her father was really gone. No more searching. Just the memories she had formed on their long walks and the repeated story he had seared into her mind. His grave was as he had directed, set directly below the pole bearing the family crest, and overlooking the valley below Hawksbill Mountain. Her thoughts turned to her future. It had been over a year since she had left Jeremiah to find her father. The servants had become her family, helping to care for her father, and providing comfort when she struggled with his fading mind and weakening body. And, while she felt close to them, she knew this would never be her home.

"I'm going to go back to Mitchborough to find my son," she told them as they walked away from the grave. "And I want to take Isaiah to the pasture he enjoyed for so many years."

The next morning, Phoebe helped Hope pack her few belongings in the haversack and loaded the haversack onto Isaiah's back. Hope then mounted Isaiah and headed east intending to find the trail she had ridden when she followed the Carsons a year earlier. "This trail is fresh," she noted aloud as she rode. She was relieved to see branches had been cut along each side of the trail's edge and stones had been cleared from the ground. She had ridden nearly half a day when she passed a fence framing a familiar small pasture. It had been carefully placed with alternating logs and branches to form wide 'X's' marking the property and a trail that led to the owner's cabin. She rode past the fence, determined to make it to Mitchborough before dark. But she couldn't resist the temptation. *I must see Hawksbill Mountain one more time as I may never travel this way again.*

She turned Isaiah and rode up to the cabin and over to the side where she could see the treasured rock. "Do you plan to stay on your horse all day, or would you like to come in for tea, or perhaps a cup of wine?" a familiar voice inquired. "I killed a rabbit this morning and there's fresh stew simmering over the fire. There's more than enough for both of us if you wish to join me," Will said as he took her hand to help her down. "Go ahead in. While you get settled, I'll take Isaiah to get some water."

Inside, Hope felt a sense of warmth and comfort. Perhaps it was the books, or could it be simply sensing the owner's surroundings -- the familiar smells, the belongings he had carried when they were riding in search of her father -- his haversack tossed against the wall next to the door, a pile of clothes in need of washing, the wide-brimmed hat that covered his face when he was sleeping.

Her wandering thoughts were interrupted when Will stepped inside and over to the small oak table to pick up a large decanter. "This decanter has been in my family for generations. Colonel Avery brought it to me last time he stopped by. I trust you will like the wine. I planted the vines when I was building this place and they finally produced delicious red grapes. The barrels are in the barn and this wine has only aged a little over a year, but I could not wait to taste it any longer. It would be a great pleasure to share it with you this afternoon."

Hope took a sip, and then another, savoring its flavor and the way it made her feel warm inside. "This is my first taste of wine. It makes my tongue tingle. My father is dead," she said without hesitation.

"I am sorry he is gone, but also grateful you had time with him." Will reflected. "Each day since we parted, I have taken in the site of what you call Hawksbill Mountain with a new meaning. Our time spent searching for your father was at times agonizing, but most often delightful. Our talks about books lingered in my mind. I believed you would head back to Mitchborough one day so I returned to the edge of your father's trail. I trusted not to enter his property but I began clearing a path as the entire trail was overgrown. I must also confess that in your absence, I did a bit more clearing of trees and brush along my own trail. I prayed you would stop, so I could see you just once more."

"Isaiah's gait is not what it was when I first rode him. He is my best friend, as he has seen and heard many moments of my life. Moments even I can't recall. I am truly grateful you made his journey an easier one for I am taking him back to the pastures below the grist mill, where he can run as fast as he desires and graze in the finest fields, as even though he is a horse, he truly is my best friend."

"I understand. My mare and I have fought hard battles together and traversed difficult trails," Will paused to refill both cups with wine. "I know you have had a trying few months and you are anxious to get Isaiah to Mitch's pastures, but I'm wondering if you would consider staying the night. You could resume your journey after a good night's rest. And I will, of course, respect your privacy. You can stay in my room, while I sleep outside, just as before."

"This wine is very good," Hope said, taking another sip. "And, I am tired and a little sleepy, so I will accept your offer to stay. I will go to Mitchborough in the morning. But, if you have more wine, another cup would be nice before I retire for the evening."

As daylight broke, Will was not surprised to find Hope sitting in the rocking chair facing Hawksbill Mountain. Her hair was loose, falling in ginger ringlets across her shoulders. She did not look up from the book she was reading. When she situated the fingers on her left hand to mark her place on the page, the sunlight bounced shards of light from her ring.

The light caught Will's eye, again calling attention to what he took to be a wedding ring, but he decided this was not the right time to question its origin. "Good morning. I see you found one of my favorite books, Shakespeare's tale of *Antony and Cleopatra*. Cleopatra is a complex and vain character, I would say."

"I am not vain, but I may be complex," replied Hope looking up from her book with a smile.

"Complex? It will take time for me to determine whether you are so." Will pondered, thinking it would be wise not to pursue this point of view, he continued. "Please, take your time and enjoy the play. You can borrow the book if you wish, with the promise that you will return it one day. For now, I will bring you some biscuits and tea so you'll be well-fed before you head to Mitchborough.

Hope was again totally immersed in the book when Will returned with a plate of biscuits and two cups of tea. She carefully widened the book to the pages she had been reading and placed it upside down on her lap.

Will handed Hope the tea, pulled his other rocker next to hers and set the plate of biscuits on his knees so they could share. "Before you leave, I must concede that I also re-traced the trail that the Carsons originally followed to bring you here. It was not well-traveled, so I cleared it nearly all the way to Mitchborough so that when, or if, you were to return to the mill, your journey would be without obstacles. But, if you wish, I'm also happy to ride with you to keep you company or perhaps you prefer to be on your own. I do not want to assume you care for my company or impose myself into your travels."

Hope sipped the tea and took a biscuit from the plate. "I will consider your offer. However, before I leave, I would like to see the wine barrels in the barn. Would you show me how you turn grapes into wine? I am curious how your wine differs from the wine that dissolved Cleopatra's pearls."

"I am honored to show you my wine-making provisions. And, rest assured that Cleopatra's wine is not my own. Her wager with Mark Antony was intriguing indeed. It is said that her wine had turned to vinegar and that's how the pearls were destroyed. That won't happen here, I promise. I'll show you how I protect my wine to keep it from going sour."

When they arrived at the barn, Hope ran over to Isaiah, embraced his cheeks and rubbed her nose against his. She then removed her haversack and a large heavy leather bag intertwined with its ropes. She carried the haversack and dragged the bag to the barn door thinking she would go through them later. Will helped her remove Isaiah's saddle and hung it on the stall's fence. They spent the rest of the morning sampling wine, brushing their horses, and discussing the nuances of the relationship between Antony and Cleopatra. After he had explained his wine-making process, Will said, "I want to show you my springhouse where I store some of the wine. And, as we're headed that way, we can take my mare and Isaiah to the spring for some fresh water."

"This springhouse is somewhat smaller than the one where Jeremiah and I stayed after the fire," Hope said when they opened the door.

"Jeremiah? Who is Jeremiah?" Will asked.

"Oh, forgive me. I know not what I said. It seems the wine has made me a bit light-headed," Hope shoved her cup toward Will and darted past him, stumbling forward. Will dropped both cups and leaped forward to catch her.

"There now," he said as he placed his arms around her waist to steady her. "Let's take the horses to the barn, then go back to the cabin. I'm afraid I may have been a bit too generous when we were tasting the wine, forgetting you had only nibbled your biscuit this morning. Another biscuit will probably help you feel better."

Hope sat with both arms resting on the table watching the fire's mesmerizing flames shoot upward to disappear in the draft. Her muddled thoughts drifted as she contemplated her situation, unconsciously twisting the ring with her right hand. She had spent only a few days with this person who was no longer a stranger. In a way he had become her only friend. Except for her time at the grist mill, she had never been close to anyone other than her father and perhaps Matilda. Hope's mind was rapidly spinning, twisting her thoughts. *Matilda is probably dead, so those secrets are safe unless her spirit chooses to share them. Even my father went to his grave without knowing he had a grandson. Mitch knows more about me than anyone,* she thought. *If I share my secrets and memories with this man, he will think less of me. And then he may not want to be my friend. Yet he will not trust me unless I share. And I want him to be my friend. The wine is weaving through my head. This man has stirred my memories, the memories I keep packed deep inside behind my heart. Memories that only surface in my nightmares, memories shoved deep inside me when I wake. Can I separate my past and find a way to thrive in the present. This man has set my mind ablaze with memories. Or maybe it is the wine. I wish all the sad times, the terror I've endured would drift from my mind and up the chimney to disappear into the sky like the smoke, never to be seen again.*

Will stood silently, watching her fidget with her ring, so caught up in her thoughts, he doubted she knew he was there. He moved slowly over to the table, sat down across from her and placed his hands on hers. "You are complex, my friend, and I can see you are struggling with how much you want to share. I respect and I think I understand your independence, though I do not yet know what makes you so. You have not fought battles with guns and swords—swift movements that left a man haunted by the souls of the slain, wounds of the mind that will be forever stuck, only to repeat again and again. Yet I sense you fought your own battles and you are wounded just the same. I am here to listen whenever you wish to talk. Yet I want you to know I also understand your need to hold your pain because you fear your heart will explode should you share your secrets. When you have killed someone, that person never leaves you ever ever ever." Will squeezed her hands and leaned forward. "The Carsons brought you here and we found ourselves in an awkward moment. But I was compelled to help you find your father and I am grateful you had your time with him. I know you have a strong faith and so do I. Perhaps the Lord brought us together to be friends. That must be. There is no other explanation. So please know I am here for you. I will listen without judging. And I will be your friend no matter what you say."

Tears streamed down Hope's cheeks, but she did not speak. *This man speaks without knowing he stirred a truth, a truth that is bubbling up to be heard. Truth I have never spoken or accepted even to myself. Truth that has shattered my soul and locked itself within my hardened heart.*

Hope looked into Will's eyes and he nodded to let her know he was listening.

"I was very young, just fifteen. After the fire at my father's home, I rode Isaiah, stopping only to walk down a hill to the stream. It was very hot that day. I woke the next day. My legs were bruised inside. A bone was pushing against the skin of one leg, but my stockings held it in place. Isaiah was gone," she sobbed harder, shaking but continuing through the tears. Suddenly, she jerked her hands from Will's grasp and suddenly stood, pushing the air away with both arms. It was as if she was in the forest, searching. "Isaiah! My Isaiah is gone! Take the stick and make a cane to walk. Follow the river. Crawl. Jake and Jared ran down the hill. Their father, Henry… Henry built me a cabin and we married. Matilda told me how babies were made for I did not know. I did not know! It hurt so much when Jeremiah came. Henry said it was not his. So he came to my bed and hurt me. I stayed silent. I held my screams inside me so Jeremiah would not wake. The river was my safe place. One morning I saw the dark man leaving -- saw him leaving the burning cabin. He had Henry's scalp in his hand." Hope reached into her pocket and showed Will her sling. "I used this to kill the dark man." She paused to show the sling to Will then stepped back, shouting, whirled the sling in the air, jerked it back, then forward as the imaginary rock fled its cradle. Will ducked as her hand just missed his cheek. "He fell. Hard. The dark man is dead. His knife is on the ground beside him. I knelt to pick it up. That scar. Jeremiah! Jeremiah!" Hope embraced her chest with both arms and held tight. "A horse! Isaiah! I killed the dark man and rode away with Jeremiah … Oh my God. He was the same! His scar, the black hair hanging over my face. He took my horse! The dark man had Isaiah all that time! He was the same -- the same! I can see him clearly now! He sowed his seed inside me. He's the same! That's how Isaiah came to be at the tree. And my son. My son Jeremiah looks just like him, except he has no scar."

Will stood, walked over to Hope, pulled her to his chest, and embraced her tightly to stop her from shaking.

He leaned his head against her and whispered. "You words sting, I know. But they do not change how I feel. You are more than a friend. Only time will tell how deep our friendship will become. I will take care of you if you let me. I will be here to listen. I will stand by your side quietly when you want to be silent. You may stay as long as you wish. Or, if you must go, go knowing that I will be here waiting. Waiting with prayers for your return."

Hope jerked away, pushing her hands against Will's chest, then leaned her head against his shoulder. "That was my nightmare. My nightmare just passed through me." She stood back to face him. "I never saw it before. Not in my waking hours. Oh Lord Jesus. Forgive me. The wine released all within. The strings that bound my heart are loosened, falling free. But now I must heal." Hope felt faint and sat back on the bench. Will sat beside her, and took her hand. She pulled her hand back, took a breath, then grasped Will's wrists with both hands and held them tightly. "I can't face Jeremiah now. My mind must clear. He is my son and I love him. But now I have seen my greatest fear. I buried the truth deep inside. I loved him. Cared for him from his birth. I taught him to read and write. And to kill squirrels with his sling. But Jeremiah is the son of the evil dark man. I dare not go until I can see my son as he is -- not as he appears. I must stay. If you will let me."

Hope was awakened by loud chopping sounds coming from outside the cabin. She quickly splashed her face, pulled up her hair, and stepped down the stairs and outside to find Will cutting branches from an oak tree.

"How long have you been up?" she asked, seating herself on the top step of the porch.

"I rise before dawn every morning, my friend. Today I'm making myself a new bed. I'll keep it under the window near the foot of the stairs. So, if you decide to stay, you can have my room as long as you like."

"I hear your words, but I do not know even my own mind. Here, you are my only friend," Hope paused to gather her thoughts. "I am so very ashamed of my ways, the way I rambled on last evening. It seems the wine chased through my soul and pushed words out into the room with a fury I did not expect. And now the night is a twisting blur, much of which I cannot remember. Except I know I shared many things, secrets I had kept even from myself. I am sorry. Please do not hold last night against me. I beg and pray you will find it in your heart to forgive me."

Will put down his ax and stepped over to sit beside her. He crossed his arms atop his knees and clasped his hands to indicate his decision to sit quietly and just listen.

Hope continued as if speaking only to herself, her eyes staring blankly into the air in front of her. "Until now I had not allowed myself to see the dark man that dwells in the face of my son. And now I fear his face will always be a reminder of the terror I harbored deep within me for so long. So, I am torn apart with sadness, my emotions ripping through me. No. I cannot go back to Jeremiah just yet. My heart aches for him, but I must wait until my mind is clear. I must wait as long as it takes to find enough peace and forgiveness to know I can look at my son with the unconditional love he deserves. A love unbound by lingering shadows. A love that he can feel when I hold him, just as I did from the day he was born. Jeremiah was all I had to hold onto until I left him." Hope turned to look into Will's eyes. "And yes. I could go back to my father's home. But it belongs to the servants now. They cared for him through many difficult years and I wish it to remain their home and the home of their children in years to come. So, it seems that for now I have nowhere else to go. But I have also disrupted your life and you … you must long for things to be as they were before."

Will turned to face Hope, took her hands in his and pulled them to his heart. "My friend, it has been a disruption that brought me great joy. Would I be building this cot if I wished you to go?" Will stood and helped Hope up from the stoop. "Now, let's go check on the horses and I'll help carry that heavy bag up to your room. Then perhaps you can help me finish building my cot."

Chapter 21

Jared lost count of the winters and springs that had passed. Days alone. Jesse was his only companion. That is except for the occasional rabbit or squirrel he allowed to live. He stepped through the barn's narrow doorway and rubbed his eyes with his knuckles to erase the vision of his father rising from the ashes to sharpen his switch. Soon, the sunlight burned away the night's dreams. He could see clearly now. But he still wondered if the frightening spirit lingered only to haunt him because he and his brother had not given their father a proper burial. The ashes had turned to mud. Wildflowers peeked through what had once been the floor of his family home. A squirrel scurried up the oak tree and across the branches under which Henry and Hope had taken their vows. He ran his fingers through his beard and twisted its ends together where it hung just above the knotted rope of the breeches hanging loosely from his hips.

"C'mon Jesse!" Jared shouted as he shoved the heavy door aside just enough for Jesse to saunter through. Jared followed Jesse as he galloped across the trail, past the oak tree, and down to the river for his morning ritual. Jesse ran into the water and down the stream to his favorite pool where pebbles formed a solid floor so he could stand and drink to his heart's content.

"It's time!" Jared spoke aloud to himself as he climbed to the top of the diving rock and jumped in. When he surfaced, he struggled to remove his shirt and breeches, only then questioning whether his plan was the easiest path to a cleaner body and clothes. He pulled his shirt across the water and folded it into a rough square so he could rub it against his body to wash away the soil that had coated his skin since his last trip to the swimming hole before the snow came. Then he loosed his shirt and swiftly swished it back and forth in the water hoping to release the stains from the fabric. He swam over to the shore and threw his shirt over a tree limb, then repeated the swishing motions with his breeches. After throwing his breeches onto another branch, Jared tumbled back into the water and dove to the pool's bottom several times to ensure his hair was thoroughly rinsed. Next he swam to the river's edge and leaned into the water, pulling his fingers back and forth through every strand of hair to clean it best he could.

Jesse followed Jared back up the hill then cantered off to graze in the fields. Jared stepped back into the barn, grabbed his sword and walked down the hill to stand in front of Hope's rock. With an abrupt motion, he tossed his head forward, clasped his wet hair, raised his sword up then swiftly downward, missing his head by inches. A large chunk of hair fell to the ground in front of the rock. He repeated this motion until he had cut his hair to a length just hitting his shoulders. Then he pulled his beard forward and swiftly cut it to a length just hitting his upper chest. *Some bird or animal will make a good nest of them hairs,* he thought.

He brought his thumb and index finger to his mouth and blew a hard, loud whistle to call Jesse back from the field. "We're goin' back to familiar parts buddy," Jared muttered as he led Jesse back to the barn. "It's been too long since ya wore a saddle, but it's best fer both of us as I dunno when, or if, we'll be comin' back." After Jared hitched Jesse's saddle and loaded his belongings, he placed his sword in its sheath, led his horse back outside and tied the reins to the oak tree. "No more grazin' today boy. If'n my clothes is dry, we'll be on our way." Jared pulled the heavy barn doors together to close them, then heaved his shoulders then his hips against the wood to align them. "Ouch!" he yelled. He reached down to pull a splinter from his bare buttocks. He then placed three long narrow logs into the slats he had hung at the top middle and bottom of the door's frame. *Sho' hope this keeps th' big critters out!*

Jesse took to the trail as if he had traveled the path every day. As Jared dismounted, a light mist was drifting through the glade near the shores of Sycamore Shoals. He decided to make camp along the river in the exact spot where he and Jesse had waited for Jake that night years ago. From here, he would try to think like his younger brother, to seek the path Jake would have taken in search of the girl, Melissa.

As Jared slowly navigated Jesse through the town just west of Sycamore Shoals, he watched well-dressed men and women scurrying along the dusty streets, entering and departing structures like he had never seen before. Some structures were constructed with logs, but their size was much larger than the one that had been the home he knew before the dark man burned it down. Other buildings were of stones stacked and sealed together with a white dirt unlike the mud they had used to seal Hope's cabin. Others were framed in smooth, flat-cut logs of a white color, topped by steep roofs. The stoops were of the same flat-cut logs, set against the front walls the entire length of the buildings. There were railings where folks had tied their horses. Just the site of so many buildings and such busy people stirred uncertainty and fear through his mind. He rode on through, past the last building and onto a wide, dirt trail that twisted aside large farms bordered by split-rail fences. Ahead, he paused, puzzled by a sharp split in the trail. Jesse snorted in the direction of a rushing river and they took the path leading down another hill and stopped at the water's edge.

Dismounting, he took Jesse's reins and led him alongside the riverbank. "That thar settlement's ain't nothin' I never seen afore, Jesse. I ain't spoke t' no other human since Jake rode this-a-way. I fears I kin only talk to ye -- a horse. So's we's gonna have t' wait til I kin figure how t' ask strangers 'bout me brother. N' maybe a girl called Melissa."

Jared studied the land around him until he found two trees where he could make camp. He gathered long limbs and stacked them across branches between the trees, then covered them with branches, leaves, and brush to form a makeshift roof. Next he built a small campfire in hopes of finding a squirrel or even a fish for supper. The fire dwindled and sleep quickly embraced a tired soul with dreams of food that never came.

The next day Jared rode further west along the riverbank. Across the meadow, far up on a hill he saw a single log structure with a steep roof. He decided to ride up to the ridge to get a better view of the farms in the valley below. He observed wagons rolling toward yesterday's village and its wide range of structures. His mind's eye blurred as he tried to imagine himself inquiring of his younger brother while navigating the crowded streets. *Too many. Too many.*

Back at his camp, he found himself walking in circles and speaking aloud into the settling fog -- a dark fog packed with shadows of strangers. "Ma'am. Sir. Ya seen my brother?" He thought back to his time with the militia, with Charlie, and his commander, Colonel Shelby. *Them wuz strangers at first. They became me friends. They wuz from these parts,* he pondered, shuffling his feet back and forth to draw a line in the mud. The mud's line soon became a ditch. *If'n Jake wuz here, he wuz a stranger too. I'm stronger n' tougher'n him. I kilt bears n' fought wolves whilst he wuz here, prolly with that girl, Melissa. He's prolly sippin' fine whiskey n' rubbin' her leg rat now. I'mma gonna find 'em n' show that girl wut a real man is.*

A gust of wind pushed a twig from the lean-to's roof onto Jared's face. "No! No!" He grabbed the twig and threw it, scratching his hand against the brush above him. The sharpened switch fell to the ground. He sat up rubbing his cut fist hard against his eyes, then sucked the blood from his knuckles. He squinted to fight the sunlight as he crawled out from under his shelter and over to the river's edge.

As he rode into town, heads turned and men shook their fists in protest as Jesse's hooves threw dust onto skirts of ladies scurrying out of the horse's path. Jared guided Jesse to a sudden stop in between two other horses and rolled off Jesse's back landing both feet hard on the ground. He cocked his head up and looked around with his nose high to show the town folks he was better than they were. After quickly tying Jesse's reins to the post, Jared stomped up the steps onto the long stoop, placed his hands on his hips and turned to survey his options. Groups of men and women whispered while they huddled conspicuously pretending he didn't exist. He decided to duck through the nearest door and found himself in a large room bordered in shelves boasting jars and sacks of unknown goods.

"Kin I help ye Sir?" Jared peered around to find the man behind the voice. "Over here Sir! Ye looks like ye ain't been here afore."

Jared gathered his confidence and walked to the man standing behind the counter. "Lookin' fer me brother. Last

I seen him he wuz headed this way. Ain't seen him fer years, ya see." Jared placed both hands on the counter and mustered the courage to look the man in the eyes.

"Wut's 'is name?"

"Jake. Jake Greer. Skinnier 'an me n' his nose is broke. Broke from afore he wuz ten years old."

"Yer's in luck sonny. I knows him if'n he's th' one Imma thinkin' about. Broken nose fer sure. He's married to th' Warner girl n' he works fer th' Doc. O'er yonder, jest up th' hill, in th' buildin' with th' blue door," the man raised his arm to point to the back of his store. "Jest walk around to the back of this here building n' ye'll see it. Ask fer Doc Taylor's place if'n ya gits lost."

Jared ignored the angry stares following him as he took Jesse's reins and led him around to the back of the store. Up the hill, he saw a small white-washed building with a blue door. Approaching the building, Jared fought the doubts churning through his mind. As he looped the reins across the post, Jesse's nose nudged hard against his back, pushing him forward. "Ya's hurryin' me buddy. I knows ya wanna see him too. I knows."

Inside, Jared was surprised to see a room packed with a dishevelled woman coaxing her three children to stop their cries, a man holding a dirty rag atop his bleeding scalp, and a small boy curled up on the floor next to a cedar chest. Across the room a closed door stood between the main room and agonizing screams on the other side. He had not heard such screams since just before Charlie fell at Kings Mountain. He nodded to the woman and gradually backed himself out the door to sit on the steps overlooking the town.

With his elbows on his knees and his head in his hands, Jared watched the townspeople scurrying about their deeds. He scooted aside each time a patient left the Doc's office heading he knew not where. The screaming children left quietly and he watched as the man with a wide bandage afixed to his head mounted his horse and rode away.

"Ya been waitin' a long time, I hear," said a familiar voice. Jared stood and turned to see his younger brother holding the door open as if to invite him inside. He was taken aback by his brother's stance, his grinning face boasting a confidence he had not seen before. The two stood, each stunned by the sight of the other.

"Jared? Is that you?" Jake said, now standing with arms outstretched, both hands pressing hard against the sides of the doorway, as if to keep from falling forward -- or backward.

Jared turned away and began walking down the steps toward his horse.

"Wait!" Jake shouted.

Jake ran down the steps smack into his brother, bumping him into Jesse's side. There was a quick embrace. And then the two brothers held each other tightly as if a strong wind was rushing toward them.

"Who's that? Do you need me to help you bring him up the steps?" Doc Taylor yelled from the door.

"This here's my brother Jared. Th' one I told ya 'bout. He's my only family -- next to Melissa and Wash, that is."

Jared grabbed Jake's arm and pulled him toward him. "Wash?" Who's Wash?"

"Why Jared, he's my son. He's almost six now. We named him after General George Washington."

"I don't know of any General Washington. Did he ride with Colonel Shelby?"

"His name is Jared George Washington. Jared -- named after you, my big brother! And George Washington, the general who finally won the war. Wash was born just three months after the war ended. Everyone was celebratin' and we were blessed with a son! Jared George Washington Greer. We just call him Wash."

"You boys have a lot to catch up on," the Doc shouted. "Go on ahead Jake. I'll close up for the day. I know you'll want to get on home to get re-acquainted and prepare for church tomorrow. Just be here the usual time Monday morning."

Melissa had imagined Jared to be as skinny as Jake, but perhaps a bit taller. After all, for the past eight years, he had lived alone in the back woods with no human contact. They had assumed he was dead, probably from starvation or a wild animal attack. Now she worked to calm herself as she stood on the porch holding Wash in her arms and watching this strapping, ruggedly handsome man remove his belongings from the back of his horse. He had obviously spent a lot of time in the sun. *His golden skin paints a stunning frame for his sky-blue eyes … and his hair with highlights of a raging fire … he must've gained his strong body living alone and fighting for his life,* she mused. *Heaven forbid! I must compose myself. This man is my husband's brother. My son's uncle.* A flash of heat rushed to her face causing her to quickly turn her head to hide her embarrassment.

Jared had never seen a place like this before. The boards on the walls were two hands wide. Very thin decorated boards connected the walls to the ceiling. The floor was wood, but the boards were wider and shinier than the boards of the general store and Doc's foyer. Everywhere he looked there were colorful rugs, some braided, some tightly woven to form patterns of large and small flowers. There were doorways leading to different rooms crowded with furnishings for sitting, tables for dining, and even large cabinets boasting shelves set with beautiful plates, cups, and saucers. He ducked, his head narrowly missing a squiggly configuration of candle holders hanging from the ceiling. But his thoughts of furnishings quickly dissolved into the captivating image in the room beyond. The home's mistress -- his brother's wife. As she leaned forward to tend the kettle on the fire, an open door released the sun's light through the threads of her skirt, revealing the curves of her plump hips. His eyes traced the skin along her muscular thighs to the shapely calves of her legs tucked into the daintily laced strings of her boots. A strange longing seared through his entire body as he inched forward.

"Jared! Come on! Let me show you the barn and our horses!" Jake shouted from the open door.

"Jad! Jad! Come with papa! I show you my pony. He's black as tar!" Wash ran into the parlor and took Jared's hand pulling him through the kitchen and out the back door.

Jared followed his brother's son to the barn, acknowledged each animal, and feigned admiration for the fancy woodwork of the barn's frame and stalls. But as he walked along the path of the little one eagerly showing his many belongings, Jared's thoughts remained with the boy's mother. *No wonder Jake hurried to return that horse so many years ago.*

After supper, Jake went to the porch, picked up Jared's belongings, and walked inside to the dining table where Jared sat alone, staring into the fire. "Melissa is putting Wash to bed and then we'll be settling in for the night. Let me show you your room."

Jared followed Jake up to the third floor and watched as Jake tossed his belongings to the foot of a large bed. He reluctantly accepted the pat on his shoulder and watched as Jake headed back down the stairs and out of sight. It had been a long time since he had seen, let alone laid in a bed. This one was high off the floor, unlike the mattress he had shared with Jake long ago, and much higher than the bed that was his for the short time papa slept entire nights with Hope. He crawled up onto the feather-stuffed mattress and laid on his back with his arms bent and his hands behind his head. He looked down at his boots, the boots he always wore when he slept under brained and softened blankets of skinned deer and rabbits. Moonlight painted a wide stream of light across his chest to the wardrobe sitting against the wall. He heard distant sounds of frogs and crickets announcing their evening's ventures. But closer in, from the room below, he heard giggling and squeals from his brother's wife.

He quietly rolled off the bed and tiptoed out of the room and down the stairs. The door to the room of giggles and squeals was slightly ajar. He slowly stepped over to peer inside. She was sitting atop his brother's belly, moving slowly back and forth, tossing her hair and emitting sounds of extreme pleasure. The silhouette he had seen earlier was now clear and vivid as she wore no clothes. The image of her breasts bounced intensely across his mind as he rushed downstairs through he kitchen and out the back door to the barn.

He found Jesse's stall and settled beside him, relieved to be snuggled within the familiar scent of dirt and straw. But this time, the familiar scent could not calm his mind, now filled with images of his brother's bride, bare breasts, curves and movements that stirred his senses. His thoughts swept back and forth between Melissa's overwhelming sounds of pleasure and memories of the sounds he had heard from Hope's cabin whenever his papa left his bed. On many a night, he and Jake had slipped outside to listen, aiming to learn how a man took his wife for pleasure. On many a night they heard sharp sounds of fists hitting flesh. The sounds from Hope were nothing like what he had heard from Melissa on this momentous evening. He spent much of the night awake, thinking of how it would be with Melissa, what sounds she would make once he took her for his own.

The next morning, he woke to the sound of Jake taking the horses out of the barn to hitch them to the carriage. He snuck around the barn and walked up to Jake to help him with the harness. "Did you sleep well brother?" Jake asked.

"Yep."

Jake looked at his brother's well-worn clothes and roughly cut beard. "You've never been to church afore, have you?"

"Nope."

"Well, I know ya well enough to know you probably want to think about it before ya meet a bunch of strangers. So's we'll go on without you this morning, if that's okay," Jake reached out his hand to help Melissa step into the carriage. Wash jumped up beside her. "We'll be at Melissa's folks for Sunday dinner after church. You'll meet them one day. They live just a few acres down the road." Jake climbed to his seat and gave the reins a quick jerk. "We'll be back around dusk."

"We'll see you for Sunday supper tonight, won't we?" Melissa's voice rang through Jared's soul like a sweet sparrow's song as he watched her whisked away until she was out of sight.

Melissa sat across the table watching Jake and Wash eat the large breakfast she had prepared. "Your brother has not stirred. He must be very tired."

"I can only imagine how tired he must be. Years of tired. Alone, with no one to hold. Howls of wolves disturbing his sleep. I am glad he is here, safe in his own room. Let him be. I'll see him tonight after work." Jake said as he brushed Melissa's face with a soft kiss.

Melissa set Jared's plate of food on a stone shelf just inside the fireplace, hoping it would stay warm until he came downstairs. Wash followed his usual routine, taking his plate to shove its uneaten bites into the scrap bucket near the door. "Gonna go feed the chickens mother!" he shouted, running out the door.

"Good boy! I'll see you back here for dinner when the sun is high noon! Don't be late!" Melissa watched Wash running to the chicken coop, knowing he would be headed to the creek with his fishing pole just as soon as he finished his chores. She cleared the dishes and placed them in the large slate sink to soak.

I need to check on Jared's horse, she thought, hoping their finely bred horses had not been disturbed by a strange animal in their midst.

Jared woke to sounds of whinnying horses. Jesse began pawing his hoof into the ground near Jared's head. "Shhhhh. Jesse." Jared whispered, slowly pushing his arm back to raise himself.

"Jared! What're you doing here? Your breakfast is in the kitchen!" Melissa exclaimed as she opened the stall door and walked toward him.

Standing before him was an image of perfection, the breasts no longer bouncing, but presenting themselves, tightly held and slightly pushed up by her stay, teasing his senses. He reached out his hand as if seeking assistance to stand.

Melissa reached toward him and within seconds she was pulled tightly against his body. His strength overpowered her efforts to pull away.

Jared kissed her hard on the mouth, imitating the hard kisses he had seen his papa give to Hope. His entire being wanted to consume the body he held with all his might. He ripped away her skirt, flipped her over beneath him, loosened his breeches, and entered her forcefully. She shoved her knees up against him to push him away, but his weight was more than she could handle.

Down by the creek, Wash heard screams coming from the barn and ran toward the sounds, dropping his fishing pole along the way. Inside the barn, he slowed down fearing any surprise would bring him harm. He inched along the wall, then peeped around the corner of the stall door. His mother was struggling under his uncle's large body, unable to move as her wrists were pressed firmly to the ground. Wash watched frozen in fear, wondering if they were playing or fighting. The sight of his mother's naked legs thrashing against the bare legs of his uncle were more than he could bear. Suddenly, the struggling stopped. His mother was crying and he started to cry too. He pressed his hands against his mouth, listening helplessly. Jared's voice cut sharply through the silence. "Yer mine now," he said, brushing twisted hairs from Melissa's face. "Keep yer silence or I'll kill yer son." Wash turned and ran toward the house as fast as he could.

Jared rolled over, leaned slightly back on his right side then hovered back over his conquest tightly holding her arms with his left hand. "Be here tomorrow morn after breakfast. If'n yer not here, I will come after ya wher'er ye be."

Jake stared at his brother across the dining room table. "Jared, I still can't believe you're here. But it's a blessing you found us. How long do you plan to stay?"

"As long as yer wife'll have me," Jared smirked. "I don't mean no extra trouble fer you'n's."

Melissa stepped over to pick up the dishes, forcing a smile to hide her true feelings. She turned quickly to place the dishes in the sink, hoping no one noticed her wincing from the searing pain shooting across her wrists. She walked back to Jake's side and brushed his cheek with a kiss. "I'm going to check on Wash, then go on to bed. It's been a long, tiring day."

Jake and Jared stayed at the table talking old times well into the night. On turning in, Jake found his wife wrapped tightly in the bed covers at the far side of their bed. He leaned over to kiss her on the cheek. She did not stir. *Caring for an extra person in the home can be quite tiring,* he thought.

Morning came with Jared again missing breakfast. Melissa and Wash stood on the porch waving until Jake was out of sight and then returned to the kitchen to finish their morning chores. "Scoot along Wash. The chickens are waiting. I'm going to tend to the horses now."

But this morning, Wash didn't run toward the creek. He cautiously followed his mother to the barn's entrance, fearing Jared would be waiting for her. She sensed his presence and turned, placing both hands on his shoulders to stop him. "Mother, let me help with the horses," he pleaded. "No son. This chore is mine alone. I'll come to the creek when I'm finished. Maybe we can catch a fish for supper."

Melissa went into the barn determined to make this a quick encounter. So this time, she did not resist his advances. This time, there was no need to hold her wrists. But her plan to force herself to submit willingly slowly wilted into moments of unexpected pleasure. Pleasure that turned into an all-consuming desire. With each passing day, Melissa found it harder to leave Jared's side and each day's encounter lasted longer than the day before. By Saturday evening's supper, Melissa found herself avoiding Jared's eyes, as the intense feelings that had come at the first sight of him now surged through every vein in her body with a passion she had never felt for her husband.

Sunday morning Jake was relieved to see Jared fishing by the creek, clearly avoiding any interest in church, so he went about his Sunday routine of preparing the carriage for the short journey into town, gladly leaving Jared behind. The afternoon's family dinner at the Warner home was filled with talk of Jake's brother -- when could they meet him, how long would he stay, where would he find work? With each question, Melissa's thoughts strayed beyond her husband's answers to contemplating ways to hide her growing desire to run away. As the family's farewells moved to the porch, Melissa sat in the swing watching her husband, listening to his fine words, a language far from the fragile unpolished words he had uttered when they first sat in this spot. A way of speaking that was wild and free, teasing her with wild images of an unfamiliar life, one she was challenged to tame. One that became boring, too polished, too familiar. A boredom that was freshly broken with the arrival of the young man whose recklessness ripped away her sensibilities.

When they returned home, Jared met them in the kitchen proudly boasting a bucket of trout noisily flipping about, creating a dilemma for Melissa as she stirred the simmering pot of chicken stew she had prepared before leaving that morning. "I can make do," Melissa said. She took a knife from the shelf, wiped it clean with her apron, then picked up the bucket of fish and headed to the kitchen door.

"Jared, come with me. We can prepare the fish and keep them in the springhouse until tomorrow's supper. Jake and Wash'll tend to the horses, won't you Jake?"

Jared took the bucket from Melissa and followed her to the springhouse without a word. Once they were inside, Jared stood at the door and watched as she whipped the knife through the cold spring water. He was greatly relieved when she began cleaning the fish. He peered outside to see Jake and Wash leading the horses into the barn, then ambled over to embrace her tightly from behind. Still holding the knife, Melissa shoved herself backwards to gain space between them. "Jared, I have to talk to you," she continued to scrape the scales from the fish, intentionally keeping her back to him. He stepped back and sat down on the low rock ledge near the spring.

"I no longer want to come to the barn to be with you -- you need to understand!" Jared eyed the knife as she skillfully maneuvered it across the fish, swiftly removed its guts, tossed them into the spring, and loosely swished the knife in the water as the guts floated along the current to the larger creek outside.

"I want you to sleep in the room we gave you. The straw itches -- and my skin is scratched until I can no longer tolerate it. Your bed has a very fine down mattress." She turned and began waving the knife and a perfectly-cleaned fish in his face. "I expect you to sleep in your bed and I will join you there after breakfast in the morning." Jared sat stunned while Melissa continued talking. She laid a large clay jar on its side, placed the fish inside, turned back to the bucket, picked up another fish, and continued without looking at him. "Now go find Wash. You told me you would teach him how to make a sling. I left some flax hanging on the fencing near Jesse's stall."

The next morning, after Jake left for the Doc's, Melissa took Wash outside. "Wash. Listen to me. I tended to the horses before breakfast and I'm not feeling well. I need to rest so I'm going stay inside. After you feed the chickens, why don't you run along to your grandmother's. She'll be so happy to see you. Just come back before suppertime."

Wash didn't hesitate. His grandmother let him do anything he wanted. And she always made her raisin oatmeal cookies whenever he visited. "Bye mother! I'll see you for supper! Maybe I'll bring you some cookies!" Forgetting the chickens, Wash ran straight toward his grandmother's house. Melissa stood waving from the front porch until he was out of sight. She too forgot about the chickens.

At Doc Taylor's, Jake spent the morning anxiously waiting for their dinner break. After ushering the last patient out the door, he moved quickly through his assigned duties preparing for the afternoon's patients, silently rehearsing the words he would use, peering back to the Doc's desk until the time was right. "I think there's something wrong with Melissa," he blurted loudly.

"Come here and have a seat son. I could see something's been bothering you all morning. What's her symptoms?"

"She goes to bed early. Maybe she's more tired than usual. During supper, she stares at her plate and eats very little. Then when I get to bed, she's swaddled up in a blanket, fast asleep with her back to me. And in the kitchen this morning when I went to kiss her good-bye, she was shivering. And it's not even cold, especially with the kitchen fire burning. Do you think I need to bring her in for you to examine her?"

"Is your brother still there?"

"Yes. I think maybe his presence is making her unhappy. He doesn't seem to be much help with the chores and all."

"Well, maybe it's nothing but exhaustion, but definitely sounds like I need to take a look to be sure she isn't coming down with anything. She could've caught the chills from one of the folks at your church, Why don't you go now and check on her. I'll just work her in between patients as soon as you get back. And if you can't get her back here, I'll come to your house after work."

On the way home, all Jake could think about was how much he loved Melissa. She hadn't been herself lately. He prayed hard for the Doc to find out what was wrong. To make her better, back to the loving passionate wife he had cherished for the past six years.

"Melissa!" Jake shouted as he entered the kitchen. "Melissa! Doc sent me home to check on you!" He went through the dining room into the parlor and stopped at the foot of the stairs. The sound of Melissa's laughter made him smile. *They're probably cleaning* ... he thought ... *but Jared's never been one to jest.*

"What's so funny?" he inquired as he reached the third floor landing. He heard another familiar sound. Melissa's soft sigh of joy. Jared's slow measure of pleasure "Ahhhh my Me ... liss ... a."

Seconds after he peered inside, rage surged through Jake's body sweeping him across the room to swiftly seize Jared's sword from its sheath at the bed's edge and whip it across the back of his brother's neck. Jared's head narrowly missed Melissa's nose and landed on her breasts, his body collapsed, its full weight pinning her to the bed. Blood gushed across her struggles to move.

Jake's mind began spinning recklessly to form commands. "You've got a mess amongst you. Wrap him in the quilts. Drag him to Jesse's stall where a shovel awaits. Scrub this bed with a vengeance. That is, unless you want to sleep in his blood." Jake didn't look back as he fled down the stairs to the bedroom he and Melissa had shared for six years. There he grabbed a clean shirt, headed down through the kitchen, dashed into the barn, threw the shovel into Jesse's stall, and pulled Jesse by his mane out through the gates to release him into the pasture. Blinded by his anger, he didn't see his son chasing him as he mounted his horse and galloped away.

"Father! Where you go?" Wash shouted, running as fast as he could to catch up. "Grandmother and I saw you riding to the house. She let me come to meet you for dinner."

Wash ran down the road shouting until Jake disappeared in a cloud of dust. Not knowing if his father had heard his pleas, Wash turned back to the house to find his mother. "Mother. I'm home!" he shouted as he entered the parlor. "Why did father go so fast? I'm hungry!"

Loud thumping sounds stopped him in his tracks. Thump, thumping down the stairs. A long lumpy quilt landed at his feet. His mother pushed past him and picked up the end of the bloody quilt. "What's that?" She turned her back to the quilt and pulled it behind her, oblivious to her son's presence. "Mother?" Wash made his best effort to step around the trickling streams of blood that followed her out of the house and into the barn.

Once she was in Jesse's stall, Melissa raked the straw aside with her hands. After the straw was cleared, she took the shovel and began digging a long, deep hole in the ground closest to the far wall. It was almost dark when she rolled the bloody lumpy bedding into the hole. When it was completely covered with dirt, she raked the entire stack of straw back over the grave. Exhausted, she collapsed onto the straw and cried herself to sleep.

Wash had situated himself just outside the stall door, in the same place he had hidden the day his mother had screamed under Jared's heavy movements. Now she was lying in the same place, crying. He longed to go to her, but his own fears stopped him. She was covered in blood, blood that had begun to dry on her face, arms, and clothes. The harrowing stench was unbearable. Gagging, he rushed outside and fell to his knees just in time to release his breakfast cookies. Soft drops of water trickled down his neck, bringing much-needed relief from his queasiness, until sharp pellets of rain began stabbing his back. He pulled himself up and stumbled in and out of the now diluted crimson trail of blood that led back to the house.

Drenched and shivering, he stopped to throw some chips onto the fire, then decided to set the table for supper. His mother would be back soon to prepare his meal. He sat down in front of his usual plate, rested his elbows on the table and grasped his head to quiet the terror and confusion churning through his mind.

Hours later Melissa returned to the kitchen, took off her clothes, threw them in the fire, then stepped outside to be washed by the rain. Naked and dripping wet, she pulled rags from the wash bucket and headed upstairs, not noticing her son asleep at the table, his head face down in his empty plate.

Chapter 22

A loud banging on the door woke Hope from a deep sleep. A sleep that was much more sound and less frightening than the disturbing nightmares that came before her confessions under the influence of Will's wine. She sat up on the edge of the bed and listened.

"Why Waightstill Avery. As I live and breathe!"

"Why Will Spenser. Aren't you a sight for sore eyes?"

Both men laughed at the sound of their teasing words. Words they had exchanged as far back as they could remember.

"Wait here cousin," Will stretched both arms across the door frame to block his cousin's entrance. "I must check on something before you enter."

Will eased the door shut, then walked back to the foot of the loft's steps. Hope stood at the top of the stairs tying her apron. "Is that your cousin Waightstill I heard at the door? I can't wait to meet him! I'll be down in a minute."

When he turned back toward the door, Will saw it was wide open. Waightstill had already stepped inside. "I believe I heard a woman's voice. Have you gone and married without informing me?"

"It's not what you think cousin. We have a lot to discuss."

Waightstill settled himself in a chair across from the fireplace. "Yes, we do have a lot to discuss. It's been awhile," he pondered a moment. "Almost four years, I believe."

Will pulled his chair near the fireplace and angled it so he could watch the staircase and listen at the same time.

Waightstill continued, anxious to address the purpose of his visit. "Yes, over four years. Much has happened since we last spoke. I'm sure you remember when the Cherokee signed my Long Island treaty ceding much of their land to our settlers. But despite my treaty and best efforts, it was the settlers not the Cherokee who broke the treaty. They continued to attack the Cherokee towns, leaving the natives no choice but to reciprocate."

Will nodded. "Yes. You and I have debated how peace could have been achieved had our people not been so greedy and aggressive." Will stood and placed his hand on Waightstill's shoulder, indicating Hope was approaching.

"Ah! Here she is." Will reached his hand to Hope, and walked her over to his cousin. "Waightstill, I'm pleased to introduce you to my friend, Missus Hope O'Connor." Will noticed Waightstill staring at Hope's ring. "And no, we're not married. She came this way searching for her father and I helped her find him. After he died, she returned and has been my guest for some time." Will stopped and gave Waightstill a stern look to indicate there would be no more information shared about his ginger-haired friend.

Hope smiled warmly. "It's a pleasure to meet you Mr. Avery. Will has spoken of you often. I know you have much to catch up on, and I'm sure you must be quite hungry after your journey."

"Thank you ma'am. But I don't have much of an appetite except for bringing you some important news. Please come sit and join us."

"I'll at least make us some tea," Hope said, hanging a kettle of water above the fire. She pulled a stool up to sit next to Will. "Please. Continue your story. We don't get much news here and I understand you are well-traveled."

"Yes, my travels have been extensive. And, as I said, much has happened. Once we Patriots defeated the British and gained independence, our interests turned to achieving peace through treaties with the Cherokee and tribes of the Chickamauga. But it took many years. Will, I'm sure you remember our near skirmish with Dragging Canoe at the Toe River."

On hearing the words 'Dragging Canoe', Hope gasped. Her eyes widened. Then, eager to hear more, she tightly clasped her fingers and placed her hands on her lap.

Waightstill continued. "Dragging Canoe lost many men after the attack on Fort Caswell. After Colonel John Sevier's militia destroyed eleven Cherokee villages, Dragging Canoe relocated his towns further down the Little Tennessee River. Much of his focus turned to defending his own people's villages and intercepting the white settlers efforts to move downstream. And he managed a massive victory in the attack at the bluffs of Fort Nashborough.

"After fighting the white man in battles from the foot of the Unicoi mountains to the southern mountain called Lookout, he settled near Nickajack just west of the Lookout and made a new home called Running Water Town.

"As he aged, his attitude changed, amazingly -- moving from the position of warrior to that of diplomat. He worked to establish an alliance with the Creeks and Shawnees. And after a successful diplomatic mission with the Chickasaws, he returned to Running Water to celebrate. It is said that he had a heart attack after dancing and drinking whiskey all night. I came to tell you that Dragging Canoe is dead."

Hope sat astonished. The name Dragging Canoe had haunted her since her father spoke his name moments before her home was destroyed. She had heard stories of his attacks from the patrons at the grist mill. And deep inside, her fears had lingered, always wondering if he and his warriors were near. Now he was dead.

"He was a legend and I followed his actions closely. Some consider him a military genius. A year ago, our new President, George Washington, made a new treaty with the Cherokee signed by Dragging Canoe's successor. It is significant and should help maintain peace, especially in this part of the country. But, I must say, my thoughts and concerns remain with the Cherokee and Chickamauga, as they were pushed westward while we claimed their land, land that holds this very home ... your home. And my home south of here. Land that was once theirs. I sometimes feel a twinge of guilt. For while we celebrate our independence and hold assemblies building a strong nation, the natives are struggling, pushed westward, seeking their own freedom and praying to the Creator for land of their own. We are the reason they struggle. We should pray for them in their journey."

The room was filled with a deafening silence before Waightstill stood to indicate his planned departure. "I came to let you know that the land I gave you is now secure and we are at peace under the leadership of our nation's president -- our first president," he paused and turned toward Hope.

"Missus O'Connor, it was a pleasure to meet you. I can see your friendship is a blessing to my cousin. But now I must continue my journey if I'm to make it back to my own homestead before dark. Perhaps the two of you will come visit me in the near future." Waightstill gave his cousin a quick embrace, and with a friendly bow to Hope, he slowly backed out the door. Will looked at Hope and shrugged his shoulders before he turned to watch his cousin ride away.

The rest of the day, Will and Hope focused on their separate chores, with a mutual understanding that they each wished to indulge their individual thoughts, reflecting on Waightstill's visit -- and his words.

And that night, Hope's dreams were intertwined with visions of Dragging Canoe. He was running, running away from firing muskets, his people following behind him. Her family had thrived on his people's land. Strings of stolen land. Stolen farms of flax that became weapons and clothing. Blurred visions of lavender turned to running pools of blood. Blood that flowed from the natives and her own people. Blood of the same color for the dark man and her own. Blood of indefinable pain. Blood that flowed down river, westward into the unknown.

Chapter 23

1794

Jeremiah gazed longingly at the white blooms of the dogwood trees, their branches arched over the wide shallow stream that flowed beneath the wooden bridge. Each spring, his mother had reminded him that the dark spots along the blossoms' edge represented the blood of Christ. Blossoms that also reminded him he was a year older. *Am I seventeen already? Why does my mother not care enough to return even if just for a day?* He leaned back in his mother's rocking chair and closed his eyes. He recalled the prophet's words she repeated from the Bible. "Blessed is the man that trusteth in the Lord … for he shall be as a tree planted by the waters, and that spreadeth out her roots by the river." His thoughts drifted to the days he crawled along the cabin's plank floor marking new letters with charred wood from the fire, then the long rides holding to Isaiah's mane while tucked safely between his mother's arms, listening to the spring waters as his mother cut apples using the knife with a deer-bone handle now tucked away in the sheath hanging from his hip.

"Father will you cut another apple for me?" The small fingers of his daughter placing the fruit in his hand startled him into the present. *This is my gift,* he thought.

"Amity, did you eat the other slices already?" Jeremiah lifted the red fruit from her tiny hand and began slicing it thinly, the same way his mother had sliced his own fruit years ago, with the same knife.

Jeremiah and Mitch had learned of Hope's absence when a neighbor ran into the blacksmith shop yelling "No one's at the mill! I need me grain!" Ten-year old Jeremiah dropped the bellows and ran to the mill and upstairs to see if his mother was still asleep. Her bed was empty. Her haversack gone. He then ran to the pasture barn to find Isaiah missing. That day changed everything in Jeremiah's world. Mitch shut down the blacksmith shop so he and Jeremiah could manage the mill together. Over supper, they pondered over where she might be. Jeremiah was convinced she had only gone to visit the Carroll's and see the Table Rock Mountain. That was seven years ago.

Jeremiah had bravely harbored his sadness and assumed his mother's duties at the mill. Each evening, he and Mitch reviewed the day's business, and Jeremiah began developing his own method of bookkeeping. His records copied the style of his mother's, but his writing was much less refined. Days into his new duties, he had found the deer-bone knife where his mother had left it on the lower shelf.

"It's almost time." Jeremiah looked up into the eyes of Abby, Amity's mother. Abby had been his one true friend, though making her a friend had taken great effort on his part. He had ignored the many local girls who flirted with him while he tended to his duties in the mill. Until he saw Abby. Abby had not flirted at all. And that was what caught his attention. Her quick trips in and out of the store, paying the exact cost of the goods with coins she deftly counted as she pulled them from her tiny leather pouch. No words, just a subtle smile. A smile that lingered in his mind throughout the day compelling him to spend his evenings and nights thinking of ways to engage her in conversation. Then one evening as he was locking the door to the entrance, she ran into him headfirst, in a rush to buy some tea leaves for her mother. It was getting dark and he convinced her she needed protection on the mile-long walk back to her home. That first walk became one of many, and soon they were taking long walks on Sunday afternoons and her last-minute trips to the grist mill occurred most frequently in the evening. When he learned she was pregnant with his child, he was overcome with a determination to make her his bride, despite her papa's frightening threats that his grandchild must be raised far from its dark-skinned father. Threats to ensure his daughter would raise her child alone turned to action when her papa jerked her out of bed in the middle of the night and tied her onto a straw mattress in the wagon that carried her to relatives in Jamestown, far from the boy whose dark features reminded everyone of the natives who had terrorized them for a lifetime. But Abigal Whitfield Turner had persisted, sneaking out of the house while her relatives slept under the spell of way too many brandies and finding her way back to Mitchborough, back to the grist mill where Mitch stood bravely by their side once he found a preacher who would marry them. Amity Mitchell O'Connor was born just two months after the wedding.

"I know," Jeremiah sighed, pushing himself up from the rocking chair. He walked back into the mill, laid the knife in its place on the shelf beneath the counter, picked up his mother's Bible and adjusted the vest he wore under the long black coat that had belonged to the finest man he had ever known. "He was a father to me from the day we saw him standing in this very spot," Jeremiah said as he pulled the door closed. "Now I must strive to fill his shoes the best I can."

Mr. Carson's arrival interrupted what had become a reasonable life for Will and Hope -- one that no longer involved Hope's emotional breakdowns as Will had continued to listen without questioning. They found comfort in Waightstill's words. The threat of attack had disappeared with news that the country had evolved into a more peaceful nation -- at least for the white man. Still, on afternoon rides through the forest and on this evening, as she watched the sun fall behind the mountains, she thought about the natives. Her view of Hawksbill Mountain was once a cherished spot for those who came before her -- and a view the natives would never again explore. Her son, Jeremiah, was one of them. Now, she tried to understand his heritage. Not a day passed when she didn't find herself searching for the words. Words that still brought a stringing memory. Words she may never find to share with her son. And until she found the words, she would postpone the reunion she longed for.

But the sound of a familiar voice shattered her drifting thoughts. She had not seen Mr. Carson since he first led her here -- to a place that had become her home. So, at the sight of him, her instincts kicked in, fearing the worst. "Jeremiah?" She asked.

"No. Jeremiah's fine, except for Mitch," Mr. Carson had reported. "Mitch died peacefully two days ago and th' entire village is in mourning. I thought ye would want to know."

Hope only nodded as she watched Mr. Carson ride away within minutes of announcing the news. Mitch had been a father to her at a time when she thought her own father was dead. "Prepare Isaiah for my ride!" she shouted, rushing past Will and up to her room to quickly throw the same clothes she had worn to her father's graveside into her haversack. She had forgotten how heavy the haversack was, only remembering its weight as she dragged it down the stairs and out onto the porch.

"I'll be just a moment," Will said, handing her the reins to both horses and running inside to grab a few belongings. When he returned, his own horse was standing alone and only a trail of dust signaled Hope's departure.

Mitchborough's mourners assembled in the church and onto the field outside to show their love and respect for the community's founding father. After the service, Jeremiah held Amity's hand tightly as he and Abby led the congregation to Mitch's graveside, ignoring the whispers and shunning frowns of those who disapproved of their bond. During the graveside service, Jeremiah's focus on his wife and daughter was so intense that he did not notice the ginger-haired woman standing at the far end of the graveyard. Jeremiah began to sing.

Hope stood, listening to Jeremiah singing the 23rd Psalm, just as she had sung it to him many years ago. Her memories rushed forward with images and sounds from the past. Jeremiah had been only ten the last time she saw him. Now he stood, holding a small child who was the mirror image of the little boy she had held in her arms long ago. Tears streamed down her face as she turned to walk away, determined not to interfere in what appeared to be a good and happy life for the son she had abandoned. Her mind was flooded with memories, memories of a little boy who had been her entire world, whose needs and activities had helped block the terrors that only surfaced whenever she slept. That is, until she had left, just for a day to see if she could find the Table Rock and perhaps see Hawksbill Mountain.

That was nearly seven years ago. Seven years beginning with her father's journey into death, then a wine-stirred release of buried memories. A wine-inspired evening that led to nearly every moment shared in a spiritual closeness that she would always cherish. These moments had led to many hours of holding each other tightly, sharing kisses and lingering touches which, after many tears and anguishing conversations, eventually led to an unspoken place where warm feelings evaporated into a calm understanding. She knew Will still loved her despite her rejection -- a rejection she held firm in fear of unleashing the evil that all men, even Will, must harbor, especially when passion overtook their very soul. Despite a diligent effort, Will ultimately realized he did not have the key to unlock the barrier that held this fear intact.

Hope prayed silently for Mitch's soul, confident that the Lord was celebrating his arrival in heaven, then walked back across the wooden bridge and loosened Isaiah's reins from the dogwood tree that loomed over the water. She took one last look across the river to the grist mill and the porch where she had first seen Mitch and where she had spent many Sundays reading. *Mitch is gone. Jeremiah is now in the care of another woman. His daughter, my granddaughter, may never know me. At least not now.* Her thoughts reflected on the words from the book of Matthew: *There are two paths before you; you may take only one path.* She realized she was standing on the road she and Jeremiah had traveled. The same road that could take her back, perhaps all the way to the home she knew as a child. Or, she could take the narrow trail on the other side of the pasture and return to Will.

Will watched the funeral procession from the ridge above Mitchborough. It had taken only a few minutes to saddle his mare and follow the trail that led to the grist mill that had been Hope's home. He felt as if he had been there before as Hope had filled his mind with vivid descriptions of the mill and tales of the local folk who traded their goods for the flour and meal that she had produced when working the grindstone. Now he stood as a silent observer hidden within the tall trees anchoring the bluff that loomed over the village. It wasn't long before he caught sight of Jeremiah, the tall dark man, holding the hand of a beautiful dark-skinned girl who walked between him and a young fair-skinned woman whom Will assumed to be the girl's mother. But it took awhile for him to catch a glimpse of Jeremiah's own mother, for not-surprisingly, she had kept her distance from her son and his family.

When he finally spotted her, she was standing in the shade at the edge of the cemetery, protected by an isolated cluster of trees, far from the mourners, safely guarding her own need for privacy during what must be a very difficult time. This was the Hope he now knew well, possibly better than she knew herself. A woman who could not let go and share the love he desperately desired.

The mourners dispersed to their individual lives. Jeremiah seemed to be singing to his daughter as they maintained guard over Mitch's grave. Will placed his arms across his chest to still his heart. Hope had crossed the bridge and now stood next to Isaiah staring at the road, then looking back almost as if she knew he was waiting.

I've given everything of myself to strengthen her … if I give her more of me, will I grow weaker? I have little more to give, he thought. *But I pray she will return, for though I am weak of heart, I am not complete without her.*

"I will be your Sancho Panza, your servant, your friend. We will chase windmills, be they your fears or your wine-kissed smiles, as long as we're together, we can conquer whatever comes our way."

Hope took one last look at the grist mill, then mounted Isaiah and headed down what was now a well-traveled road. *Perhaps I can get to the springhouse before nightfall.* She paused to let Isaiah partake of the water in the brook below the waterfall where she had found Jeremiah that terrifying morning. This time there was no hurry, no reason to hide. She recalled the stories of the Overmountain men, the hundreds that had ridden on this very road the last time she was here, some of whom had settled in Mitchborough after the battle. Most had retraced this road to return to their home not far from Sycamore Shoals. She felt a sudden urge to follow their trail, to see if she could find the Watauga settlement and perhaps visit that first grist mill she had seen when she had gone to the fort with her father.

She was relieved to see the springhouse had not changed, except for grass that had grown taller above the roof. The door was as she had left it. As soon as she dismounted, Isaiah began lurching forward, then shaking, snorting, blowing and pawing at the ground. She sighed, acknowledging his plea. Hope grabbed his reins and stopped him long enough to remove his saddle and untie her haversack. Isaiah ran out into the pasture celebrating his freedom and within minutes he returned again pawing at the ground, circling, and then slightly bending at the knees coming to rest on the ground with a satisfied grunt. Leaning over to one side he then began to roll, vigorously back and forth, writhing and wriggling. Hope was thrilled to see Isaiah rolling around on his familiar grassy mound next to the spring. *He loves his freedom,* she thought. *He didn't have room to play in the land surrounded by the many trees near Will's cabin, though I wonder if he misses Will's mare.* Happy to let Isaiah roll to his heart's content, she turned to the haversack, pulled it into the springhouse and began rummaging through it to see if she had remembered her sling. That was when she discovered the leather pouch, a pouch she had not packed. The pouch that had made her bag so heavy she had barely been able to heave it onto Isaiah's back when she left Will's cabin. When she opened the pouch she was overcome with emotion realizing it was dozens of gold and silver coins that had made the bag so heavy. Under the coins was a short note, written in the familiar hand of her father. She stepped outside to read it.

> *By the time you read this, you will know I am dead. I trusted Phoebe to get it to you and now you know she has.*
>
> *These are the coins that I held after I sold my gem piece and built my new home by Hawksbill Mountain. I saved them for you, for your future.*
>
> *You should want for nothing. But I also pray you will find happiness beyond the riches.*
>
> *You will always be my princess.*
>
> *Love,*
> *Your father,*
> *Patrick O'Connor*

The next morning, Hope dragged the haversack outside and began sorting the coins from the pouch. She took several coins and placed them inside one boot and then the other and put five coins in each of her pockets. She tightly rolled other coins inside different articles of unpacked clothing, then tucked the clothing back into her haversack. Hope saddled Isaiah, then hung the haversack across the front of the saddle where she could protect it. She lifted her skirt and tied the leather pouch to her waist, then scooted it around to sit in the arch of her back.

Mounting Isaiah, she reflected on the day ahead. This would be the most difficult day of their journey. A day Hope had dreaded from the moment she took the road leaving Mitchborough. They rode back through the apple orchard and onto the trail they had followed from the farm they had escaped fourteen years ago. While Hope sensed she would pass that haunting land, she was determined to get past it quickly. She took a deep breath. The soothing scent of fresh pine took her back to the night she sang Jeremiah to sleep snuggled amidst the pine needles near the waterfall. The same song she heard as the last clumps of dirt fell on Mitch's grave. She let Jeremiah's voice fill her mind, her soul. *The Lord is My Shepherd, I shall not want.* Placing her head downward, she pushed Isaiah into a rapid gait and rode without glancing at anything but the narrow stretch below until it turned into a wider road. Confident she had passed that dreaded site, she raised her head, and pulled Isaiah's reins to turn westward. This was an unfamiliar path, but it was beautiful, with long winding trails heading down the mountain. As they rode through a meadow of blooming yellow ragwort, Hope began to relax, knowing she would soon return to the place that held fond memories with her father, but aware the journey held one more challenge.

The sun's bright light beamed directly in front of them as they traveled along the ridge high above the Doe River. Suddenly, Isaiah slowed and snorted, as if he sensed lurking danger. Hope had known she must also pass this point, yet she was determined to again use her well-practiced skills to block her way past it. She closed her eyes tightly and nudged Isaiah with a swift kick that moved him into a fast gallop, past the ravine where he had been seized by the dark man, past the terror rushing through her mind at that very moment. A terror she was determined to leave behind by moving quickly toward the Watauga settlement. Toward a new life in a place that only held good memories.

As dusk began to embrace their surroundings, Hope abruptly pulled Isaiah's reins to a stop in the middle of the road. "There it is!" she shouted. "The grist mill I saw as a child!" A horse-drawn buggy narrowly missed them as it rushed toward the village ahead. "We'll come back and visit the mill another day," she told Isaiah. "This village looks much larger and busier than Mitchborough. And many more buildings than the village I remember." She leaned forward and patted Isaiah's shoulder. "For now, we need to find a place to stay. A proper place that I heard folks talk about. It's called an inn, I believe. I heard they have nice beds with fine mattresses framed with fancy wooden posts and canopies. Some even have a stable where you can eat all the grains you desire. And now. Now I have the means to pay for the finest inn and stable this place can provide -- thanks to father."

Hope took her time, preferring to survey the entire village before settling in for the night. She noted the church high on the hill above the village and rode up to its long row of hitching posts which she assumed were for horses ridden by the church's guests. She counted room for tethering at least forty horses in that one area. "This must be a very popular church," she told Isaiah, recalling Mr. Carson's mention of his daughter's marriage to a preacher in Watauga. "I think her name was Caroline. Maybe we can come back here one Sunday. Though I've never been in a church with so many people."

She rode back down the hill to the center of town. Several horses were tied to another long post in front of a building with a sign that read "General Store". The store had smaller signs in its windows boasting a variety of goods including canteens, lanterns, and candles. There were about twenty buildings in all scattered about the village. Among them she had spotted two inns or ordinaries. One was packed full of loud men shouting and drinking what she assumed to be cider or wine. The other was in a much quieter setting not far from the church. A sign posted in its window read:

"*Hot Dinner - 2 Shillings
*Supper or Breakfast - 1 Shilling
*Stable for night - 1.4 Shillings
*Lodging in Feather Bed - .8 Shillings"

"This looks perfect Isaiah. A stable for you and a feather bed for myself. Now, I just have to think about my coins and how to barter for our boarding." She felt confident as she dismounted and pulled her haversack from Isaiah's saddle. After all, she had spent more than seven years bartering with the customers at the grist mill. And now, she had more shillings than she could count. Most of her coins were Spanish silver dollars each of which she knew had a value of at least six shillings. She reached into her pockets and took out five silver dollars. *This will be enough for one week's boarding for me and the stable for Isaiah,* she thought.

Hope was relieved to find the innkeeper was a woman, short and thin-faced, with high cheekbones, quite talkative and friendly. "This here's my inn. I own it. My captain wuz killed at th' Battle of Brandywine. I didn't know it til th' war wuz over n' they come to tell me I got a nice pension. I ain't one to set around pitying myself so I got busy n' invested his pension in this place. I turned it into a very fine inn, if'n I say so meself. We ain't like that other place with th' loud tavern," the widow allowed as she counted Hope's coins. "I 'spect me guests to mind thar manners n' respect th' requirements n' privacy of th' other boarders. If'n ya kin abide by these rules, ya kin stay fer one week and we'll board ya horse. Of course ya kin stay longer if'n ya find ya have more coins fer me. Fer now, just sign th' rej'ster n' my boy will show ya yer room n' take care of yer horse." Hope signed her name on the registry then followed the boy out to the water trough where Isaiah was quenching his thirst. Just as she had heard was the custom and with great relief, she watched as the boy lifted her heavy haversack and signaled her to follow him upstairs to her room where he set her bag on a low table and turned toward the door. "Wait!" She reached into her pocket and gave the livery boy one shilling. "Take good care of my horse. His name's Isaiah and he's my only friend." After he left, she ran to look out the window and watched him lead Isaiah to the livery stable.

Hope stood in the dining hall doorway brushing the front of her tattered skirt with both hands in a futile effort to hide its stains. The innkeeper wore a beautiful linen gown imprinted in a purple iris with long thin green leaves. Slim purple ribbons criss-crossed the bodice of her long green apron to form a tiny bow behind her neck. Fine lines stretched upward from her eyes to meet shimmering silver hair pulled tightly to the top of her head and covered by a tiny violet cap that highlighted her blue eyes.

"My room is very nice -- and this room -- it's absolutely breathtaking!" Hope said, seating herself at a small table covered in the same lace that trimmed the window curtains. *I pray my dirty clothing will not spoil this fine table covering,* she thought. *I wish I had spent more time twisting and pinning my hair.*

"Glad ya like it. I worked hard to git it to my suitin'." Hope admired the innkeeper's graceful hands pouring tea into a fine gold-gilded porcelain cup that matched the beautiful plate of pastries and blackberries before her. The woman's nails were immaculately cleaned and finely trimmed.

"Ma'am, I must apologize for my rude behavior last evening," Hope said trying to hide her own ragged nails while raising the cup to her mouth. "I arrived after a very long journey and I must admit I failed to remember your name."

"Me name's Madelyn Montgomery. Maddie fer short. Ya wuz quiet but not th' least bit rude last evenin'. I know'd ya wuz tired. Most travelers is. But I kin also see ya's a young woman of fine upbringing count of how ya speak, tho' ya seems jest a bit worn from a life that's not been easy of late. Me own husband wuz from a respected family of these parts n' I been tryin' to live up to thar expectations, tho' I ain't seen 'em in a month of Sundays. N' my son married n' went to live up north 'bout a few years back. So, it's jest me n' my inn now. What about yer'n?"

"I'm a widow too," said Hope, unconsciously turning the ring Mitch gave her. "I grew up not far from here. My father was Irish and I was privileged to his wise guidance until I was fifteen."

Maddie sauntered over to the cupboard and returned to Hope's table holding another porcelain cup and saucer. "I reckoned ya must've been quite weary since ya's jest gittin' down to breakfast. Most of my guests left at th' break of dawn having had a hearty breakfast. I already served all my breakfast fixin's, so's I hope ya don't mind jest havin' th' pastries n' berries. Mind if I join ya fer a cup of tea?" Maddie seated herself before Hope could respond.

Hope took another sip, certain her own appearance was unsightly, especially to this impeccably-dressed woman. "I pray not to offend you, but what I am wearing is all I have with me, and as I'm sure you can see, I'm in great need of time for mending and washing. Everything I have, including my shift, short gown -- everything -- is in need of repair. And, to be honest, I have never owned anything new, at least not since I was fifteen. For many years I managed a grist mill -- it was the heart of the land where it sat. My clothes were those traded by women who no longer wanted to wear them, in exchange for corn meal or flour."

"It would be my pleasure to introduce ya to me seamstress, if ya like," Maddie said. "We kin go soon's ye finish yer pastries n' berries. Jest be sure ya locked yer door." Hope quickly finished her meal and dashed upstairs to gather coins, then pulled her door to lock it, placing the key alongside the shillings and Spanish coins in her left pocket, then patted her right pocket to ensure her sling was still there.

The older finely-dressed innkeeper walking alongside the ginger-haired maiden in tattered, dirty attire made a unique pairing as they walked past the tavern and up the hill past Doc Taylor's place. "Don't mind the townfolk a starin'. They's used to me walking with folks they ain't seen afore. And besides -- here we are!"

Hope's eyes grew wide and her mouth dropped open at the sight of the seamstress' wares. Finished corsets, petticoats, and underpetticoats were neatly laid across wide tables. A long rod hung across the back of the room boasting both modest dresses and fancy gowns. Another table held fabrics of linen, silk, and cotton featuring printed patterns of every color and flower imaginable. "This here's my new friend Hope O'Connor," Maddie said as she escorted Hope to the back of the room where the seamstress sat.

"Hello ladies," she said, deftly moving her shears across a piece of fabric. "I'll be a moment. Can't stop now. Jest be lookin' to see what ya like."

Maddie helped Hope select several ready-made pieces and stood outside the dressing room while Hope shed her old garments and replaced them with fine creations from the dressmaker's skilled hands. Stepping out of the dressing room, Hope beamed with new-found confidence, turning round and round and gleefully glancing Maddie's way to seek her approval. "My! My! Ya jest gone from th' look of a pauper's daughter to a king's princess! Now, we'll need to work on yer way of walkin'. Yer not walkin' like a princess. Ya's been walkin' like yer pushin' a plow! Yer a beautiful woman. So, from now on, I want ya to walk as though th' sunlight depends on yer head held high. Like this!" Maddie grabbed a book off the dressmaker's shelf and walked a few steps with it atop her head. She then placed it atop Hope's head. "Jest always pretend ya got that book on yer head n' ya'll be jest fine."

After a few minutes of book balancing, the two new friends spent several hours inspecting every single bolt of fabric in the dressmaker's possession and after much consultation, left the seamstress happily ladened with several weeks' projects, a pound sterling plus fifteen shillings richer, and images she would not soon forget. It would be several days before she stopped giggling over the young lady's struggle to find a purse large enough to hold that ugly flax sling.

Each afternoon thereafter, Hope accompanied Maddie on her errands and Maddie made it a point to introduce her to every shopkeeper in the village. Soon they noticed a significant change in the townsfolks' behavior. Instead of snickering and turning their heads, they greeted Hope admiringly and after she passed, they speculated as to whether the beautiful ginger-haired lady had come from a wealthy upbringing in Boston or Philadelphia.

Hope was awakened by loud banging on her door and Maddie's voice, shouting. "Hope! Hope! Come quick!"

As soon as Hope turned the key to unlock her door, Maddie pushed it open and rushed in. "I need ya! I need ya to help me!" Maddie sat on the bed and began sobbing. Hope handed her the thin towel by the wash bowl. "Anything! What can I do? What happened?"

"A horseman jest brung me a note from me son's wife. He's very ill. I must git to him fer fear he's dyin'!" Maddie wiped her face with the cloth then took Hope's hands in hers. "I knows ya purty well now n' I trust ya with my life. I also trust ya with my place, my business. It'll be much easier than runnin' a grist mill, I tell ya. I knows ya kin do it. Please!" She squeezed Hope's hands tightly, pleading. "Please! Please! Take care of th' inn fer me whilst I go to him. I took all my money from th' safe, but ye kin have all ya brang in whilst I'm gone. 'Course they's gonna be supplies to git, but ya'll do jest fine usin' yer own good judgment. I'll send ya word once'd I get thar n' I'll be back soon's I kin. Tho' Lord knows how long I'll be."

"Go! Be with your son!" Hope let go Maddie's hands and embraced her tightly. "The inn will be fine. Send me your location once you get settled and I'll be sure to send word as to how it's going with the inn. And, I'll also send you word of any interesting tales of the townsfolk."

Hope quickly dressed and as soon as she arrived downstairs, Maddie gave her a hurried embrace and rushed out the door.

In the kitchen, Hope emulated Maddie's preparations to the best of her ability and the guests seemed to enjoy their breakfast. After they left for their individual endeavors, she tended to the laundry and refreshed each of the six rooms, just as she had seen Maddie do on many mornings prior to this day. Afternoons were spent carefully following Maddie's recipes to prepare supper, following Maddie's meticulous step-by-step routine of making puddings and baking pastries and pies, along with ironing napkins and other linens. Supper often lasted much later than she wished, with the inn's guests immersed in discussions and debates over the issues of the day, lingering long after the tables were cleared. She often found herself torn between retreating to the kitchen to complete the day's last chore of polishing silver or tarrying to hear the latest news as she filled their mugs with ale. Enforcing the inn's curfew grew more difficult each evening as the hearty discussions gave her unique insight into the community and its people. Each evening after the last guest's departure, she gave the stable boy his day's earnings, along with an extra shilling in appreciation for tending to Isaiah and a reminder to release him to pasture a few hours each day. After settling his wages, she sorted the day's receipts and balanced the ledger, a process she found immensely simpler than keeping trading records at the grist mill.

Retreating to her room, she turned to her father's Bible, happy to have time to herself to begin recapturing her faith -- a faith that had carried her through the past eighteen years, and one she now embraced in peace, no longer threatened by evil doers. Now the words of the Bible held new meaning as the perils and pleasures of God's people were not unlike those of Watauga's townsfolk. She closed the Bible and held it to her chest, smiling contentedly. *The inn holds my family. Strangers are now friends. No matter how tired I am, their laughter warms my heart. Hearing their stories, their worries, their wishes are a blessing in this place, my past is lost in the present. I have unraveled the strings of my memories. My new family only knows me as I am today. Here I can be myself. Find myself.*

She began experimenting with new recipes, getting ideas from the farmers who brought her their freshest crops. And, after several efforts, she mastered the recipe for Matilda's sweet potato pie. Watching her guests' faces as they savored each new dish made her blush with pride and joy.*The Lord brought me here. This is where I belong.*

She found herself anxiously awaiting her guests' arrival and the news of the day. The news of their lives. She listened thoughtfully to the boastful stories of the powerful and consoled them through their tales of tribulation. And over time, with each new story, she longed to learn more -- beyond the confines of the inn.

On this particular Sunday, she was pleased to find every single guest departing the inn after finishing a rushed breakfast. Some spoke of long journeys to their next destination. A few were determined to seek the Lord's blessing by going to church. To Hope, church was what the apostle Paul referred to as a body of believers. But the folks of Watauga referred to church as a building. She was curious to see for herself what compelled men and women to seek such a building every Sunday. It was time to explore this ritual they called worship. She hung a sign indicating the inn was closed until supper, grabbed her new bonnet, walked to the stable, mounted Isaiah, and headed to the Methodist church high on the hill above the town.

Chapter 24

1795

Each time Jake harnessed the horses for the carriage ride to church, he thought of his friend Charlie. Charlie's horse. Charlie's shoes. Charlie's friendship. How he wished Charlie was alive now. He needed a friend now more than ever. But all he had was Charlie's horse. The horse he had ridden into Watauga to search for Melissa. The horse that was the only thing he trusted, other than Doc Taylor.

He had found happiness with Melissa. A happiness unlike anything he had ever known. That is -- until his older brother came to visit. Jared had been Jake's best friend until that day -- the day Jared died by his own sword -- at the hand of his brother. *My hand. My anger. My brother. My wife. My rage*. He finished harnessing the horses just in time to see two boys running toward him. Wash, now thirteen, was followed by his six-year-old brother, Carter. Carter, the son who was not his. Or was he? *Carter's eyes are blue and his hair is the color of acorns, like my brother's. Yes, it's possible the boy is mine … I'll never know.* Jake's hands clinched into fists as he could not help but cringe at the very image of Jared running toward him.

Wash took his perch on the bench for the privilege of driving the family to church. Carter ran back to his mother, took the violin she was carrying, placed his hand under her arm and held her steady as she ambled toward the carriage. He gave her a boost to lift her in, then took his usual place by her side.

Jake hopped up beside Wash, nudged him sharply, and handed Wash the whip. "Is this the same whip you use to punish mother?" Wash asked.

Jake answered with a wink. "Shhh … she's lucky I let her out to go to church. But we have to keep up appearances with her folks, so we can keep this fancy home." Jake snapped the whip to stun the horses forward. "Look at the clouds. A big storm's coming. What're you waiting for? Let's get on before the preaching starts." At the whip's crackle, Carter screamed, flinging himself into his mother's arms to protect her -- and even though they were safely inside the carriage, they clinged tightly to each other until the carriage stopped on the grounds of the church.

This was the first time Hope had set foot in a church. She recognized several townsfolk wearing their finest and chatting loudly amongst themselves. Holding her father's Bible tightly in her arms, she wondered how worship would emerge within this bustling environment. She seated herself at the end of a bench at the back of the room, hoping to maintain a respectful distance from the rather chubby middle-aged man seated at the other end, but she soon found this goal impossible as latecomers urged her to move down the row closer to him in order to make room for themselves.

As she was settling in, the room suddenly became silent. She looked up to see the preacher taking his place, placing both hands on the pulpit. "Welcome to the…" he paused, frowning with a harsh stare at Jake and Wash rushing in, followed by Melissa slowly shuffling with Carter's assistance. They sat on a bench directly in front of

Hope. The preacher continued sternly "…Lord's place. Where those with respect arrive early so's not to inconvenience th' others. Let's bow our heads."

Hope was impressed with the way everyone present knew words to each song they sang whenever the preacher allowed. The guests listened politely as he read from the Bible and spoke about Jesus. After several more songs, the preacher's words became louder and more intense emphasizing how each person should be grateful for their blessings.

She watched as a young boy stepped to the end of the row in front of her. He held a fiddle to his shoulder, then placed the bow against the strings. The music was unlike anything she had ever heard. Not like Henry's fiddle. Not at all. This music was soft and soothing, so stirringly beautiful it made her heart sing. As the music played, two men walked forward then waited by the first row, then the next row, while guests carefully placed coins in platters they passed along to each other to the row's end where another man gathered the platter and took it to the next row for the same ritual. Hope reached into her new purse and set two shillings on the platter when it passed her way. Then four men carried the platters forward and placed them on a table in front of the preacher. The music stopped and the young boy sat down at the end of the bench in front of her. *The Lord must be very pleased with these generous people,* she thought. Then everyone bowed their heads while the preacher thanked the Lord for their gifts and began praying together when he said "as the Lord taught us to pray." With her head bowed, Hope forced back tears, overcome with emotion and the immense power of every single person praying the words she had read and silently prayed throughout her life. Everyone's loud "Amen" and spirited singing brought her back into the moment and the realization that she was standing among many of the townsfolk she had served at the inn.

Looking around, she began thinking anxiously about how to exit without engaging in conversations with individuals she hardly knew. The young blonde-haired man in front of her was also looking around a bit nervously. His back stiffened while he watched the frail, dark-haired young woman next to him scoot across the row to embrace a woman who was her spitting image, except the older woman seemed stronger, more robust, her dark hair pulled tightly back and braided to her waist. Hope noticed the younger woman also appeared to have a few more grey hairs than her older likeness. Hope tried not to stare, then gazed back past the two young boys to the one who had led them in. Her eyes caught his, striking her like a bolt of lightening. Could it be? The young man had a broken nose, just like Jake's. Hope froze in place, staring, as he edged along the bench to get closer.

Jake's mind flashed back to the two cabins, sitting so close that he heard nearly every movement next door. The sounds of fists hitting flesh. The muffled screams. Memories burned like a fire surging through his veins. His papa's vocal resentment of the dark-skinned child mothered by this woman. The ginger-haired girl Jake adored. The one his father called a harlot. Words and actions he now mimicked with his own wife.

"Hope? Are you Hope, Jeremiah's mother?"

Riding Isaiah, following the carriage in front of her, Hope reflected on the morning's events. Church had been one of the most powerful experiences of her life, one she intended to repeat every Sunday. Church was no longer just a building. But while church was in itself a new and unexpected experience, it was overshadowed by the shock of seeing Jake -- a ghost of one she had assumed dead after the fire fifteen years ago. And the beautiful, but frail woman was his wife, Melissa. The busty woman Melissa embraced upon hearing "Amen!" was Mrs. Warner, Melissa's mother. The two boys were Jake's sons. They looked a lot like Jake, although the younger boy reminded her of Jared. The whirlwind of greetings and revelations had ended with Mrs. Warner's insistence that Hope join them for Sunday dinner. Hope had reluctantly accepted, noting that she had to be back at the inn in time to prepare supper for her guests and any locals that might pop in.

What had been a light mist, turned into torrential rain as Hope approached the Warner home. The house stood out as one of the finest, if not the finest, of the houses Hope had seen in the Watauga community. On her arrival, Mr. Warner ran to her with an umbrella and helped her dismount, taking her hand and leading her up the steps where Mrs. Warner welcomed her with a courtly, but friendly voice, insisting that Hope call her Bernice. "We are so pleased to have you as our guest," Bernice enthused. "You probably know our Jake better than our own daughter knows him. Although Jake has become like a son to us. He's such a hard worker, with the Doc and all. And so busy. These days, we hardly see them except on Sunday at church and for Sunday dinner. Thank God they make the time! Melissa is skinnier every time we see her, and Sundays are our chance to fatten her up, and see the boys, of course. Please join us in the dining room and sit next to me." Bernice lifted the tiny porcelain bell from the table and rang it gently. Within seconds, a plump black woman rushed in carrying a silver platter boasting a small roasted pig with an apple-stuffed mouth. She set it in front of Mr. Warner, who after a swift word of prayer, resumed his usual stern demeanor and focused on the task at hand, slicing the pork. Bernice picked up Hope's plate and passed it to him so he could place a thick slice on her plate. At Mrs. Warner's signal, the black woman presented a large silver bowl of steaming vegetables. "Help yourself to as much or as little as you wish," Bernice allowed while the woman held the bowl to Hope's left and lowered it so Hope could spoon a portion onto her plate. "Tell me about Jake's father. I see you still wear his ring."

"Jake takes after him. Yellow hair," Hope said, scooping a spoonful of vegetables to her mouth, then another, and raising her finger to her face to indicate she was too polite to talk with her mouth full.

"And Jake's brother Jared," Bernice continued, rambling. "We didn't have the pleasure of meeting him. He was here only for a week or two, so Wash told us. Then he traveled back to the homeplace where he and Jake grew up. And I assume that's where you married their father? Have you been back there to see Jared?"

"No ma'am. I lived in Mitchborough before I came here."

"Hope, I want you to see my place!" Jake interrupted, then awkwardly attempted to recover his blurting rudeness. "You can come back here for dinner next week after church, that is," he turned to the head of the table, "if it's okay with you, Mr. and Mrs. Warner."

Hope was relieved to excuse herself upon Jake's insistence and, at Bernice's urging, agreed to return for dinner the following Sunday. Jake tied Isaiah's reins to the back of the carriage, and held an umbrella to protect Hope from the driving rain, helping her inside to be seated next to Carter and Melissa. Though it was a short ride, it was long enough for Hope to notice Melissa's thin, hollow cheeks. Her dark eyes held a weary sadness, sadness not camouflaged by a forced smile.

The carriage stopped in front of a house distinguished by a knee-high porch that wrapped around three sides of the house. Rocking chairs sat on the porch's left side, facing a nearby creek, its waters now raging. Carter took the umbrella and helped Hope out of the carriage and onto the porch, then quickly returned to help his mother up the porch's two steps. On entering their home, Jake immediately took charge, loudly boisterous in his lengthy descriptions of how each and every piece of furniture was acquired, making it seem as though it was all a result of his own doing. Melissa, on the other hand, remained quietly demure and cautious, following closely behind Jake and nodding subserviently when she felt compelled to do so. After describing each of the paintings in the parlor, Jake ushered the obviously bored boys out to the front porch. "What're you still doing here! Get the carriage and horses out of the rain and into the barn and make sure Hope's horse gets some oats." On returning, he took Melissa's hand with a jerk, and began leading her up the stairs. "Follow us, Hope!" After the first step, Melissa quickly let go of Jake's hand to lift her skirts in order to climb freely while also holding the railing tightly as she inched up the steps. Following behind, Hope gasped, then quickly caught her breath, her mind splashed with alarming visions of her own legs some seventeen years ago. Streaks of swollen red welts circled Melissa's calves, a vision Hope struggled to dismiss when Melissa released her skirt and stepped onto the upper landing, barely lifting her feet to scoot painfully across the floor.

Hope smiled politely, using few words to compliment the beautiful canopy that hovered above the large bed in the master bedroom. They quickly viewed the boys' room, then headed over to the third floor steps. "Wait!" Jake stopped abruptly, placing his arm back to halt their movement. Hesitating awkwardly, his voice reflected a noticeable loss of confidence. "No need to see the rest of the house," he said, stepping backwards. "Upstairs is just for storage." The look on Melissa's face told a different story.

On leaving, Hope spoke directly to Melissa, taking both her hands in hers. "It is a lovely home. But I'm especially honored to meet you, Melissa. I pray you will come visit me at the inn soon. We'll have tea and I'll share some of my special pastries. You are always welcome." As soon as Carter brought her horse around, Hope left without a word to Jake, who stood on the porch holding an umbrella, weakly waving in her direction until she was out of site. He stormed inside, slammed the door, and stomped back into the parlor, yelling.

"She's my friend. Not yours! You don't have friends! You're no better than the worms in the privvy. And you're beginning to look like it too," Jake jerked her to him, then threw her to the floor, rubbing her face into the coarse tapestry until her body fell limp.

"Yer a harlot. But yer my harlot as long as I live!"

Hope gripped Isaiah's reins so tightly the leather cut into her hands, her entire being consumed with concern for Melissa, mixed in with memories she had successfully buried since arriving in Watauga. This was not the Jake she knew. Frightening thoughts whirled through her mind until the raindrops trickling from her hat turned to another torrential downpour. She held her hat tightly with one hand, fighting the wind's efforts to take it away. It's brim filled with water causing a stream to run down her face. She tilted it back so the water ran down her back, urged Isaiah into a fast gallop into town, straight into the stable, dismounted, removed his saddle and guided him to his stall. Drenched and shivering, she tucked her purse under her arm and pulled her Bible from her saddlebag holding it close to her chest to cover her soaked, clinging clothing. With her free hand, she lifted her skirts, waded through the rapidly rising water and rushed up the steps into the inn, past the guests and upstairs to change into dry clothes.

Sounds of rain hammering the tile roof drowned out the words of her guests. Hot tea replaced the usual mugs of beer, diners moved their tables to get closer to the fireplace. Hope prayed there was enough dry wood stored in the barn to outlast the storm. Then she realized the water she had waded through had surely covered the barn's floor by now. Isaiah would have to stand or sleep on wet hay through the night. But this wasn't just any night of pouring rain.

Thunder stirred Melissa. The nightmare lingered as she hovered between consciousness and sleep's escape. The rug beneath her was soaked. A flash of lightning revealed water rushing across the parlor floor and for a moment, its coolness felt good, soothing the burning skin of her face. In the next second she knew this was no nightmare. The creek was rising. And rising fast. She found the stairs' railing and pulled herself up the steps to wake the boys. "Get to the horses! Swim if you have to!" she commanded, now standing, holding the door knob to support herself. "Bring them to the front porch."

After what seemed an eternity, the two boys arrived at the front of the house, riding their own horses and leading two more up to the porch where their mother stood holding her grandmother's quilt above her head to keep it out of the rising water.

"Where's papa?" Wash shouted, leaping from his horse to the porch.

"I don't know. We have to ride out of here now!" Melissa threw the quilt across her horse, grabbed its mane, and pulled herself onto its back. "Come on boys!" Carter rode up beside her. "Come on Wash!"

"I'm gonna find papa!" Wash replied. Melissa watched as he used the door handle to pull himself through the water and back into the house. His shadow disappeared up the stairs. The water now covered the porch. She had no choice but to save her youngest.

"Carter! Hold on tight and follow me!" she yelled. With her head down close to its mane, she hugged her horse tightly to guide it through high water, past her parents' home, and up hill to the road toward town. The fog was so thick she couldn't see Carter behind her. Only the sound of his horse's hooves sloshing through the mud assured her he was not far behind.

Hope rose early to complete tasks last night's weather had delayed. She was moving slowly, her mind muddled by the previous day's events and lack of sleep. It was still dark when a guest brought her a bucket full of water from the leaky roof in his room. She pitched the water outside and handed him extra towels to dry the wet floors, not asking, but assuming he would be willing to help under the circumstances. Without a thought, she picked up twelve china plates and headed into the dining hall, almost dropping them at the sight of a muddy, soaked Melissa and equally drenched Carter standing before her.

"What happened?" Hope queried, still holding the twelve plates, yet trying to focus on the moment at hand. "Just a moment!" Hope hurried to set the plates on a table, then returned. "Never mind. You need dry clothes! I'll take you to my room and we can talk later." Hope took Melissa's arm and Carter followed with both hands behind Melissa's back to give her balance as they slowly climbed up the stairs and into Hope's room. Hope pulled some extra towels from the hall closet and handed them to Carter. "Please! Get out of those wet clothes and take anything you need to get comfortable. I'll be right back."

Anxiety kicked in, giving Hope more energy and enough mindfulness to run across the road to the stable to find help. Fortunately the livery boy was there, cleaning up the flood's debris. She promised him a big tip if he would run to the general store to find Carter some breeches and a shirt. "Tell them to charge it to my account. Go quickly and bring the clothes to the boy in my room," she ordered. She then hurried back to her room, knocked on the door, and told Carter to wait for his clothes. "And tell your mother I'll be downstairs tending to the guests' breakfast. There'll be plenty of food if you're hungry. Or you're welcome to rest in my room as long as you like."

Breakfast was served a little late, but the guests understood, especially since they were in no hurry to venture out to the flooded streets.

Exhausted, Hope forced herself through the motions, scraping, washing, rinsing, drying each dish, one-by-one, so immersed in repeated drudgery that she didn't see Carter come into the room. Not until she whirled around to take the clean plates back to the dining room, bumping straight into him.

"Mother asked me to tell you she's seated in the dining room, wearing one of your hats." Carter muttered shyly. Hope smiled and nodded her head in that direction, indicating he should follow. She set the plates down on a table and walked slowly over to the same corner table by the window where she had dined her first morning at the inn. Melissa was wearing a wide-brimmed hat, tipped down, nearly covering her eyes. Hope sat in the chair across from her and signaled Carter to sit in the chair between them. Melissa slowly raised her head to acknowledge Hope's presence, revealing a face awash in tiny red bumps, raw flesh exposed from the side of her left eye to her chin. An emerging scab marked the tip of her nose.

Melissa tipped her head back down as she spoke. "Thank you for letting me wear your clothes. I picked your largest hat so I could hide my face from your guests, though we waited until we thought they were gone. I didn't want to embarrass you. You see, I had a bad fall shortly after you left yesterday. It seemed only moments later that the creek was rising, flooding our house."

"Let me get you some tea and I'll bring you some pastries. Carter, you must be starving." Hope said forcing a slight smile from the grimace she wished to hide. Hope's anger at Jake surged within her, her hands shaking uncontrollably as she assembled the pastries, piling them high, knowing the boy would devour them. Unable to go straight to the dining room, in an attempt to halt the shaking, she sat down and prayed for relief from the distress and anger that had suddenly sapped her energy to the point that she doubted she could recover in time to prepare dinner for the guests. "Jesus, I pray to you for calm and inner strength. Please hold Melissa close to help her heal. And give me wisdom to do thy will and to help her." Hope sat still, her hands folded loosely in her lap, listening for the Lord's whisper of support. Through her silence she felt the familiar presence of Jesus behind her, with His hands placing reassurance on her shoulders, replacing her distress with the confidence that He would guide her through. A sensation of peace settled within her. "Amen," she sighed. With a deep breath, she placed her feet firmly before her, stood, picked up the pastries and teapot, and headed into the dining room.

Carter was sobbing, wiping his tears with his sleeve. Hope leaned over and gave Carter a big hug. "Carter. I'm so sorry. I know this is hard. Your mother will get better, I promise."

"My violin." Carter's shoulders moved up and down with his sobs. "My violin. It's gone. I know it's gone."

"Oh Carter," Hope put her hands on his shoulders to calm him. "Never you mind. I'll get you another violin. We can't have church without your beautiful music, can we?" Hope paused to show Carter a platter of pastries. "Try eating one of these. It'll make you feel better."

Carter took three pastries, hungrily shoved one in his mouth, and dropped the other two on the plate. "Thank you, Miss Hope."

Hope poured Melissa's tea and placed a pastry on the plate in front of her. "Maddie, the inn's owner, has left me to handle things until she returns. I haven't heard from her and I don't know when she'll return. Most of the guests are regulars and some have even paid me to hold their rooms for weeks, and even months, in advance. But there's Maddie's quarters on the third floor. I know she wouldn't mind if you and Carter stay there for now, as long as you keep it as you found it. So, after breakfast, I'll take you there where you can rest, as I know you haven't slept." Hope continued, "Carter, after we get your mother settled, will you help me get lunch ready for the guests?"

"Yes mmmmm," Carter mumbled, his mouth open, cheeks brimming with pastry crumbs.

Carter's manners, or lack thereof, amused Hope, reminding her of a young Jeremiah. "I'll be right back, young man." Hope went back to her room, grabbed her purse, and returned holding it in front of her with both hands. "I have a son who was about your age when we last spent time together. We used to play outside whenever no one was around. But this is taking up too much room in my new purse." She handed Carter her sling, smiling, wishing she could pull him to her and hold him as she had once held Jeremiah. "My son has his own sling so I have no use for it here. But, if you like, I'll show you how to use it. I used to be very good at killing squirrels, and …" she paused, reflecting on the last time she had used it. "Anyway, maybe tomorrow or the next day, we can go outside and see what we can find!"

Carter took the sling, held it tightly to his chest and without warning, hopped up on his chair nearly knocking Hope off her feet as he leaped into her arms to give her a big hug. "Thank you Miss Hope! I love you!"

Bernice Warner had made every attempt to heed her husband's demands that she stay out of her daughter's life, acquiescing to the once-a-week church and Sunday dinners, as the only time she could see her. But it had been two days since the creek crested high above its shoreline rushing through the fields, flooding the barn and the sawmill, stopping within feet of her own home. On this morning she had begged her husband to go check on Melissa, but, as always, he had insisted on putting his work ahead of family. "I'll get the sawmill up and running and then check on Melissa's house later. I'm sure she's fine. After all, she has Jake and the two boys there to take care of her," he had reasoned.

Emma, the cook, followed Bernice as she paced back and forth between the front porch and the back stoop stepping in and out of the rain in an attempt to see Melissa's house across what now was a field of water. Finally, the rain stopped and the water began receding back to its basin, allowing her to see her daughter's home. Since marrying Mr. Warner, Bernice had proudly upheld the family's prominent status, managing the household help, relinquishing her own opinions in deference to her husband's. It angered her that Mr. Warner put supervising the sawmill's clean-up before his daughter's well-being. She was running out of patience, filled with anxiety over the unknown. "Emma, bring me my horse and mind you, be alert. Don't let anyone see you. Bring it to the far side of the house, out of site from the sawmill." She had not ridden her horse in over a year and had often longed to go back to the days of her free-spirited youth, long rides along new trails, leaping over fences, racing her friends. Now she took charge of her own wishes, and rode through the muddy fields to her daughter's home. Or what was left of it.

The stone steps were all that remained of Melissa's porch, its landing now collapsed into loose boards drifting in shallow currents toward the creek. Pieces of furniture floated in the front yard. The entire house leaned toward the creek, giving way to the pressure pushing against it to follow the receding waters. She perched up from the stirrups to peer inside, shouting, "Melissa!...Jake? Wash! Anyone home?" Clearly, no one was. It took all the strength she could muster to guide the horse through the current to the back of the house, where it became more difficult, as she cautiously guided him around floating tree limbs and bones. "Bones!" she gasped aloud. "Bones! Watch out! Careful!" She pulled the reins, guiding him to stop so she could take a closer look. Floating below her were remains of a skeleton, remnants of shredded cloth tangled amongst its ribs. A small wedding ring glistened from bones of a dangling finger. A few feet away, a skull bobbed face up twisting back and forth in the water.

"Oh my God!" Bernice turned the horse and kicked it into a gallop, splashing through the water, toward her house, her thoughts racing. *I must find Melissa! But there's a dead man floating in her yard! ... No time to dally at the sawmill. Doc needs to know!*

With fierce determination, Bernice rode past her house and up the hill to the road into town. She threw the reins over the hitching post and dashed up the steps, through the door, past the waiting patients and straight into Doc's office. "Doc! Thank God you're here! Is Jake here? I can't find Melissa!"

"Bernice! Calm down now! Jake and Wash are upstairs in my quarters. They got here before dawn. Said the creek ran over and the house was overcome with water. They were lucky to get out. I'm sure they'll be down shortly. I'd let you go up but they might not be decent, if you know what I mean. I told them they could borrow my clothes until theirs dried," Doc stepped around his desk and pulled a chair aside, gesturing her to be seated.

"I can't sit Doc! There's a dead man's remains floating in Melissa's back yard! I came straight here! Melissa's missing and there's a body. His head is floating!

He had a ring on his little finger! I was so upset, I rode right past my husband's sawmill. Came straight here. I knew you'd know what to do!"

"Okay. Okay. I see. Best you wait here for Wash and Jake. I'll get the sheriff and we'll ride on down to see what's up." Doc Taylor closed the office door behind him, told his patients they'd have to wait a little longer, and headed down the hill and across the street to the sheriff's office.

Dressed sharply in the vest, waistcoat and trousers he had pulled from Doc's wardrobe, Jake had approached the back door to Doc's office, touched his hand to the handle, then stopped abruptly and placed his head against the door. He heard everything. Jared's skull … granny's ring … Bernice was the last person he wanted to see. And he had no interest in finding Carter and Melissa. He ran back up the stairs to Doc's quarters. "Come on Wash. Grab our wet clothes! No time to lose. We gotta get outta here! Now!"

He led Wash around to the side of the clinic and peeked around the corner to make sure Doc's horse was gone. "Run! Follow me!" he waved his hand forward signaling Wash to follow. Within seconds, they were both riding their horses, heading east, past Maddie's inn, past the grist mill, and up the same road Jake had ridden, alongside Charlie, and not far behind his brother Jared. Once the settlement was far behind them, he sided his horse up alongside his son's. "Wash, my son. It's time I showed you my homeplace. Where Jared and I grew up. It's beautiful there, and there's a wide river, the Doe River, filled with trout, and … I can't wait to show you my swimming hole!" Jake paused and smiled thoughtfully. "And the best thing … the very best … is … it's my very own property. It can be yours one day. A place where we don't have to account to nobody!"

Bernice waited, relieved to have a moment to recover from the morning's discoveries. But the longer she waited, the more she worried about Melissa. *Did the dead man have anything to do with her disappearance? Could Carter have fallen into the rushing water? Could she have drowned trying to save him?* Worrying thoughts churned through Bernice's head to the point that her chest hurt. *I'm going to have a heart attack and that won't help anybody,* she thought. *I need to be strong. For God only knows what's to come about next. A cup of tea. I need a cup of tea. I'll go to the inn and see if that young lady Hope is there. I bet she'll help me find my girl.*

Bernice led her horse down the hill, deftly dodging large puddles in order to maintain her fine appearance. In her anxious state, she was totally unaware that splotches of mud had painted her from head to toe on the ride into town.

Mid-day at the inn found Hope serving dinner to only a few guests. Hope raised her eyes upward for a moment to thank the Lord for a quiet day. Tuesdays were usually quite busy with local businessmen taking advantage of meals hosted by visiting salesmen and ladies stopping by after a morning of shopping. But this Tuesday was not a normal business day as many of the locals had stayed at home to tend to their farms, or their neighbors' farms, cleaning up debris and wrangling lost livestock. But the laid-back undemanding service did nothing to buffer her shock at Bernice's appearance in the dining hall doorway.

"Good afternoon, Mrs. Warner. What a pleasure to see you here today," Hope garnered her thoughts in an attempt to compose herself and determine how to handle Mrs. Warner with grace and discretion. "Why don't you come into the kitchen with me and I'll make you a cup of tea."

Mrs. Warner followed, deferring to her host's guidance.

"You must be exhausted. Did you ride in on your own, or is Mr. Warner with you?" Hope asked, gesturing for Mrs. Warner to sit at the small round table in the kitchen.

"I rode in alone."

Bernice's answer told Hope what she needed to know. "Here's a damp towel, if you'd like to freshen up a bit." Bernice took the towel and wiped it across her face, straight down her nose, missing much of the mud. "Let me help," Hope said as she gently touched the towel to the missed splotches on Bernice's face, used her fingers to remove several chunks of mud from her hair, then handed the towel back with a slight wipe across Bernice's muddy wrists. "There, that's better, I think." Hope left Mrs. Warner to tend to other spots on her own, then took the steaming tea pot from the wood stove, and poured two cups of tea.

"How's your home? Did the creek rise up that high?" Hope asked, determined not to betray Melissa's confidence by revealing what she already knew.

Bernice's shaking hands lifted the cup to her mouth. She took a long sip and sighed longingly, fighting back tears. "Melissa's home is destroyed. I don't know where she is. She could've drowned for all I know. I left without telling Mr. Warner. You know he's more interested in the sawmill than his own daughter. I rode straight to the Doc's and he went back to look around … I waited for Jake. But he never came down. My heart hurts so much. I needed a cup of tea. Thank you. I can't …" Bernice was now sobbing helplessly. Hope stood and leaned over to give her a hug.

"You stay here. I'll be right back."

Hope went up to the third floor. Entering Maddie's room, she carefully stepped over Carter sleeping on the floor, and tiptoed over to the bed where Melissa lay holding a damp rag over her face. Hope gently touched Melissa's arm and whispered. "Melissa. I don't know how to tell you this, but your mother is downstairs."

Chapter 25

Moaning winds marched through the trees, tossing red and yellow leaves to dance with those of lesser colors along the grist mill's pathway. Wagons loaded with wheat were lined up, waiting their turn to get their produce milled. This was Jeremiah's busiest time, working from dawn until hours past sundown, depending on lanterns to hold the light throughout the building. Four-year-old Amity had posted herself at the counter to practice writing her letters while her parents labored through the fast-paced, repetitive tasks of milling and bagging the grain.

A familiar face approached her this afternoon. "Good afternoon, Miss Amity, I hope yer having a good day. Not much time for play this time of year, I see."

"I don't mind, Mr. Carson," Amity replied.

"I have news of yer grandmother. I must see yer father to tell him right away."

"My friends have grandmothers. I don't," she mused. "But if you can find me one, I would be very pleased. Grandmothers are a special gift for those who have one. So please sir, hurry upstairs and tell him as soon as you can. But I hope you have time for waiting. When he's milling, he moves pretty fast and it's hard for him to stop, if he can."

Mr. Carson climbed to the second floor and patiently waited until Jeremiah could turn away from the milling wheels. "What is it Mr. Carson? It must be mighty important for you to stand there waiting all this time until I could speak to you."

"It's yer mother, Missus Hope. I jest got back from seein' me daughter, Caroline. She lives in Watauga, ya know."

"I knew you had a daughter. But I know not of Watauga," Jeremiah responded, growing impatient, anxious to get back to the mill.

"Watauga's 'bout two day's from here, I reckon, if ye head west down 'cross th' river. Anyways, Caroline's husband's a preacher at th' Methodist church in Watauga. Me n' me wife gone to thar church some weeks back n' I seen yer mother, Missus Hope, settin' a few rows across from us. 'Course I ain't seen her since she wuz livin' with that Will fella, 'bout a year ago when I wuz by his cabin n' my travels. He said she left n' he didn't know her whar'bouts. But I'd know that red hair anywhar. She wuz lookin' good, tho' I must say she wuz dressed fancier n' I e'er seen her. She left afore I could say hello, but me daughter says Missus Hope's at thar church most ever' Sunday n' she's runnin' an inn down th' hill from thar."

Jeremiah sat speechless on a barrel next to the millstone. Not a day passed that he didn't think of his mother, wondering where she was. The pain still lingered in his heart. Constant questioning. Why she left. Why she had not returned. It had been nine years since she went missing, without so much as a word or reason he could think of. "I thought she was dead."

1796

Dogwood blooms peeked out from their buds, waving in the peaceful spirit of soft spring breezes. Jeremiah walked through the mill one last time before locking the door and securing the sign: "Closed Til Summer Harvest". Two years had passed since the community had bid farewell to Mitch, its founding father, and it had been ten years since Jeremiah's mother had gone missing, with no farewell to bid. The winter had brought brutal snow storms, leaving Jeremiah isolated for almost two weeks, with only his wife and daughter to talk to. In many ways, they were the best weeks of his life. A time to tell stories, roast chestnuts, give the entire mill a good cleaning, sleep late, and learn to relax, basking in the quiet, without the constant, often inconvenient interruptions of neighbors expecting their full attention. These quiet moments brought Jeremiah time to reflect, and remember his first ten years, adventures with his mother, riding between her arms, destination unknown. Learning. Feeling loved. Now, if his mother was alive, if Mr. Carson was correct about Watauga, it was time to go see for himself. And, perhaps, find a grandmother for Amity.

In Watauga, this particular Sunday morning had kept Hope moving quickly as it seemed all the guests were energized by spring, expecting a full breakfast. So, as soon as the last guest departed, Hope left the dirty dishes on the tables, and dashed to the front hitching post, where her faithful stable boy handed her Isaiah's reins, saving her precious moments as she fervently prayed she could get to church before the preacher placed both hands on the pulpit. Thankfully, she made it in time and Melissa, Carter, and the Warners had saved her usual place at the end of their bench in the middle of the sanctuary. She sang along cheerfully, confident she now knew the words to every hymn by heart and proud of the generous donation she placed in the collection plate, happy to give voice to the final hymn, and say a silent prayer of gratitude that Melissa and Carter had reunited with Melissa's parents, seemingly happy to be living with them in their large home. *All blessings flowed.* She always looked forward to Sunday dinners at the Warners, now a tradition, so with quick hugs to Melissa and Bernice, discussing her plans to ride along behind their carriage, she headed over to where Isaiah was waiting. Waiting, but not alone.

A tall, dark-skinned young man was holding the reins, staying Isaiah, patting him on the cheek, and smiling up at a beautiful child, sitting atop Hope's horse. The child looked just like Jeremiah when he was four or five years old. Hope stood stunned, frozen in the moment, staring, checking her surroundings, certain this horse was hers, wondering if her eyes were tricking her, astonished that someone would have the nerve to place their child on her horse as if it was their own.

"I recognized Isaiah right away," said the young man. "This is my daughter, your granddaughter, Amity. And my wife, Abby. Amity, this is your grandmother. My mother." He choked back the tears, then let go the reins to embrace the one he had longed for. It was really her. She was alive.

Bernice tried to place the young dark-skinned man hugging Hope. She had never seen him at church, she was certain, as she knew everyone, having attended every Sunday since she had wed Mr. Warner. *Perhaps he is a regular guest at the inn,* she mused. *And why is Hope crying*?

Leaving her husband and Carter to tend to the carriage, Bernice took Melissa's hand and pulled her toward the small group in order to rid Hope of this intruder, if he was hurting her, and at the very least, satisfy her intense curiosity.

"Good afternoon. I pray I'm not intruding. I'm Bernice Warner and this is my daughter, Melissa."

Hope turned to her, holding tightly to Jeremiah's arm, smiling through her tears. "Bernice, Melissa, this is my son Jeremiah, his wife Abby, and my granddaughter Amity."

The look on Bernice's face was only out-done by Melissa's widening eyes and dropped jaw. Bernice struggled for words. *Hope was a mother? Her child was an Indian? And now Melissa was hugging him?*

"Jeremiah. My husband Jake told me all about you. But his stories were about your childhood and how he used to play with you. Now you're a grown man. With a little girl!" Melissa put her arm around Hope's waist, giving her a hug. "Hope! What a surprise this must be!"

Bernice regained her composure. *I must think of Hope's feelings. She has been so kind to us.* She grinned widely and clapped her hands in delight. "My! My! What a great day this is! You must join us for Sunday dinner! Hope knows the way." Bernice looked up at Amity, sitting atop Isaiah. "You'll meet my grandson Carter when you get to the house. I know he'll be glad to have someone to play with." Bernice placed her arm on Melissa's and gently pulled her in the direction of the carriage. "Your father is waiting on us. We'll ride ahead and tell the cook to set three more places at the table."

Sunday dinner was filled with questions. Jeremiah explained Mr. Carson's visit which answered the question about how he found the church. Hope told Jeremiah about his grandfather and how she found him once she spotted Hawksbill Mountain. She didn't mention Will, the details of her long absence, how her own years had passed quickly while the same years had slowly dragged on carrying sadness and distress for her son, and she still agonized over how to face him with the truth. It was certainly a story she didn't want to share with the Warners.

Melissa told about the flood, leaving out the reason she had fled to the inn rather than face her mother. Yes, Jake had gone missing, along with their son, Wash. No one had seen them since the flood. In telling this story, she tried to appear sad, fending grief for Jake's absence while silently thanking God that he was gone. And she didn't divulge her resentment of Wash and the fact that he had acquired his father's hateful ways, ways that she feared would bring her more harm.

Fortunately, Bernice held back on the obvious question, one that burned in her mind, searing to the point that she remained untypically silent through most of the meal -- *Jake's father was fair-skinned and blonde, like his son. How on earth did he parent a son who very clearly was not in his likeness. And Jeremiah definitely didn't look like his mother.*

Hope shook the crumbs off the lace covering and placed it back on the same table where she had her first breakfast at the inn. Two years had passed since Maddie left to go visit her son. Hope had received only one letter indicating he had passed away and that Maddie planned to stay longer in order to help care for her three grandchildren. There had been no further word of Maddie or her family, despite Hope's frequent letters updating her on the activities at the inn and shared stories of the townsfolk. But Hope was grateful for the extra space. Maddie's third floor accommodations were now occupied by Jeremiah and his family. Their time together had been precious and fun, with Hope keeping everyone busy, ensuring there was little time for any serious discussions. Hope wondered if or how long their light-hearted moments could delay Jeremiah's questions, questions she prayed Jeremiah wished to remain unanswered. *No time*

today, she thought prayerfully, for today's light-hearted moments were already well-planned.

Abby was in the kitchen, washing plates and cutlery in preparation for the evening's meal. Jeremiah was outside replacing loose boards on the inn's front landing.

Amity had raced across the way to visit her pony at the inn's stable. As soon as she arrived, Amity reached into her pockets, pulled out the sling her father had given her, waved it in front of her pony's nose, then raised it above her head to twirl it. "You know my grandmother Hope made this sling. I'm the best rock slinger around," she boasted. "When they finish their chores, we're going to ride over to Carter's house and as soon as we get there, Carter and I are going to sling rocks at the squirrels! He knows I'm better than he is!"

Amity's playful jabber was interrupted by loud thumping in the adjoining stall. "Isaiah! Stop that racket!" she yelled. "Grandmother will be here real soon!" The thumping continued, only more intermittently, and slower. "That's better."

Hope held the door open while she waited for Abby to join her on the landing."Jeremiah! Thank you! Now the guests won't be complaining about tripping over loose boards!" Hope exclaimed as she hung the sign "Innkeeper Out Until Suppertime". "Now let's get our horses and head over to ride in the Warners' pastures."

"Amity! You in here?" Hope shouted gleefully, anxious to spend more time with her granddaughter. "I'll get Isaiah. He loves to follow your pony in the meadow!"

Amity ran and jumped into her grandmother's arms. "You took too long! And Isaiah's been kickin'! He's waiting for you to get here! Come on!" Amity said as she began pulling Hope over to Isaiah's stall.

Hope clasped the stall latch and peered in, surprised that Isaiah wasn't already nudging his nose against the door and pawing his hooves impatiently. Instead, he lay on the straw, his tail flapping slowly back and forth. She ran over to him and placed her head against his nose. "Isaiah. Isaiah," she whispered. "I'm here, baby. I'm here." Instinctively, Hope knew the kicking Amity heard had been his failed attempts to stand, and now he was too weak to even try, so she snuggled down beside him and began rubbing her palm gently across his ribs to comfort him.

Jeremiah stooped down and leaned over, placing his hands on his mother's shoulder. "What can I do to help?" he asked.

"You can't help. Go. Just go. He's had a good life -- most of the time." Memories flashed through her mind, tears turned to ceaseless sobbing. "Now he wants to rest," she gasped. "Take Amity to Carter's. I'll stay here as long as he needs me … or, as long as I need him."

Jeremiah kissed his mother on the cheek, then tiptoed out, placing two fingers to his mouth to indicate "Shh. Leave her be." Hope's sobbing blocked the sound of three horses being led out of the stable.

"There, there, my friend. I know you're tired. We've had a long journey, you and I. I wish you were small like Amity, so I could hold you tightly in my arms and you could feel my heartbeat like I feel yours." Hope placed her hand across Isaiah's ribs. His heartbeat was growing slower, his breathing hardly noticeable. "With you, I was brave, never alone. You carried me through forests, across meadows, and even through rising waters. And while I rode you hard and fast, it was your spirit that held me …" Isaiah's heartbeat faded. His breathing stopped. But Hope still held on, caressing his ribs, then gently moving her hands up to his cheek, and across his forehead to close his eyes. "I will stay with you as long as your spirit lingers, but I know you will soon be in heaven, running with those who passed before you. One day I will see you there and we will ride again, this time across pastures of soft golden grain near still waters, where you will never again thirst, for the Lord is your Shepherd as He is mine. And life in our two spirits is everlasting ... and you will always be my best friend."

Chapter 26

1804

Years had passed since that first visit to Watauga. Jeremiah's mother had never returned to Mitchborough, satisfied with his family's annual visits to see her. Visits that had become a tradition for the past eight years. The visits had been filled with special moments and Jeremiah was especially grateful for Amity's time with her grandmother, Amity proudly reading the Bible having learned to read in the same manner Hope had taught him when he was little, singing hymns, most especially hearing his mother teach Amity the 23rd psalm in the soothing voice that had so often calmed him. Amity had even learned to prepare his favorite dishes, just like his mother had made him when he was little. And he had shared his own memories with his mother on long walks recalling his childhood, learning to make letters with charcoal, watching her cut apples in the springhouse, cutting with the same knife he had used to cut Amity's fruit, their afternoons in the woods and along the river, twirling their slings to hit squirrels and trees, skills he passed along to his daughter, and skills his daughter, in turn, had shared with Carter, her special Watauga friend.

His questions about his own appearance haunted him, but in light of Isaiah's passing and his mother's attempts to hide her lingering heartache with forced smiles, he had reluctantly set his own needs aside. He had begged his mother to come back to Mitchborough, but

Hope had no interest, reaffirming her commitment to remain at the inn until Maddie returned, or even if she didn't. The truth was, Jeremiah knew his mother was fiercely independent. He had seen her strength and determination prevail many times when he held on tightly in fear for his life, and hers. At the inn, he had observed that guests considered his mother to be kind, but distant. Her "don't mess with me" demeanor served her well, he thought. At least it kept potential suitors at bay -- for she had made it clear to Jeremiah and Abby that she preferred to remain "on her own" without the burden of meeting a man's expectations. He held onto the thought her independence had emerged from her own life's experiences, and that it had nothing to do with him. Maybe one day she would return to Mitchborough, perhaps another spring, when the dogwoods bloomed.

Today, his thoughts turned to Amity, praying his sweet little twelve-year-old would achieve her grandmother's independent and strong spirit. Her long, coal black hair, dark almond-shaped eyes, high cheekbones, and soft, creamy cinnamon-toned skin, set her apart from Mitchborough girls her age, already attracting interest from young boys, including the strapping young man he had hired to tend the blacksmith shop. Interest he attempted to deter at every turn. From now on, Saturday evenings would be devoted to teaching Amity how to defend herself against unwanted moves. He now wore the deer-bone knife in a sheath strapped at his side.

Chapter 27

His father's homeplace was nothing like Wash had imagined. As far back as he could remember, Jake had painted his son's imagination with visions of two cabins, side-by-side, Papa Henry playing the fiddle, Granny Matilda making stew and corncakes by the fireplace, summer days with his brother Jared -- harvesting flax and corn from the fields, gathering eggs from the chicken coop, and swimming below the diving rock at the river.

When Wash and his papa arrived at the Greer farm just days after the flood, Jake had been stunned at the sight. There were no cabins. Only rocks fallen from two collapsed chimneys -- no walls, no floors, just thorny bushes and weeds. The barn was still standing, mostly. Several logs had loosened, giving access to racoons and other animals. But the roof had remained intact, missing only a few shingles. So they made the barn their home, eventually sealing the gaps in the walls, securing their shelter from invading critters and harsh elements.

The years since the flood had been filled with hard work, freezing winters, and near starvation until attempts to revive the fields yielded corn and potatoes. These were added to slain deer and rabbits to make meals. A life drastically distant from privileged days spent seeking trout in the creek and work only defined by clearing dishes and bringing the horses in from the pasture.

The romanticized visions painted by his father were now replaced by harsh realities, despite the fact that his father never diverted from his original stories, not then or now, except for the additional, but brief tale of the fire that led to he and Jared escaping to Sycamore Shoals and the story of their heroic victory at Kings Mountain. And Wash dared not ask questions, not anymore, for fear the sharply carved switch would again be unleashed to cut into his skin. His papa was firm in his limited recollections and there was no more to it.

But Wash had his own memories. Memories of his mother, Melissa. Warm memories of suppers with hearty meals at the table with his mother and father laughing and hugging each other. Nights when he heard his papa and mother laughing in their bedroom. Memories that faded into horror soon after Uncle Jared's disappearance, presumably to return to his homeplace. At least that's what his father had said. The homeplace where Wash now tried to sleep. Where there was no Jared. Wash dared not tell his father what he had seen or heard. His mother's screams from the barn, Jared atop her. Mother pulling the bloody quilt down the stairs and out the door. The night Jared disappeared. A night followed by terrifying changes in his father's behavior. Mother sleeping in Jared's bedroom. No more laughter. No more hugging. Anger and harsh words from his father. His mother's growing silence. Hiding under his bed, holding his ears to block out the sounds of a whip hitting flesh. His mother's hands shaking as she presented breakfast to her son and husband. A baby brother. Carter. So sweet, so cute, so innocent. Loved by his mother. Hated by his father.

This was the family life he knew. But yet he had seen couples holding hands at church. Looks of longing across the pews. And he himself had felt longing at the sight of a pretty girl. Longing that now dominated his thoughts. Men and women were meant to be together. They were created that way. Men took great pleasure in a woman's touch. And he had seen girls teasing boys in order to share that pleasure. *I am twenty-one years old and yet to feel a girl's breast.* The images consumed his mind and the hardness between his legs grew in his moving hand -- until wetness brought release from his self-induced pleasure. He rolled over onto his stomach and buried his head into the furry bed Jared had left in the barn's corner. *I cannot go another day not knowing … not touching.*

Jake's stomach growled loudly as he trekked up the path from his morning ritual at the river. "I'll roast some trout for our breakfast," he muttered aloud to himself. "Thank God th' coals in th' firepit are still hot." He threw some sticks on the fire, and sharpened another one to pierce the trout, carefully hung it over the fire, and waited. And waited. The smell of breakfast cooking always brought Wash out of the barn. Not this time. *That lazy boy. He'll never amount to anything. I'll show him. I'll just go ahead and eat it all!*

Jake hungrily gobbled his trout, his patience growing thin. *Still no Wash.* "You aren't gonna sleep the day away are you?" Jake yelled running into the barn. Wash was not in his furry bed. And his horse was gone.

As soon as his father had headed to the river, Wash had pulled on the vest and breeches he wore the day they left Watauga, threw the bed furs on his horse and lured it out of the barn down the trail toward the main road, knowing the rushing river waters would hide any sound he made. *I can't go to Watauga,* he thought, thinking his father's sudden disappearance would bring too many questions. *I'll go where no one knows me*. So, he headed east down the road toward what he thought was Kings Mountain.

Riding along the road, he saw a large overhanging boulder and wondered if that was the same shelving rock his father had mentioned in his tales of Kings Mountain. This made him question whether his father would try to follow. He decided to ride as hard as he could and only take short breaks, just in case. The Doe River was now a good distance behind him. Beads of sweat streamed into his eyes as the sun's rays beat down through the trees. He wiped his brow with his sleeve, relieved to see a grove of apple trees off to the right. *It will be cooler in the orchard.* Wash steered his horse slowly through the trees, pulling down apples, chomping one with his teeth, and wrapping a few more into folds of his shirt "You'll have your own apple soon," he promised his horse. He then cut across the field, past a springhouse, and onto the main road where arching tree branches shaded their trek. Just ahead he saw two streams of water tumbling from a rock bluff into a wide pool before it fell to the brook below. His horse slowed on its own, hinting this would be a good spot to rest. After indulging in their apples, he stepped aside to let his horse cool down in the brook.

He hiked up a narrow trail leading to the waterfall and stood under its misty arch to relieve himself. It was so peaceful, he wished he could stay and make camp, but fearing his father had followed, he rushed back downhill, mounted his horse and kicked it into a gallop. As dusk approached, the arching trees grew further apart, revealing narrow trails shooting out from the main road. Wash took a deep breath. These were large farms. He had reached some kind of settlement. He rode through another tunnel of overhanging trees. Shafts of moonlight lanced their way. Ahead he saw smaller farms, lanterns in small cabins spotted the land. He crossed a long wooden bridge over a wide shallow stream. Up ahead, he saw a large building next to a river. As he got closer, he saw a barn off to its side, its wide door slightly ajar. He dismounted next to a long water trough and peered inside. *This is a blacksmith's shop. A good shelter til morning,* he surmised.

A tall silent shadow loomed over him, blocking the sunlight. Wash scurried to his feet. "Morning sir. I got here early. Fell asleep while I was waiting," Wash told the blacksmith, forcing a wry smile. "My horse needs re-shoe-in', if you have time."

"Since yer th' first one here, I kin do it," replied the blacksmith. "Go to th' mill n' tell 'em to charge ye fer me service. Ye'll pay thar. Yer horse'll be fit as a fiddle when ye return."

At that moment Wash realized he had no way to pay for the blacksmith's service, unless they would accept pelts in trade. He pulled the pelts from his horse and headed around the corner and up the steps into the mill, building confidence by recollecting his visits to the Watauga mill with his father. This mill, however, was much larger. He couldn't believe his eyes. It looked more like the general store located in Watauga's center, down the hill from Doc Taylor's. He threw the pelts over his shoulder and began walking around, pretending to inspect the varied wares. *I could use a clean shirt,* he thought, pulling Doc's waistcoat tighter. Out of the corner of his eye, he saw a young girl scribbling in a book on the counter. Her hands moved with a fast, intense grace, reminding him of a hovering hummingbird. Loose strands of coal black hair fell across her forehead, hiding her eyes. He inched over her way to get a better view.

"You find what you're looking for?" she inquired, looking up from her book. He felt as if her dark eyes pierced through him, seeing him clearly, as if she knew his every thought. Thoughts he hoped to keep to himself by maintaining his distance.

He cleared his throat and glanced her way. "What's a pelt worth in these parts?"

"How many do you have?"

"Three."

"What are you trading for?"

"The blacksmith's shoeing my horse, and I was hoping to get this here shirt."

"That'll be fine. My father's kind that way. I don't have to ask him unless it's something we haven't seen before."

Wash removed the shirt from its hook, mustered up his courage, walked over to the girl, and placed the pelts on the counter.

"What's your name? I need it to make a note in my journal. Three pelts for one shirt and the blacksmith's services."

"Wash. Jared George Washington Greer."

"Really? That's strange. I have a good friend - Carter. Carter Greer. But he's in Watauga. Have you ever been to Watauga? My grandmother has an inn there. My name's Amity. Amity O'Connor. Where are you from?"

"Nope. I don't know any Carter from Watauga. My home's west of here. Probably two days' ride, but I rode hard, late into the night "

"Why were you riding so fast? Are you meeting someone here in Mitchborough? Or are you taking your horse to Alder Springs or maybe Jamestown? Watauga's west of here, two days' ride to see my grandmother."

"Maybe Jamestown," Wash stammered, thinking he had heard of Jamestown, but with no idea where he was, he could not presume to continue the conversation without embarrassing himself. Just the sound of her voice was making him nervous. He put his hands in his pockets to calm them and gain courage to speak. "But I like it here. Yep. Might hang 'round for awhile. Gotta check on my horse. Maybe I'll see you tomorrow."

Amity moved her hand in a slight wave as she watched Wash rush out the door. *I hope so,* she thought to herself.

The sound of horses' hooves hitting the planks of the bridge startled Wash, waking him from a tender embrace, the dark honey of young girl's skin tightly pressed against his paleness. He moved his hands across his thigh to calm his passion, dwindling in recognition of the reality around him, his soft bed of grass damp from the morning's dew. He sat up, brushed back his hair, scooted around and leaned against the dogwood tree to watch the mill across the deep river. The river's strong current of water rushed along a narrow channel to a large wheel, then tumbled hypnotically across its blades, turning in a constant rhythm, holding his imagination captive, pulling his thoughts back into his dream. He closed his eyes in concentration, wishing the girl was in his arms.

His horse whinnied to get his attention, shaking its head to loosen its reins slowly down the tree's trunk. Taking the reins in his hand, Wash led his horse down the stream's bank to quench its thirst while he knelt down and leaned into the water to splash his face and rinse his beard. A nearby rock offered a dry perch and a good view of the mill's entrance, its surroundings aflutter with the comings and goings of locals tending their day's needs. He pulled his fingers through the long blonde hairs of his beard, hoping to remove the dust from his journey, contemplating ways to make his dream an actual experience. Once he had his plan, he walked his horse back to the road, climbed up into the saddle, and rode back toward the arching trees where rhododendrons lined the trail. With his knife, he cut several branches, then trimmed the stems so the blooms were unencumbered by their sharp leaves. Then he removed the bark from a vine, thinning it to reveal its rich green flesh. He carefully laid the rhododendron blossoms in a flair shape and tied them together with the green vine, twisting it to form a bow. He now proudly held a bouquet -- a bouquet like those he had seen presented to pretty Watauga girls by young boys seeking their favor.

On returning to the bridge, he was relieved to see only a few horses lingering along the mill's hitching post. Wash changed into his new shirt and waited patiently until the last trader rode away. With the bouquet hidden behind his back, he sauntered over to the front of the mill, looking around to ensure no one else was coming. Once inside, he eased his way over to the counter, so quietly that Amity gasped when she saw him. He quickly presented the flowers, proudly grinning in anticipation of her approval.

"Oh my! They're beautiful. I love rhododendrons!" she exclaimed.

"They are nothing compared to your beauty. You simply take my breath away," Wash said with relief on remembering the words he had rehearsed all day.

Amity blushed. "These are my first flowers. I am not yet thirteen, you know. I fear my father would not approve."

"Is he still upstairs?"

"Yes. He usually keeps the mill running until all the day's grain is done."

"Then perhaps we have time for a short walk? We can stay close by so we'll see him when he's finished."

"I guess we can go for a few minutes but it's already getting dark so we don't have much time." Amity closed the journal, laid down her quill, scooted around the counter, and led the way onto the front porch. Wash hurried to her side and took her hand to guide her down the steps.

"There's a full moon tonight. Let's go over to the bridge. I'll show you where I camped -- and my horse, under the dogwoods."

Wash was filled with anticipation. His plan was working. As they walked, he listened without hearing a word of her constant chatter, his mind intently recalling his father's ways with his mother. He placed his arm around Amity's waist, gently lowering his hands to touch her curves.

Amity felt an unfamiliar tingling throughout her body and raised her palm to her chest, hoping to still her heart's excitement. When they reached the dogwoods, Wash firmly gripped her waist and pulled her to him, holding her tightly. With his other hand he eased across his horse's back to find his whip. *Just in case,* he thought. *Everything is going according to plan.*

Amity struggled to free herself. "That hurts! Get away from me!" she screamed. She threw her head back then thrust it forward hitting his chin, stunning him for a second. She pushed both hands against his chest to no avail. Wash tried to hold her with one arm while tugging his other hand to loosen the whip from its slip. He hadn't anticipated her strength or her determination. She kicked him in the shin of his leg, then pushed herself loose, reached into her pocket, pulled out her sling, and began whirling it above her head. Wash caught her wrist and pulled her back to him. "I have one of those - just like yours!" he chuckled, now confidently grasping his whip, raising it back behind his shoulder. "This'll calm you down!"

Jeremiah was angrily searching the store, pondering Amity's punishment for leaving without his consent. His anger turned to fierce energy as he ran toward the screams coming from the dogwoods. A flash of moonlight revealed Wash swinging the whip above his head. Jeremiah's knife whisked through the air and pierced Wash in his left shoulder, causing him to drop the whip. Amity ran into her father's arms. "Get inside!" Jeremiah yelled, pushing her toward the mill. In seconds he was on top of Wash, grasping the screaming eagle handle to pull the knife free then swiftly pressing its blade against Wash's throat. "That's my twelve-year-old daughter you're messing with." Jeremiah's free hand moved across the ground to find the whip. He pressed his knee against Wash's chest, then stood. "You'll never have the pleasure of a girl as long as you live," Jeremiah shouted, raising the whip and sharply lowering it, again and again, repeatedly slashing Wash between his legs.

"It's only by God's grace and my mother's teachings that you're still breathing. I expect you to crawl up on your horse as soon as you're able. If you're not gone by morning, I'll whip you til you're dead."

Chapter 28

Hope stepped down from the carriage and looked up at its driver. "Thank you Carter. I pray I've not been too much trouble all these Sundays. You have been such an angel, bringing the carriage into town to take me to church and carrying me back after dinner. It means so much to me. I just can't bring myself to get another horse. There will never be another Isaiah." Hope squinted to hold back the tears. Tears that came every time she thought of the horse that had been her best friend -- a friend she could not replace -- not just yet.

"I know Missus Hope. It's no trouble at all. You're like family to us. I'll be your driver as long as you need me."

"What a kind young man you've become. I can't believe you're fifteen! And your music. Listening to you play your violin every Sunday brings me great joy. I'm going to write Amity this evening and tell her how her playmate is becoming such a fine gentleman. Maybe she'll convince her father to bring her for another visit soon." Hope took both his hands in hers, giving them a warm squeeze. "I'm going now to prepare our guests' supper. I'll see you after you settle the horses."

After the last guests bid their compliments and farewells, Hope sat down on the stool behind the front desk. Taking her quill pen from the ink well, she reflected on the day's events. It had been a good day with many blessings, highlighted by her weekly dinner with the Warners. Guests had enjoyed their supper, accompanied by the soothing sounds of Carter's violin. And as had become his habit, he had stayed after the guests' departure to help her set the dining room for the next morning's breakfast. It was quiet now. Carter and the stable boy had been paid and gone their separate ways. *Time to write Amity.*

This was a special time she allowed herself each Sunday evening before going upstairs to read the Bible. Having a granddaughter was her greatest blessing, but thoughts of Amity also made Hope sad, reminding her of the days after Isaiah's passing. Jeremiah had been very helpful with Isaiah's burial and thanks to the Warners, Isaiah had a fine resting place in their meadow. *Seven years without my best friend.* Her heart ached now even more than it had the afternoon of his death. He had carried her through her greatest trials. Isaiah had been her lifeline. Now she was alone. Sundays had their blessings, but they would be better if she could ride Isaiah to church and watch him run in the Warners' meadow. Now the meadow held him -- forever.

Tears flowed down her cheek and onto the folded linen stationery, creating a small wet circle. Hope leaned over and blew on the paper to dry it.

"Good evening, Ma'am. I wonder if you have a room available, along with stable accommodations for two horses."

The familiar voice interrupted her efforts, causing her to drop the quill, spilling ink onto the paper. *But it can't be. Unmistakably British.* She raised her head slowly to confirm her suspicions.

"Will?"

"Sorry your writing paper is ruined," Will mused, pulling a handkerchief from his pocket to sop up the ink.

"Is this a good time to check in? I pray you have a room available; that is, if it's not too inconvenient. I saw your stable boy as he was leaving. He was kind enough to take care of my horses."

"No. I mean. It's not inconvenient. Y-Y-Yes. I do happen to have a room. How long will you be staying? How ... how did you find me?" Hope stammered, crossing her arms at her chest to stop the trembling.

"Mr. Carson told me he saw you and Jeremiah at his daughter's church. I was very pleased to learn your whereabouts as I have something to show you. I think you'll be quite pleased." Will reached up and touched his fingers to her face to wipe the tears. "If you'll come with me." Will gently placed his hand on her arm and guided her around the desk to stand next to him. "May I?" He glided his hand down her arm and took her hand in his.

"We'll need this." He picked up the lantern from the desk.

Her hand in his brought calmness, the trembling stopped, and with a familiar trust, Hope let him lead her outside -- until they arrived at the stable. "No, I can't go in there!" she exclaimed, letting go of his hand. "I don't go there. It's been seven years! No!"

Will turned, facing her. "Oh! Hope. I apologize. I should've been more thoughtful. Wait here."

Hope crossed her arms as the trembling returned. "I can't. I'm going back inside." She ran to the top of the stairs but stopped suddenly when she heard a horse whinnying.

"Please. Hope. Turn around. Just for a moment. I brought you a gift." Will held the lantern toward the steps, then took Hope's hand to lead her down to the hitching post. "Remember when we were picking grapes and Isaiah got loose? He ran to the pasture ... and we just let him go. You said 'we'll get him when we finish'."

"It was getting dark and we were up to our necks in grapes. We forgot my mare was already grazing. Well … that's the only time we left them together that I can recall. I believe it was the Lord's divine providence -- and Isaiah's lucky day." Will grinned. "Hope. This is Isaiah's colt -- a fine stallion. Don't you think? Look!" Will held the lantern to the horse's nose. "He has a very wide zig-zagged white blaze running between his eyes and down his nose! And he is the color of your hair. He was born about six months after you left."

Hope couldn't believe her eyes. Her heart was pounding, this time with sheer delight. "Oh Will! He's beautiful!" She ran down the steps, placed her face against the horse's nose, and gently rubbed his cheeks. "I don't know what to say. Do you think I could ride him? Maybe tomorrow after breakfast?"

Hope rushed through breakfast, picking up each guest's dish as soon as they took their last bite. Will had already finished his meal and was sitting at the corner table watching her, waiting patiently.

She scraped the dishes and placed them in the kitchen's wash barrel. *I can wash them while supper's cooking,* she thought. She heard footsteps behind her, then felt Will's arms pulling her to him. A sense of peace overcame her as she leaned backwards in his arms, savoring the moment, a sense of joy sweeping over her from head to toe.

"I asked the stable boy to saddle the horses. They're tied to the post out front."

Hope slowly turned to face him. "Oh Will. I'll need you to help me."

"Of course I'll help you. Anything you want. I've been yours since the first day you rode up to my cabin.

And it's been far too long..." Will pulled her to him, leaned down, and kissed her gently on the forehead. "Let's go see if we can chase some windmills."

Will rode by her side, consciously watching her face for any sign of fear or anxiety. As they rode through the town and out to the Warners' meadow, her face lit up with excitement. She nudged her horse into a fast gallop, leading Will through the fields. He sensed her pleasure and connection with her new friend. As they neared a large rock, she stopped and dismounted without a word, taking the horse's reins and reaching up to pull Will's hand, urging him to join her. The large rock was surrounded by daisies. "This is your father," she said to her horse, rubbing his shoulder. "He loved daisies." She patted the rock lovingly with her left hand and knelt down, pulling the reins to bring the horse closer. Leaning to the ground, she whispered, "Isaiah, this is your son. I bet he likes daisies too."

Will sat down on the ground beside her, lightly stroking her back, not saying a word, waiting patiently for her next move. *I am quite contented, just being near you,* he mused to himself. Hope's voice interrupted his thoughts.

"I think I'll name him after the prophet Isaiah's own son. Maher-Shalal-Hash-Baz. It means 'spoil swiftly'. It's the longest name in the Bible. When God gave Isaiah the name for his son, his intention was to say 'No matter how powerful and terrifying your enemies, do not fear them; rather, trust in God.' Throughout my life, the Lord has given me strength to pull through even the worst of times. Isaiah provided much of that strength. Now I have his son," she smiled and looked lovingly at Will. "I'll call him Shalal."

Riding back into town, Hope talked constantly, telling Will about Maddie, church, the flood, her new family of the Warners, Jeremiah's visits, and most passionately about her granddaughter, Amity. "I am blessed," she said.

As they dismounted, handing the reins to the stable boy, she continued. "I had to leave you in order to find myself. My time here helped me heal. I am free now. Free to care. Free to give."

She took both his hands in hers. "I pray you will stay for awhile. You won't need to rent a room."

Chapter 29

Dearest Amity,

Much has happened since my last letter. Your friend Carter was such a big help after Isaiah's passing, for as you know, I could not bring myself to ride again. Carter is such a fine gentleman. And, up until recently, Carter continued to bring the carriage into town and take me to church every Sunday. And as always, I enjoyed fine food and company at Sunday dinner with his mother and grandparents. After dinner, Carter would bring me back to the inn and help me prepare supper, then he would play his violin for the guests. They love his music.

But the best news is that while Carter continues playing the violin for my guests, he no longer takes me to church! The Lord has blessed me with a great gift. Two gifts actually. I'll explain.

Many years ago, when your father Jeremiah was only ten years old, I left him for what I thought would be just a few days. I rode Isaiah up to Hawksbill Mountain to find my own father, as I believed with all my heart that if he was still alive, he would be there. Prayers were answered. I found him alive, but his mind was so frail he hardly knew me. It was clear this would be the only time we would have together, so I stayed. Simple afternoon walks were precious. After his death, my soul was in great peril, for in addition to losing my father, I had lingering memories to sort through. So, instead of returning to Jeremiah, I chose to stay with a friend who lived near Hawksbill Mountain. Years passed as I searched my soul for answers -- reading, crying, lashing out. My friend was incredibly patient, listening to my agonizing stories, and supporting me with kindness, even though I wasn't much support to him. But we both loved reading books and we spent much of our time sharing recalled passages, discussing characters' imperfections and strengths. We also rode our horses through the forests and across nearby fields.

On the day I learned Mitch had died, I left my friend and rode to Mitchborough. I kept my distance, watching you and your father as you prayed next to Mitch's grave. As I watched, I sensed it was not yet time to reunite. And something inside my heart told me I shouldn't return to my friend. Instead, the Lord led me to Watauga and to this inn, where I was totally on my own for the first time in my life. Here, with the Lord's help, I became a strong, confident woman. Yet, in many ways, even when surrounded by guests and friends, I was alone.

That is, until several weeks ago, when my friend from Hawksbill Mountain surprised me at the inn. I was writing you a letter when he arrived at my desk. Seeing him again brought unexpected joy. But, that joy was not the only gift. My friend brought me a stallion. Yes! A stallion the color of my hair, with a wide zig-zagged white blaze running between his eyes and down his nose -- just like Isaiah! And, in fact, my stallion is the son of Isaiah and my friend's mare. Isaiah's son! I named him Shalal and I have so enjoyed riding him along the rivers and through the meadows, alongside my friend and his horse.

So, I was blessed with two great gifts.

I am very happy now, no longer alone. My forty-one years have taught me much about life. Life is like a violin, capable of stirring your emotions to agonizing irritation, or soothing you into a mellow trance that you wish to hold in your heart forever. Life's music brings each person moments of elation, but it can also bring challenges and adversity.

Sometimes we are so overcome and immersed in those challenges, that we cannot give or even accept love. Without warning, we become a puppet, manipulated by a strong-willed and evil master who wields the strings of his actions so tightly and completely into our soul that we cannot break free. And often evil begets evil, seizing the souls of its successors until they also become demons, passing that evil along from generation to generation.

For many years, my soul was possessed by demons controlling the strings of my very being, making me distant, unable to let my heart be free. It took years to re-discover my faith. Through many tears, the Lord showed me the way and, with His help and the help of my friend, I began to loosen the demons' strings. Building a life in Watauga, losing myself in my work, getting to know my guests and hearing their stories, their worries, their wishes, helped me define my own. The dark music that mangled my mind slowly faded into pleasant melodies, setting my soul free.

My dearest Amity, I pray your life will always be filled with blessings of peace and joy. I pray you will never be the victim of evil binding your soul. If you ever sense someone is threatening your spirit's freedom, seek the Lord's guidance. Listen to your heart. Tug hard against the hurtful strings, break free -- and flee into your faith.

Above all, I pray you find a companion who embodies such kindness and confidence that he frees your spirit simply by holding you.

My friend's name is Will. He is very British, but in a kind way. He is strong enough to share his life, and his love, without strings. He is going to stay in Watauga for awhile. My heart is now filled with the music of contentment and yes -- even love.

Please give a hug to your mother and Jeremiah. May the Lord bless and keep you always.

I love you,

Grandmother Hope

"A new heart also will I give you,
and a new spirit will I put within you:
and I will take away the stony heart out of your flesh,
and I will give you a heart of flesh." Ezekiel 36:26 KJV

A book takes a village . . . or many trusted advisors.

My primary editor, Alexandra Avaleen Riehl, was a passionate and conscientious proofreader. Without her keen eye and supportive feedback, this book would be incomplete.

Readers who gave me invaluable feedback and the encouragement to continue writing: Jill Murray Anderson, Chuck Creasy, Jo Doster, Kim Anderson Griffin, Ann Morton Lee, Sheila White Postell, Jeff Riehl, Steve Ricker, Paula Underwood Winters.

The staff and numerous re-enactors at Sycamore Shoals State Historic Park, Overmountain Victory Trail Association, and Hart Village were extremely patient and kind in sharing their knowledge regarding weapons, apparel, the march to Kings Mountain, and the many aspects of daily life in the late 18th century. Additional research included reading *The Land Breakers* by John Ehle on the historical background of early pioneers and *Before They Were Heroes at King's Mountain* by Randell Jones, on the Patriots' journey to Kings Mountain.

"Commit thy works unto the Lord
and thy thoughts shall be established." Proverbs 16:3

Most importantly, I acknowledge the guidance of the Lord Jesus Christ without whom I would not have been in a time and place to write. Each day as I sat before my computer, I prayed: "Dear Lord, I commit my work to Thee. Please establish my thoughts." Many days I prayed with no idea of words to come. But, by the time I was ready to type, the inspiration would come, and the Lord established my thoughts. Without a doubt, it is His guidance that led to the completion of this book.

"For ye have need of patience,
that, after ye have done the will of God,
ye might receive the promise" Hebrews 10:36

PATRICIA ANN LEDFORD

Patricia Ann Ledford grew up in Kingsport, a small town in eastern Tennessee. An early career in politics evolved into managing marketing campaigns for corporate clients and ultimately into working on film projects and producing television programming.

After forty years of copywriting for clients in Nashville and Chattanooga, she finally achieved a lifetime goal of writing stories of her own creation. *Strings – The Story of Hope* is her first novel.

She divides her time between writing in her North Carolina hideaway and enjoying family and cultural activities in Chattanooga.

www.palinks.net
Jacket Design & Illustration by Chuck Creasy

Interior Layout by Paula Underwood Winters

CPSIA information can be obtained
at www.ICGtesting.com
Printed in the USA
FFHW020032231119
56122718-62227FF

9 781733 524216